LIA ANDERSON
DOG PARK MYSTERIES

# FUR BOYS

**LIA ANDERSON MYSTERIES**
by C. A. Newsome

A SHOT IN THE BARK
DROOL BABY
MAXIMUM SECURITY
SNEAK THIEF
MUDDY MOUTH
FUR BOYS

# FUR BOYS

LIA ANDERSON DOG PARK MYSTERIES 6

C. A. NEWSOME

This is a work of fiction. All of the characters, places and events portrayed in this book are either products of the author's imagination or are used fictitiously. Any resemblance to actual events is coincidental.

FUR BOYS

Two Pup Press
1836 Bruce Avenue
Cincinnati, Ohio 45223

Library of Congress Control Number: 2017907566
ISBN 978-0-9963742-9-3 (paperback)
ISBN 978-0-9963742-6-2 (ebook)

*For Ducky. You will always be my favorite heroine.*

# PROLOGUE

## WEDNESDAY, NOVEMBER 2

"No, no, no, no, no!"

The words echoed from the rafters of the chapel, harsh in the chill air, each punctuated by the violent slash of an elegant male hand. If there had been doves in the rafters, they would be swooping down in response, like a scene from *The Birds*. Or bats. Really, bats would be so much more appropriate.

Geoff Lawrence stood in the center aisle of Spring Grove Cemetery's Norman Chapel and raked frustrated fingers through blond, wavy hair suitable for a Regency era poet. He glared at the performers jammed behind the miserable excuse for a chamber orchestra like terrified penguins in their concert blacks.

"Have you joined in a conspiracy to ruin my reputation?" he screamed. "Fauré's *Requiem* has been performed thousands, hundreds of thousands, a million times in the past hundred years. This has to be the absolute worst of the lot. Homeless schizophrenics banging on garbage cans would do better. No one will touch it after you massacre it tonight. You're an embarrassment, each and every one of you. I'm canceling the concert."

Geoff's ex-wife Constance sat, a prim and diffident mouse at the seat of the third-rate organ he'd had to make do with.

"Don't you think we're at the point of over-rehearsing?" she asked. "The doors open in forty-five minutes."

She said this as if she were asking a petulant child if he preferred a popsicle or a lollipop. Her calm demeanor infuriated him.

Geoff snorted. "And no heat. They promised me heat." He raised his face to the vaulted ceiling and opened up his legendary throat. "Where is the God damned *HEAT!*"

Getting no answer, he eyed his terrified chorus and growled, "No matter, there's *nothing* to be done at this point. Everyone out of here! Out, out, *OUT!*"

The group scattered from the dais, grabbing coats from the pile strewn across the front pews. They headed for the side doors, keeping their distance from Geoff.

"Toby, just a moment," Geoff said.

A slender young man with lush, dark curls halted. Toby's lips twitched as other members of the choir brushed past him, casting speculative looks in his direction. Geoff caught Constance out of the corner of his eye, shaking her head as she followed the last of Geoff's students out.

"Come here," Geoff said.

# WEDNESDAY, NOVEMBER 2, CONTINUED

LIA ANDERSON RUBBED HER ARMS AGAINST THE FRIGID NIGHT air while she waited for Peter Dourson to lock the door of his ancient Chevy Blazer, a vehicle more suited to logging trails than urban streets. She and Peter, along with their friends, Brent and Cynth, stood in the Spring Grove Cemetery parking lot. The lot was packed with cars of other concert goers, whose dark shapes migrated toward the original, post-Civil War buildings. Arriving vehicles drove cautiously down the unlit cemetery roads looking for places to park, their headlights providing the only illumination.

Lia's beau, Peter, was tall, with a runner's build and pleasant looks. He seemed perfectly ordinary until you noticed his extraordinary, twilight-blue eyes, so often hidden by the mud-brown hair that constantly fell in them. Those eyes held a wicked glint as he looked at her. "Tell me again why we're doing this?"

Brent Davis, Peter's partner and District Five's pretty

boy, adjusted the knife-edged crease in his slacks and examined the sleeves of his new overcoat. "You may be allergic to culture, but pointing out your sacrifice destroys the value of pleasing the ladies. Please stop. I don't want it to rub off on me." He plucked off an offending dog hair. It was long and black and formerly attached to Peter's temperamental chow mix, Viola. "I don't know why we had to drive your embarrassment on wheels."

"Because there's no leg room in the back seat of your Audi. You should have thought of that before you tossed away the price of a house on a toy car."

A wheat-colored braid long and thick enough to classify as an appendage slipped over Cynth McFadden's shoulder as she whispered to Lia. "They act so married sometimes." Cynth was another District Five detective, whose computer skills earned her a special position and an office of her own, even if it was a maintenance closet in the basement.

Lia snorted and whispered back, "Everyone says that when people bicker. Sure makes me want to put a ring on it." She raised her voice. "Peter's pulling your chain, Brent. He thinks if he admits he wants to be here, it won't count in his favor during March Madness."

They fell in with the procession on the sidewalk. Lia leaned into Peter's arm while Cynth and Brent trailed behind as they passed silhouettes of the original, Romanesque Revival buildings. Ahead, a soft glow emanated from Norman Chapel.

"I've been dying to see the inside of the chapel for years," Lia said. "It's never open to the public. We're lucky one of the professors at Hopewell couldn't use his tickets."

"Spooky out here," Peter said.

"Cemetery. Spooky. Duh," Cynth said.

"A hundred years ago, you had to have tickets to get in on the weekends," Lia said. "Crowds of people would ride horses and drive cars through the grounds to see and be seen."

"Sounds like *American Graffiti*," Brent said.

Faint, colored lights bled through the magnolia trees shielding the near end of the chapel from view. Lia stepped off the sidewalk, tugging Peter along with her as she headed through the trees. "You've got to see this."

"Oh, look!" Cynth cooed. Christ, flanked by angels, ascended to Heaven above his amazed apostles on a magnificent hand-painted stained glass window, brilliantly illuminated from the inside.

"Pretty," Peter agreed.

Lia nudged him with her elbow. "It's more than pretty. It's fabulous. They don't make work like that anymore."

Peter shrugged. "I like your flowers better."

Lia walked up to the building and traced a reverent hand over the intricately carved stonework. "And that's why I love you. I wish I'd brought a flashlight. The detail in the masonry is wonderful. When we get around to the front we should be able to see some of it in the porte cochère. The pattern for every window is unique. All the rosettes are different too. I could spend hours looking at it."

"What the bleeding Jesus is a port co-chair?" Brent asked.

"It's a covered drive-through so coaches could drop off passengers in bad weather. Someone as *cultured* as yourself should know that." Cynth sniped, getting in her first zinger of the evening at Brent.

Lia considered the pair. *Talk about married. There's a story there and one of these days I'm going to dig it out of her.*

They rounded the side of the chapel to find more than a hundred people packed into the porte cochère and spilling onto the drive.

"The doors should have been open fifteen minutes ago," Lia said, rising on her toes to see better. "I see Hannah up front. I'll find out what the problem is."

Lia squeezed through the growing crush to the steps where Hopewell Music Conservatory's administrative secretary stood, her breath visible in the frigid air. A frown pinched a vertical line between Hannah's eyes as she spoke to a security guard. Lia thought she recognized a few students from the school. The crowd muttered as the guard leaned over and inserted an ancient key into the lock.

A small, elegant woman named Constance DeVries stepped forward. Lia knew her slightly, and that contact had led to her current project at Hopewell. Constance was the organist for tonight's concert and she sounded worried. "Better let me go first. There's no telling why he locked us out."

The guard pulled one massive door open. Concert goers responded by flowing around the guard and through the door as if sucked into a vacuum. A wave of people carried Lia through the narthex, into the nave, and down the aisle toward the giant glowing Jesus floating overhead. The initial rush played out as Lia neared the altar. She ducked into a pew, followed by a pair of matrons. *At least we'll have good seats.*

From the front of the scrum a woman's voice erupted in a scream, the sound echoing off the chapel vault. The matrons froze, their hands stilled in the act of unbuttoning their coats. Chill silence followed. Then came panicked female cries. "Geoff, Geoff! Oh, my God, Geoff!"

*That sounds like Constance.* Lia bolted out of her seat, uttering incoherent apologies as she brushed by the matrons. The packed aisle roiled in confusion. Lia forced her way through the throng to the foot of a dais.

Constance lay in a sobbing heap by an electric organ, one hand clutching the leg extending from behind the instrument. Lia stepped around her, bringing the body into view.

Dr. Lawrence stared heavenward, eyes fixed and mouth agape in a macabre echo of the awestruck apostles in the stained glass window overhead. Blood matted wavy gold hair and congealed on skin whiter than that of saints in an El Greco painting. *No blood circulating. Taking his pulse would be pointless.*

Crimson smears painted the base of the four-foot-tall brass candle stand crossing the body. More red pooled and glistened on the floor. A fat pillar candle lay several feet away.

"Leander killed him! I saw them arguing!"

Lia turned, her eyes searching for the source of the voice. It came from a curly-haired Hopewell student named Toby. His pretty face wrenched in horror while people turned in all directions, looking for Leander.

Toby knelt by Constance and took her free hand. "I can't believe I left him alone with Leander," he cried. "If only I had known—"

SECONDS TICKED by as Peter struggled to make progress through the mass of bodies separating him from the source

7

of the scream. He didn't have to look to know Brent and Cynth followed in the path he opened.

He scanned for Lia as he fought his way through a crowd as packed as any he'd worked at the WEBN fireworks, where it could take ten minutes to move ten feet.

He broke through to open space, almost tripping over a standing harp at the foot of a dais filled with folding chairs. Low moans came from a woman on his right. She sprawled on the floor, weeping over a man's leg, the rest of the body blocked by an electric organ. A young man with a mop of wildly curling hair comforted her.

Lia stood on the far side of the bizarre trio. Relief washed color back into her face as their eyes met. She stepped aside as Peter made his way around the grieving woman, giving him room to survey the body hidden behind the organ. It took him a fraction of a second to assess the scene: a Caucasian male, supine with a crushed skull; a giant, bloody candlestick the obvious weapon. Peter crouched by the man and pressed his fingers against the cool throat, searching for a pulse he knew he wouldn't find.

He stood and surveyed the onlookers, his height enabling him to see to the back of the chapel. Newcomers pushed in from the entrance while people still jammed the center aisle, unable to move forward or back and uncertain what to do. A few slid into pews and were unbuttoning coats.

He searched for someone who was out of place: someone with a flushed face, someone without a coat, a jittery someone looking for a way out. The crowd continued to shift and murmur, now with a tone of annoyance seeping into the confusion. More people moved into pews.

Brent caught Peter's eye and shook his head. *Nothing.* That didn't mean the doer was gone. They'd search the building, but first they had to get a hundred people under control. Peter jerked his head at the dais, knowing Brent would understand. He then nodded at Cynth, wagging his fingers by his chin in the universal "call" sign.

Brent slipped between the harp and several folding chairs to mount the platform while pulling his badge out of his pocket. He climbed on a chair, facing the crush of people as he held his badge high, shouting to be heard. "Police! Remain exactly where you are."

The muttering stopped. All eyes trained on the dais. Brent continued. "This is a crime scene. In a minute we will give you instructions. Until then, please stay where you are and stay calm."

Cynth spoke into her phone while urging people away from the dead man, creating space so they could function.

Peter's mind raced. *What are we going to do with all these people?*

He felt the press of Lia's hand on his arm.

"Not now," he said. Hurt flashed across Lia's face, making Peter wince. He deliberately softened his voice. "Sorry. I have to focus."

"Peter, you need Hannah. She knows everybody. She can help."

"The admin? Find her then." He had a new thought and touched Lia's sleeve before she could leave. "Wait here. I have an idea."

Peter joined Brent on the dais. He waved his arms, raising his voice over the renewed din. "May I have your attention. I'm Detective Dourson with the Cincinnati

Police. We're going to take your names and move you out of here. It will take time. Please be patient."

He beckoned Brent to follow him and rejoined Lia and Cynth by the organ.

"What did dispatch say?" Peter asked Cynth.

"Heckle and Jeckle are on rotation, ETA twenty minutes. If they're at their favorite nude bar, it will be twice that. Backup in five."

"That's just perfect," Brent groaned. "We've got 40 minutes to solve this thing before they take over and screw it up."

"We do what we can." Peter reassessed the situation. Any evidence in the aisle was now ground into dust. "Cynth, Lia's going to point out Hannah to you. She'll help you sort out who needs to stay and who can go. Get contact information on everyone. Brent, meet our backup outside and get ID on as many people as you can before they disappear."

Lia turned away with Cynth. Movement behind the pair caught Peter's attention. A blue-haired woman edged down the front pew. *Wants to see the body so she can report to bridge club.* "Ma'am, go back to the aisle."

"Constance needs me," she whined.

"We'll take care of her," Peter said. "I need you off my crime scene." The woman hesitated. Peter glared. "Now." He stared long enough to ensure the blue-hair was leaving, then knelt down beside the prostrate woman. He placed a gentle hand on her shoulder. "Are you Constance? We need to move you somewhere else." He jerked his chin at the young man. "You, too."

"You bastard," Constance moaned. "Stupid, stupid, stupid bastard."

*Talking to a corpse.* A hand touched his arm. *Lia.*

"There's a family chamber on the side. Maybe they could go there?" she asked.

"I can't let you into an unsecured area. Whoever did this could be in there." Peter rubbed the bridge of his nose. Brent and Cynth were now heading back into the crowd.

He yelled. "Brent, hold up a minute."

Brent turned.

Peter nodded to the chamber. "Check that out, will you?"

Brent held one thumb up. He turned into a pew, heading for the chamber door as he drew the gun he always carried, keeping it low to his side. Brent edged into the chamber and returned an instant later. He caught Peter's eye and mouthed, "Clear."

Peter spoke to Lia, nodding at Constance and the young man. "Get junior to help you take Constance in there, and wait for me. Don't let them talk to each other."

"I'll do my best," she said. She bent over Constance while speaking quietly to the young man.

Peter returned his attention to the body. It had fallen between the organ seat and the wall, as if the man had been sitting on the end of the bench and someone knocked him off. There were drops of blood on the side of the organ and a puddle on the floor by the man's head. Spatter on the floor indicated part of the beating took place where the man lay. The candlestick looked clean except for the bloody base. Closer examination revealed smears where the brass had been wiped. *Something for crime scene to sort out.*

Peter stood and cast his eyes around, ensuring that people were in fact leaving the building. He continued to scan the area but saw nothing of obvious significance. He got out his phone to record the scene. He knew full well the crime scene techs would duplicate his efforts, but evidence could disappear. *Better two photos than no photos.*

BRENT TAMPED down irritation as he pressed through the throng. It would have been so much simpler to have everyone sit down while they sorted this out, but Peter was a stickler for preserving the scene. Nothing that had not yet been trampled was going to get trampled under Peter's watch, though Brent thought it unlikely that there was evidence to be found in the pews.

A woman tugged on Brent's sleeve. "What happened?"

"I'm sorry ma'am. I can't say just yet."

He spotted Cynth ahead of him, in the vestibule. She had one hellacious task, collecting all those names. He pulled a notepad from his inside pocket and ripped off a blank page, giving it to the woman. "Write down your name and two phone numbers. Show your driver's license to Detective McFadden at the door."

He raised his voice, repeating the instructions before he pushed onward, handing a page to everyone he passed.

"Then we can go?" a man asked.

"Then you can go," Brent said. "Unless you're special."

Hands swarmed him, grabbing for pages faster than he could rip them out.

"Dourson," Brent muttered under his breath, "You ass. Come with us, you said. You'll get to sit next to Cynth. Some fun evening, Dourson."

LIA SAT on a stone bench in the family chamber, Constance clutching her like a life raft on the ocean. Toby, stalked angrily around the small room in a disconcerting change of mood.

*I shouldn't be here. I don't know what I'm doing.* She considered the way Peter, Brent, and Cynth had snapped into action. *They're a well-oiled crisis machine. I'm just a clueless lump.*

"I don't understand," Constance moaned into Lia's shoulder. "He was fine an hour ago."

"He was not fine," Toby said. "He was in a vicious rage."

"Please," Lia said. "You can't talk to each other. It will mess up the case."

"What case?" Toby scoffed. "Leander did it."

"Who's Leander?" Lia asked.

"A colleague," Constance said. "Geoff's best friend."

Toby snorted.

CYNTH SPOTTED the auburn-haired admin inside a circle of people standing in the porte cochère. *Everyone is too calm. They must not have heard the scream.* She approached, deciding to start with her authoritative voice. "Ms. Kleemeyer?"

Hannah turned away from a sharply dressed man with John Lennon glasses and the thin, blonde woman beside him. Hannah's face was smooth and expressionless, except for a worried vertical line between her eyebrows. "May I help you?"

"I'm Detective McFadden with the Cincinnati police. We need your help."

"Excuse me, Detective, Ms. Kleemeyer is my assistant," the man said. "What's going on here?"

Cynth ran through her options. Expediency won out. "Geoff Lawrence's body was discovered inside when the doors were opened—"

"Geoff?" The woman gasped. "What hap—"

Cynth interrupted, turning to Hannah. "We've got to clear everyone out of the chapel except the folks who may know something. Lia Anderson said you would know who we should talk to and if anyone is here that shouldn't be."

"Geoff's dead?" The man said. He nodded briskly at Hannah. "Go, go. Suki and I will talk to the parents."

"What a disaster," the woman named Suki moaned as Cynth led Hannah up the steps. Brent guarded the door, politely urging a fur and diamond draped matron at the head of a long line to be patient.

"Was he murdered?" Hannah asked.

Cynth cocked an eyebrow at her.

"Sorry. Stupid question." Hannah drew in a deep breath, the line between her brows digging in. "I'll do what I can. What do you want to do with your witnesses?"

Cynth scanned the chapel. "Let's sit them in the back pews, four feet apart so they can't talk to each other."

"Excuse me," the diamond-draped matron said. "Here is my driver's license. I'd like to leave."

"Just a minute." Cynth quirked an eyebrow at Hannah. Hannah nodded. Cynth took the card. "Just let me photograph your license, Mrs. Ah–Derwintmeyer."

Flashing red and blue lights pulsed as a patrol car pulled through the crowd, into the porte cochère.

"Our backup is here," Brent said. "I'll get them

canvassing the grounds. Is there anyone outside who needs to talk to us?"

"I saw a few members of the chorus floating around," Hannah said. "They were all here for warm up, before Dr. Lawrence kicked everyone out of the chapel."

"They might have seen something, then," Brent said.

"And if you can give Dr. Wingler and Dr. Thomas a few minutes, it would help," Hannah said, nodding at the dark-haired man and the thin blonde.

"On it," Brent said, already out the door.

BRENT TROTTED DOWN THE STEPS, pausing for a moment to assure Hannah's bosses he would give them what information he could as soon as the scene was under control. Officers Brainard and Hinkle worked their way toward him, along with a pair of rookies Brent didn't know.

Neither Brainard nor Hinkle was a brain trust, but both were reliable. Brainard, a former Marine calendar pinup, fancied himself a ladies' man, while Hinkle was earnest and followed directions well.

Brent decided to put Hinkle to babysitting the witnesses, some of whom would be college women, and put Brainard to identifying the mostly middle-aged patrons milling around. That would prevent Brainard from hitting on the girls and keep him away from Cynth as well. He sent one of the uniformed officers to photograph license plates and the other to ensuring people went straight to their cars and did not trample evidence hiding in the dark.

Assignments given, he returned to the entry with Hinkle in tow. A now orderly line of disappointed music lovers

passed between Kleemeyer and Cynth in an admirably efficient manner.

"Ms. Kleemeyer, this is Officer Hinkle. He'll monitor our
witnesses until we can take statements."

Cal Hinkle bobbed his head. "Ma'am."

"How goes it?" Brent asked.

"I think all Detective McFadden will need to do is pull
the performers. You can't miss them. They're the youngest
people here and they're wearing head-to-toe black. No one
else was here earlier, except Constance DeVries ... Oh, and
Leander Marshall. ... Maybe if I made an announcement we
could direct the performers to the back pews?"

"That works." He glanced at Cynth who was snapping an
ID with her phone.

"Go on, I'll be fine." She didn't look up.

"Ms. Kleemeyer, if you could come with me for a
minute?"

Hannah followed Brent and Cal into the nave. More
than a dozen college students sat in the rear pews. A
quartet of girls in long black dresses leaned across the
mandated four-foot separation, whispering to each other
while the boys slouched and stared up at the vaulted
ceiling.

Brent leaned to Hannah, speaking quietly, "Is anyone
missing?"

Hannah paused and did a mental head count "There
should be another half dozen floating around."

Brent cleared his throat, loudly. The girls snapped
upright, putting on guileless faces.

He planted his feet, aware the girls were now sending
him coy looks. *God save me from children.* He turned to
Hannah. "Can we get the security guard to open up one of

the other buildings? We can't keep these kids at a live crime scene."

"I'm sure Marty will do that for you."

Brent directed his gaze to the students, who looked back at him with baby owl eyes. One of the girls had undone the top two buttons on her otherwise prim dress. She inhaled deeply when she realized Brent was looking at her.

"I'm Detective Davis, this is Officer Hinkle, and you know Ms. Kleemeyer. As soon as we round up the rest of your group, Officer Hinkle is going to escort you to another building and stay with you. I know this is a hardship, but it is crucial that you not talk to each other until after you have all given your statements."

Two of the girls pouted. A studious blonde with too much hair and oversized glasses raised her hand. *She's in college? She can't be more than twelve, surely.*

"Excuse me, Mr. Detective, sir?"

"Yes?"

"You won't be able to get everyone together."

"Why is that?"

"One of the guys left."

"And who was that?"

"Leander Marshall. The one who did it."

Brent felt his grip on the situation slipping. "What part of don't talk about this until you get interviewed did you not understand?"

A tubby boy with a flap of hair hanging over one eye raised his hand. "Sir? I'm not leaving unless I can take my violin."

"Where's your violin?" Brent asked.

Hannah whispered in Brent's ear. "There's a hundred thousand dollars in instruments on stage."

He stared at her. "Just laying there?"

She nodded.

He addressed the group. "Your instruments have to stay where they are for now."

He held up both hands to ward off their understandable cries of outrage. "They're part of a crime scene. I can't do anything about that except to make sure we keep a close eye on them until we can release them." He silently apologized to Cal before tossing him to the wolves. "If you have an instrument onstage, please give Officer Hinkle your name and a description of your instrument."

"And no funny business," Hannah said. "I know what's supposed to be up there."

"Then why don't *you* tell him?" someone muttered.

Brent left the students with Cal and headed back to Peter, Hannah in tow. The aisle was almost clear, most of the crowd having passed through Cynth's improvised checkpoint.

"Why did Maggie say Leander killed Geoff?" Hannah asked.

"I can't say," Brent said. "We're too busy getting this circus under control to take statements."

"Leander couldn't have done it," Hannah said. "He was with me."

Brent found Peter photographing Dr. Lawrence's body with his phone.

"I figured I might as well document as long as I was stuck here," Peter said.

"You'd better shoot those instruments while you're at it. You could buy a nice house or three with what's on stage."

Peter grimaced. "Any sign of Hodgkins or Jarvis?"

"Not a peep. It's only been—" Brent shoved back the sleeve of his coat and checked his watch. "eighteen minutes."

"Feels like eighteen years. Is the morgue wagon here yet?"

"I told them there was no hurry since the star of our show won't be going anywhere until Heckle—I mean Hodgkins and Jarvis—arrive."

Peter nodded at the wall, addressing Hannah. "You're Hannah. That bronze door behind you, where does it go?"

"There's a bathroom and a utility room back there."

"It hasn't been cleared yet. I'm having nightmares that our doer is back there with a stockpile of automatic weapons." He looked at Brent and jerked his head toward the door. "Check it out, will you?"

"On my way."

PETER STUDIED HANNAH. She looked away, her eyes following Brent as he worked his way between the pews. *Doesn't care to think about what's behind the organ. No picnic for any of us.*

Hannah spoke, her back to Peter. "One of the girls said Leander killed him. I was just telling Detective Davis that was impossible."

Peter scanned the chapel. The performers were filing out of the pews under the direction of Officer Hinkle. *Brent must have found somewhere to put them. Good.* The rest of the nave was empty. Cynth was visible through the door to the narthex, processing the last of the concert goers. He thought about the hell he was going to catch for what he was about to do and mentally shrugged it off. Hannah shouldn't have to deal with Heckle and Jeckle's bad cop/worse cop act during her initial interview.

"We need a statement from you. I'd like to get it now, and I'd like to record it."

Hannah turned back, looking at Peter with large, hazel eyes. "Whatever I can do."

He put a hand on her arm, gently steering her away from the body to a pew halfway down the now vacant aisle. He scanned it to ensure there was no obvious evidence. "Have a seat."

He brought up the recording app on his phone. "What happened here?"

Hannah bit her lip. "I don't know. The last time I saw Geoff, he was sitting at the organ."

"When was that?"

"A little after seven. We have a final rehearsal, then we break for an hour before the performance."

"The doors were locked when we arrived. Lia said they were supposed to open at eight. What went wrong?"

"Geoff had the key. It's probably still in his pocket."

"Shouldn't the performers be inside before you open the door to the audience?"

"Everyone was going in and out the back door, the one off the family chamber. There was a shim to keep it from locking. It was in place when Leander and I left. It was gone when I got back."

"Tell me about Dr. Lawrence. How was he before you left?"

"He was his usual pre-concert self."

"Meaning?"

"Threatening to rip the vocal chords out of the students so as not to punish the world with their musical ineptitude."

"Sounds like a fun guy."

"He's a very important man in the world of classical music," Hannah said. "He told everyone to leave, though he did ask one student to stay."

"Who was this?"

"That was Toby, the soloist."

"What happened after he asked Toby to stay?"

"I went to use the restroom—it's in the hall behind the bronze door. It was occupied. Leander came out and I went in. Someone was yelling when I came out. I didn't want to walk into the middle of an argument between Leander and Geoff, so I waited in the hall. I finally decided to hell with it and went into the nave. They'd finished yelling and Leander was glaring at Geoff. Leander saw me and followed me out."

"What were they yelling about?"

"That door is solid bronze and two and a half inches thick. I couldn't hear what they were saying. Leander told me they were arguing about Toby."

"What about Toby?"

"Leander and Geoff have been in a relationship for years. When Leander came out of the bathroom, he saw Geoff and Toby kissing and blew up."

"What happened after you and Leander left the chapel?"

"We walked to the waterfall, the one with the wall of cremation vaults. He needed to get himself together, so I left him there. When I came back, all the students were huddled by the front door because they couldn't get in. I called Marty to open the door and everyone rushed in. That's all I know."

Peter looked at the dais. Folding chairs jammed side by side on risers below the stained glass window. The risers were blocked by a maze of abandoned musical instruments:

kettle drums, a harp, and a standing bass, along with a pair of violin cases. It looked more like a junk shop than a stage setting.

The altar hid behind the risers like an afterthought, its purpose of no matter. It was something that Peter, a not exactly lapsed Lutheran, found offensive. Three tall brass candle stands lined the wall on the left side of the stage. Two more stood behind the organ, their mate lying on the floor next to the victim.

"Are those instruments really worth a hundred grand?"

"That's a conservative estimate," Hannah said.

"I'd better get pictures of them, too."

Brent returned after several minutes, accompanied by an older man in a gray uniform, his face grimy and his hands blackened with grease. There was a nasty streak of grease on one leg of Brent's new suit.

"What did you fall into?" Peter asked.

"I had to check out the attic, didn't I?"

Peter turned to Hannah. "You didn't mention an attic."

"There's a ladder in the utility room and a trap door in the ceiling," Brent said. "Meet Nigel Porter. I found Nigel working on the furnace," Brent said.

"You know anything about this?" Peter asked Hannah.

Hannah gave Peter an apologetic look. "They were supposed to turn the heat on, but it wasn't working so they brought Nigel in. I forgot all about it."

"And you were working on the furnace?" Peter asked Nigel. He turned to Brent. "There's a furnace in the ceiling?"

Nigel stepped in front of Peter "Yeah, the furnace is in the ceiling. It was built that way and I'm the only one who knows how to fix it. What's this about? Pretty boy grabbed me and frisked me and didn't say boo, just dragged me down here. I have to get that furnace on or there's going to be hell to pay."

"I wouldn't worry about that," Peter said. "The concert is cancelled."

Nigel looked at Hannah. "You got me working overtime to get heat in here and now there's no concert?"

"There's been an accident—" Hannah began.

"How long were you in the attic?" Peter asked.

"I got here at five-thirty. Then maestro pitched a fit about my truck being out front, so I had to unload it and move it to the parking lot. That took twenty minutes I could have been working. I went into the attic and I stayed there until your friend decided to roust me."

"What did you hear while you were up there?"

"Nothing. I was working on the furnace like I said."

"You can do better than that," Brent said. "There was a rehearsal. Could you hear that?"

Nigel sighed. "Yeah, I heard singing and music. Then it stopped and I could hear Maestro screaming about the heat. Then it was quiet until I heard the scream."

"What scream?"

"The woman, a few minutes ago."

"And you didn't come down?"

"I had to get the heat on before eight-thirty, scream or no scream. You still haven't said what happened." Nigel stepped to the side and ducked his head so he could see beyond Peter. "Jesus, what happened to the maestro?"

"That's what we want to find out."

"Is he dead?"

"Yeah he's dead," Brent said. "Now what did you hear?"

Nigel scrubbed his face with one hand, smearing grease across his suddenly pale cheek. "I heard nothing."

Peter sighed. He gestured to the fourth pew. "Take a seat, Mr. Porter. You're in for a long night."

"Dourson!" The voice boomed from the entry. "What the hell did you do to my crime scene? First you let a hundred people trample on evidence, then you send all my witnesses away. Next you're going to tell me you deputized your girlfriend." Peter winced, thinking of Lia guarding her charges in the family chamber as a pair of running-to-fat detectives strode up the aisle like they owned the place.

Hodgkins and Jarvis were former District Five detectives recently promoted to the newly created city-wide homicide unit, a position Peter had turned down. They were dressed in mafia-style suits with dark shirts and ties. Their dress and mannerisms were so much alike people mistook them for brothers.

"Here come Hot and Shit," Brent muttered to Peter before addressing the taller of the two detectives. "Decide to do a little work tonight, Hodgkins?"

"What's the matter, Ken?" Jarvis jibed. "Barbie have a headache?"

"I thought we got rid of you," Brent said. "Why couldn't you just stay gone?"

Hannah looked confused.

"Hannah," Peter said. "Detectives Hodgkins and Jarvis have been assigned to Dr. Lawrence's murder. They're in charge now."

LIA WATCHED STEADILY SEEPING tears migrate down Constance's face. They washed furrows into the woman's makeup and dripped off her chin, spotting her black, floor length gown. Constance gripped Lia's hand so tightly her bones hurt. *Thank god it's not my left hand. I'd never be able to paint again.*

Constance moaned and uttered incoherent words as she slumped back against the wall. *I should sympathize, but I want to slap her silly.*

Toby Grant paced jerkily across the floor, his hands fluttering about like a pair of canaries on Adderall. "I can't believe it! My debut! My big night! My solo! Ruined! Geoff was going to cast me as Faust. Now that will never happen. My father donated millions to Hopewell, and *this* happens.

"Toby," Lia said, her voice quiet but firm.

Toby stopped in his tracks and looked at Lia as if he'd forgotten she was there.

"Detective Dourson asked that you not talk. It could hurt the investigation." This was the third time she'd interrupted Toby's tirade and she expected no better results. *I need to get Peter to show me how to make "strong commands" like they teach in the academy. Then maybe I could get him to shut up.* She rubbed the base of her skull with her free hand, in the vain hope she could massage away the headache brewing there.

"Then why can't I give my damn statement so I can leave? I don't see why it matters. I already told you Leander did it. Leander was jealous of me. Anyway, I'm not saying anything that has to do with your investigation." He tilted his head at Lia. "You can take my statement. Then I could leave this miserable little room."

*Where's a Taser when you need one? Peter is so going to owe me after this.* "It wouldn't be official. They'd just make you do it over again."

"This sucks. Sucks! Sucks! Sucks!"

"They'll get to you as soon as they can. They need to protect the crime scene and take care of Dr. Lawrence first."

"You don't understand. This was supposed to be *my* night! My father must be pitching a fit outside."

She looked up in relief when a shadow fell across the doorway, then groaned when Hodgkins walked in, followed by Peter. It *would* be Hodgkins. It hadn't been so long since the detective dismissed her when she reported she was stalked by a man whose prior target wound up dead.

"I can't believe it Dourson, your girlfriend is taking witness statements. You're even stupider than I thought."

"I'm not taking anything," Lia said. "He's spewing and won't shut up."

Constance raised her head and blinked, her face wrinkled in concentration as if she weren't quite sure what she was seeing.

"Geoff, is he dead? Really dead?"

"Yes Ms. DeVries," Peter said gently.

"I don't know what to do. We have a concert to put on and I don't know what to do."

"There isn't going to be a concert tonight, Ms. DeVries," Hodgkins said. He stood over her, high enough that Constance couldn't see him roll his eyes. Still, it was as close as Lia had ever seen the man get to being compassionate.

*A bleeding heart, that man is.*

"I don't know why I have to be here. *I* didn't kill anyone." Toby said. "My father—"

"Will get to bail you out of jail if you don't shut your pie hole, Junior," Jarvis said.

Toby's expression was so affronted Lia had to stifle a laugh.

Lia caught Peter's eye. He gave her a minute shake of his head. *A warning? What's going on, Peter?*

"Lia, we're going to be here for hours. The school admin has agreed to take you home. Her name is Hannah. She has auburn hair and she's wearing a green coat. You'll find her out front."

She opened her mouth to speak, but Peter was giving her a hard look. She shoved the questions out of her head. "That's nice of her. So I can leave?"

"Hold your horses," Jarvis said. "We may want to talk to your girlfriend. I think she should stick around."

"Don't you have more important things to do? She has nothing to do with this and you know it."

"Whatever," Hodgkins said, narrowing his eyes at Lia. "We know where to find you. Scram."

Lia stood up, but was pulled back by the death grip Constance still held on her hand. She bent over and stroked the woman's fingers until they relaxed, then placed the hand gently in Constance's lap and made her escape.

LIA FOUND Hannah pacing under the porte cochère, one hand rubbing the opposite arm in a gesture of self-consolation. Her green duster was buttoned tight against the cold. The woven jacquard of her black silk dress caught the light as it skimmed over classic pumps. *Those shoes have to be killing her by now.*

A morgue wagon waited just beyond the circle of the exterior light. One attendant leaned against the vehicle and smoked while her partner sat inside the open rear doors, hands shoved in his coat pockets. *They look bored. No telling how long they'll have to wait for the go ahead to remove the body.*

A crime scene van and three police cars pulled in the drive. *Everyone wants in on this one.* "You look like you're ready to get out of here," Lia said. "Let's go before someone changes their mind."

The women walked past the influx of officers. Hannah stared out at the black maw of night that was the cemetery grounds. "I gave you those tickets thinking you would see one of our shows. Instead we saw one of Peter's."

"Funny how that happens. At least he got us out quicker than I expected."

Officers walked through the magnolia trees surrounding the chapel, flashlights sweeping back and forth in an eerie dance of lights as they searched for clues. It was like an art performance, except for the scratchy voices erupting at random from their radio handsets.

Light glowed through the windows of the gatehouse. At one time it had been a ladies' retiring room. Now it was an office for the security guards. Cal Hinkle's haystack hair was visible amid a cluster of young people in black clothes. *Poor guy. I bet they're giving him hell.*

Lia was surprised to find the parking lot still packed. She could see people sitting in the cars.

"Who do you think those cars belong to?" she asked.

"Parents," Hannah groaned. "They refuse to leave until they can take their children home."

Lia and her sister had grown up fending for themselves. She wondered what it would be like to have parents that were so protective.

Hannah stopped at the edge of the lot and looked back at the guard house. "I feel like I'm abandoning them."

"They won't let you talk to them. You'll be more help tomorrow if you've had some sleep."

"It feels wrong to be leaving. I don't know how much sleep I'll get." Hannah pulled her phone out of her pocket, looked at it. "Barely nine-thirty. Do you mind if we make a stop before I drop you off?"

"Sure. What do you need to do?"

"I need to pick up Geoff's dogs. Constance won't be sane enough to remember them until tomorrow. Buddy has epilepsy. He can't be alone overnight."

Hannah pointed her key fob at a tidy hatchback and clicked it. The car's lights flashed in response.

A tall man, taller than Peter with a striking mane of white hair, stepped out of a nearby Lexus and blocked their way.

"Mr. Grant, what can I do for you?" Hannah tilted her lips the fraction of an inch necessary to signal a conciliatory attitude. There was tension around her eyes.

"You can tell me why you're going home when my son is being kept in police custody, Ms. Kleemeyer."

"I'm not sure what you want me to do."

"You can find out why they're keeping him."

"Toby publicly accused one of the other performers of killing Dr. Lawrence. I imagine they want to find out what he knows. I'm sure the police won't tell me anything they wouldn't tell you or the dean. Suki is here, have you talked to her?"

"She's with the students. They won't let me in."

"I'm sorry," Hannah said, "but there's nothing I can do. Try her cell. I'm sure you have the number."

Hannah sidestepped Grant. Lia followed, taking a wide berth around the man's other side.

Lia looked over her shoulder as she fumbled the unfamiliar seatbelt into its clasp. Grant stood in the center of the lot, staring at them. His form receded in the darkness as Hannah pulled away. "Who is that man?"

"Tobias Grant, one of our donors. He funded your frieze."

"Seriously?" *I'm glad he doesn't know who I am. I hope it stays that way.*

"What's his story?" Lia asked.

"He developed an unhealthy interest in Hopewell after Toby started taking classes in high school. All the high muckety-mucks want to keep him and his deep pockets very happy."

"He doesn't look like the kind of man who would support a dubious career choice by his gay son."

"I don't know that he knows."

"How could you miss it?"

"Parental denial is a wonderful thing. Toby's mother gave up a career in opera to marry Tobias. Toby says it was the one thing she wanted, for him to have the career she sacrificed. Rumor is, she wouldn't marry Tobias Sr. until he put it in the prenup. She died a year ago, an overdose of alcohol mixed with prescription meds. Some say accident. Dark voices whisper of suicide. Darker voices say she was helped."

"What do you think?"

"I don't know what the truth is, but the only times I ever saw her smile were when Toby was on stage. I don't think she liked being Mrs. Grant very much."

"Oh, my."

"Oh, yes. Thus the *Requiem for All Souls.* The performance was to be dedicated to her memory. Are you familiar with All Souls Day?"

"It's a Catholic practice, isn't it?"

"Mostly, though other sects recognize it. It's a day of prayers for the departed who have gone on to purgatory, so that they might go to Heaven."

"Guilty conscience?"

"Some think so. Maybe he just loved her that much."

"Dr. Lawrence's Fur Boys, what do you think will happen to them?"

"I don't know. I'd love to keep them, but Constance might have other ideas."

"They're so adorable. Is Buddy's epilepsy the reason they come to school?"

"That, and Geoff was a total diva. That man never saw a boundary he didn't push or a situation he didn't twist to his own ends. It's not surprising someone conked him on the head. It's only surprising that it took so long for it to happen. God, I could tell you stories. ..."

"He seemed like such a nice man."

Hannah's mouth hardened in a grim line. "You've only seen his ever-so-charming public face. Geoff was so vindictive that if he ever got a hint of the things I knew about him, he'd have had my job, and made sure it would be hell for me to get another one. He's a malicious and whimsical little god, making and destroying careers at will."

"He had that much influence?"

"He had enough. One word from him could open doors or close them. And poor Leander has been under Geoff's thumb ever since they got together. Geoff promotes him, but will only allow him so far from the nest. If this had to happen, at least it happened while Leander is still young enough to have a real career."

"You don't believe he killed the professor like Toby said?"

"Toby." Hannah spat the name out like a bitter seed. "I'm sure he's making this entire catastrophe about him."

Lia recalled her torturous minutes at the mercy of the young man's histrionics. "You could say that. But could it be true?"

"I don't see how. I left the chapel with Leander and stayed with him until a few minutes before I saw you."

"If not Leander, then who could have done it?"

"That conversation could take a week," Hannah said as she turned into the long drive fronting a gray stone house on Clifton Avenue. "We're here."

Unlike the Victorian era homes that characterized Cincinnati, The Lawrence mansion had an unembellished, prison-like façade. This impression was enhanced by the ten acres of dead grass that comprised the lot.

"He lived here? You could build a housing development in the front yard."

"I expect that's what they'll do with it. The only way to get new construction in Clifton is to break up one of these old estates, and this is a prime location. Geoff doesn't have any heirs. There's no family to keep it intact."

Hannah pulled a keyring out of her purse as she marched up the steps of the house. Her actions were efficient, as if she'd walked up those steps so many times she didn't need to look where she was going. Claws scrabbled across the wood floors inside, punctuated with joyful yips. Hannah swung the huge, carved door open. Three furry cannonballs burst forth, dancing circles around Hannah as she entered the house. Hannah sank onto an opulent oriental runner and the trio competed to see who could wiggle their furry butt onto her lap first. Through some defiance of physics, they all fit. She buried her head in the mass of squirming fur.

"Poor babies, poor, poor orphaned babies. Auntie Hannah is going to take care of you now. It won't be as fancy as you're used to, but you'll be together as long as I can keep you that way."

Hannah kept her head down and began sobbing. Lia hesitated, then knelt beside Hannah and ran her hand down the woman's back. Hannah shook her head, sniffed and looked up.

"Sorry about that. There's always so much stress before the concert. Then Geoff is killed and I have no clue what's going on."

Buddy—at least Lia thought the white Bichon Frisé with the pink nose was Buddy—propped his forepaws on Hannah's chest and licked at the tears dripping off her chin. Rory—a Chihuahua whose tilted, buggy eyes reminded Lia of Harpo Marx—curled in Hannah's lap in a tight ball, reacting to her stress. An apricot miniature poodle with long, floppy ears nosed under the hand currently resting on Rory's back, demanding attention. That was Dasher, always at center stage.

"How could such sweet dogs belong to such a nasty man?" Hannah sighed.

"What did Dr. Lawrence do that was so awful?"

"He specializes in poison pen. He'll very sweetly agree to write a letter of recommendation for a student who has committed some ridiculous offense such as performing in someone else's concert without his blessing, then he'll blast them as uncooperative and unprofessional."

"How do you know this?" Lia asked.

"Any decent person will refuse to write a letter of recommendation for a student they can't support. The schools on the other end are sorting through the accolades and look for consistency in the letters as well as reading between the lines for what's not being said. It's rare to get a hatchet job.

"A teacher at a school that received one of his letters found it so vitriolic, she risked her job and contacted a teacher she knew here about it. She didn't know what to do with the information and asked me. We looked at it from all sides and decided that we couldn't expose him because breaking confidentiality would get us all fired, including the woman who called."

"And yet you're telling me."

Hannah shrugged. "He's dead. I don't have to put up with his games anymore. I suppose you could tell Peter, but what can he do with it? I haven't told you the name of the student or the university, and I won't. Besides, I know you don't want me fired. Who would make your green tea lattes?"

"It must have been awful working with someone like that."

"I coordinate events and activities that require input from a number of people to reach a consensus on the best schedule for everyone, and he will neglect to respond until I give up on him and put a schedule out for everyone to review. Then he'll dress me down for not considering the needs of his students. Only he won't just send it to me, he'll copy everyone in the group and he'll send blind copies to the director, the dean and the board of trustees."

"What a jerk," Lia said.

"He tried to get me fired early on. He was after Dr. Wingler, but he tossed me into the mix as if I had anything to do with it. All I do is follow directions."

"How did you make your peace with him?"

Hannah ruffled Dasher's head. The poodle stretched his head up in canine ecstasy, oblivious to Hannah's tenuous emotional state. It occurred to Lia that Dasher's lack of sensitivity might help Hannah regain her equilibrium.

"I let Geoff think I was terrified of him. It appeased him. That, and I watch these guys for him. He still likes to humiliate me by dressing me down in those nasty group emails, but the folks who matter know what's what so I don't worry about it."

"How did he keep his job?"

"He had a high profile. He drew students and donations. That, and he was never caught doing anything they could fire him for."

"Was he really that good?"

"He was careful to surround himself with true believers. His talent was choosing students any decent teacher could turn into a star, then taking credit for their success."

A TOUCH JOLTED Lia out of sleep. She lay still with her eyes open, adjusting to the darkness and making sense of the gentle hand on her back. She rolled over, shaking disturbing dream remnants from her mind. Peter's shadowy face hovered above hers as he sat beside her, hip to hip.

Honey, Lia's golden retriever, curled at the foot of the bed. The dog raised her head at the intrusion, huffed softly and rested her muzzle on her paws. Peter's border collie-chow mix, Viola, wiggled her way up the bedclothes and snuggled her head on Peter's lap in a bid to draw his attention away from Lia. He stroked the furry head much like he'd stroked Lia's back, to her amusement. Lia's self-contained schnauzer was missing. *Asleep on the couch. Typical.*

Peter leaned over and gave Lia a weary, thank-God-that's-over-and-now-I-get-to-be-with-you kiss. "Hi."

"Hi yourself." Lia stretched and yawned. "What time is it?"

"It's after two."

He was still dressed. Usually, Peter crawled into bed without waking her when work kept him out past midnight. But he hadn't stayed over in weeks. It looked like tonight wouldn't be any different.

"You coming to bed?"

"I just wanted to check in before I headed over to the house."

Lia had bought the house a few months earlier, using a cash reward she received after inadvertently cracking a cold case. The brick Victorian had been converted into two apartments decades earlier, an occurrence so common in Northside that such houses were referred to as "two families."

Peter would live on the second floor after they finished fixing it up. Lia insisted on maintaining the division because she needed a measure of personal space. It was a need she was certain Peter didn't understand, though he accepted it. *Mostly.*

Peter now slept in the basement due to the threat of copper thieves to any vacant house in the area. Thieves would spend hours ripping out old plumbing to reap a few hundred dollars in scrap metal while incurring tens of thousands of dollars in damage. Peter had been chasing them for months.

"Stupid copper thieves. Will you stop this when I get the alarm installed?"

"Maybe. Depends. I won't be comfortable until one of us moves in."

"I hate thinking about you alone on an inflatable bed in your Boy Scout sleeping bag."

He traced a finger down her cheek. "It's temporary."

Lia sat up in bed, rearranging her pillow behind her back. "What was that business about Hannah, acting like I didn't know who she was?"

"I didn't want Hodgkins to realize how tuned in you are at Hopewell. It would complicate things."

"I'm not that tuned in. I painted Dr. Lawrence's dogs and I'm painting a frieze for the school. It's not like I know anything."

"Uh huh. And Hannah didn't spill her guts on the drive home?"

Lia gave him a sideways, bug-eyed look worthy of Rory. "You did that on purpose! You set me up so I could gather intel for you!"

"Anyone would need to talk after an experience like that. I figured she'd open up with you. Did it work?"

Lia shook her head at the strangeness of the night. "I've known Hannah for weeks and she never said boo about Dr. Lawrence. Now he's dead and she couldn't stop talking."

"Tell me about it.'"

"Nope. You set me up and you didn't let me in on the gag."

"Don't I get any points for sneaking you out before Heckle and Jeckle decided to do the Chinese water torture on you?"

"Nuh-uh."

"Not even if I ask nicely?"

"Hah."

Peter exhaled audibly. "Doesn't matter. It's their case now, and they aren't going to let me near it. If we hadn't been so overrun with witnesses, they wouldn't have let me take statements tonight. I could hand them a signed confession from the killer and they'd disregard it just because I was the one who gave it to them."

"You aren't going to coerce me?"

"You want coercion? I'll give you coercion." Peter's voice was low and menacing. He lunged at Lia, dislodging Viola as his fingers dove under the covers, tickling Lia until she shrieked. Viola slouched away in disgust.

"Stop, stop," Lia gasped, catching her breath. "Did you learn anything tonight?"

Peter sat back. "The entire world will mourn the loss of one of classical music's brightest lights. This is the day that music died. The man was a saint and his death is a tragedy second only to the crucifixion."

"Do tell."

"College girls lean to melodrama. There was also a lot of sighing about his oh, so romantic looks and personal charisma."

"Hannah tells a different story."

"Oh?"

"Geoffrey Lawrence had a dark side and liked to use his power for evil whenever possible."

"Really?"

"According to Hannah," Lia said.

"What powers could a voice professor possibly use for evil purposes?"

"Getting people fired, ruining careers before they get started, that sort of thing."

"Funny, she didn't tell me any of that."

"Did you ask her?"

"Well, no, not for a preliminary statement."

"Apparently she was ready to crack. She had a minor meltdown at the professor's house."

Peter drew back, blinking. "What were you doing at the house?"

"She needed to pick up his dogs. One of them is epileptic and can't be left alone for too long."

"How did you get in?"

"She has a key. She watched the dogs for him. They're as much her dogs as his, from what I could see. They were all over her the minute she opened the door."

"I can't believe this," Peter muttered.

"Why are you upset?"

"We have no idea who did this. There hasn't been time for anyone to search his house."

"Does that matter? He wasn't killed there."

"She could have tampered with evidence. She had no business going there without a police escort. Dammit."

"Peter, relax. She picked up some kibble, the dog beds, and Buddy's meds. Then we left. I was with her the entire time."

"Hodgkins will file a complaint."

"How can he complain about you? You didn't know."

"He'll find a way."

# 2

# THURSDAY, NOVEMBER 3

Pink clouds with a hint of peach streaked the sunrise when Lia hoisted herself on top of her favorite picnic table at Mount Airy Dog Park. It was a gorgeous color, exactly the shade of guava pulp, and it lifted Lia's spirits.

The table was already occupied by Lia's best friend. Bailey Hughes was an odd juxtaposition of graceful hands and blunt speech that Lia enjoyed. Both the woman and her hound, Kita, were lanky with reddish hair. Lia often wondered if Bailey was aware of the resemblance.

Bailey munched on an apple, feeding slivers of it to Kita while she watched Terry Dunn, a park regular bearing a strong resemblance to the elder Teddy Roosevelt. Terry dragged a fan-shaped, fallen bough while three dogs attacked the trailing ends. Terry let go of the branch.

The dogs proceeded to play tug of war and wound up going in circles. Jackson, a hound mix, and Fleece, a border collie, joined forces. They shook off a small terrier mix named Penny who followed, barking furiously.

Terry's roommate, Steve Reams, attacked another piece of dead wood with a hatchet at the picnic table nearest one of the two remaining grills at the former picnic area. The two men were alike enough that Lia privately thought of them as Tweedledee and Tweedledum.

Terry was a walking Wikipedia with a brush mustache. Steve was round and friendly and sported a Van Dyke beard. Despite similarities in age and appearance, the pair were philosophical and political opposites. No one understood how they stayed friends, or even how they refrained from killing each other.

A retired engineer named Jim McDonald layered wood in the grill. He was scruffy in both speech and appearance but his long, bearded face enfolded kind eyes. He always carried a walking stick, a honeysuckle branch stripped of bark. This habit always made Lia think of Saint Francis of Assisi when she saw him walking the park with his dogs, Chester and Fleece.

Lia nodded at the men. "I see the cold snap inspired the guys to build a fire. You're not helping?"

Bailey stuffed the apple core in her pocket, producing a second apple in the process. "Nah. Building a fire is such a nerd-manly thing to do. It would crush them if they found out I can do it better."

"You're all heart."

"Not really. It'll be more fun to burst their illusions in February, when it's too cold for an amateur to get a fire going."

"Will you be here in February?" Bailey had a small gardening business that she'd recently closed for the winter. Soon she'd head to Tennessee to spend the next several months in a Persephone arrangement with her boyfriend, a hacker who went by the nom de guerre "Trees."

"Probably not. I might make a special trip if humiliating the guys is involved. How long do you suppose it will take for Jim and Terry to start arguing over how to build it?"

Lia eyed the men. They looked peaceful enough for the moment. "Shame there isn't anyone else here this morning. You could take bets."

Bailey hopped off the table. "I'm going to freeze if I sit here waiting for them to get it going. Come walk with me."

Six of the more than 1400 acres of urban forest that was Mount Airy Forest had been fenced and dedicated to canine recreation. Though now somewhat shabby in comparison with newer parks—especially the hipster canine haven at downtown's Washington Park with its signature water feature—the presence of a picnic shelter, restrooms, year-round water pumps, tables, and numerous lichen-covered shade trees provided functionality other parks lacked.

The repurposed picnic area ran along a ridge at the highest elevation in the forest and was aptly named "High Point." A narrow parking lot ran below the ridge, with a service road at the back that curved up the rise to a brick picnic shelter wedged between the two enclosures that made up the park.

Honey raced up, presenting Lia with a Lucy ball. Lucy balls were a recent, unofficial perk at the park. Lucy's owners honored her passing with regular deliveries of a dozen tennis balls. Nobody would have known where the balls came from except for the basket attached to the notice board beneath a photo of the golden retriever and an explanation of the bequest.

Sometimes all the balls were in the basket when Lia

arrived. Sometimes they peppered the park like Easter eggs and Honey nosed among them, sniffing each until she found one that satisfied some mysterious canine criteria. Today was an Easter egg day.

Lia slipped the ball into the cup of her ball launcher, then winged it down the back slope of the park. Honey shot off like a rocket with Kita in hot pursuit. The ball was drenched in dog slobber when Honey dropped it at Lia's feet. Lia extended the launcher to pick up the tennis ball.

Bailey took a bite of her apple. "I'm convinced they invented those things so you don't have to touch dog drool. The fact that it gives you extra leverage is just an excuse."

Lia stopped to search the fence line for Chewy. Chewy was off on his daily patrol of the perimeter, ostensibly keeping the park safe from invading squirrels and aliens. Lia suspected he was secretly looking for an opportunity to taunt the coyotes that occasionally appeared outside the fence.

Lia knew every dog in the park and Chewy was in no danger. Still, that half second of worry made her think about Dr. Lawrence's dogs. What if something happened to her and Honey and Chewy had to be separated? *Not going to happen. I won't let it.*

Lia spotted a Lucy ball in the grass and popped it into her launcher. Honey dropped the ball in her mouth and readied to run instead of playing keep away with the ball she had.

"Retriever logic," Lia said. "A ball in the launcher is worth two in the mouth."

"So true. How was the concert last night?"

"You didn't hear? It was on the news."

"Like I watch the news?"

"We arrived in time to discover the conductor's body in the chapel. The only performance was given by the witnesses Peter had me babysit. One of them wouldn't stop crying and the other acted like he was the victim."

"No! Who did it?"

"My drama queen claimed the conductor's lover did it, but someone else told me that wasn't possible. The professor wasn't well liked. The list of suspects is almost as long as the list of people who were on the scene when we found the body."

"Sounds insane. How are you holding up?"

"I'm okay now. I was a bit shaky last night. I had no idea how crazy it could get."

"Some date night," Bailey said. "I guess Peter's going to be absent for a while."

"Nope. Heckle and Jeckle have it."

"Aren't those the guys who had Desiree's murder?"

"Yep."

"Good luck solving it."

Lia tossed another ball for Honey. "I don't understand why they were accepted into the homicide unit when Peter is so much smarter than they are."

"I could do a reading around it, why he's not in the unit and what he needs to do to get ahead, that sort of thing."

"You want to read Tarot cards for Peter's career? Why?"

Bailey shrugged. "It would be interesting and I need the practice."

"What do you need practice for?"

"I'm getting certified as a Tarot reader."

"You're kidding."

"Not kidding. I'll be 55 this year. Unless I want to expand and hire young backs to do the work for me—which

I don't, I need to find something else. Shame Peter isn't on that murder case, I could help him narrow down suspects."

"He has other cases. If you ask nice, he might let you help him catch his copper thieves. Then maybe he'd stop sleeping in the basement."

"Hail," Terry said, dragging the now fractured bough past Lia and Bailey while Penny, Fleece, and Jackson snapped at twigs. "Will you join us for the lighting of the inaugural fire?"

"Why not." Lia turned and tossed a ball in the direction of the grill, an iron box on a pole typical of older parks. She and Bailey fell in step beside Terry. "You do know, by the time you get your fire lit it will be time to leave."

Terry grinned. "Not true. What I want to know is, what's happening with the corpse du jour? A shining light of classical music bludgeoned to death in Spring Grove Cemetery." Terry wiggled his eyebrows at Lia. "Quite evocative."

"Lia and Peter were there when they found the body," Bailey said.

"Indeed?" Terry said. "Are detectival pursuits afoot?" He dropped the bough at Steve's feet, then headed for the grill to look over Jim's shoulder. "Ah, coming along, I see." He reached out to move a branch in Jim's carefully erected edifice, but snatched his hand back when Jim gave him a withering look.

"Not Peter's case," Lia said. She wondered how many times she would say that in the next week.

"How can that be?" Terry asked.

Jim flicked a lighter under the grate. The flame caught on wadded paper and crawled up the surrounding tinder. Then it died.

It took all three men several minutes of intense argument and consultation before the fire caught. The blossoming flames were a mesmerizing sight. *More effort than it's worth, but pretty.*

"That's District Five and Peter was there," Steve said. "Why wouldn't it be his case?"

"Because they re ... re—" Jim said.

"Restructured?" Bailey suggested.

"Rearranged the department," Jim said. "Homicide cases have their own department now."

"Bah. Bureaucratic nonsense. Peter's the obvious man for the job. What else does he have to do with his time?" Terry said.

"There are other crimes to solve besides homicides," Lia said, wondering why she felt the need to defend Peter.

"None worthy of our stalwart detective," Terry said, jabbing a gloved index finger in the air.

"You just want an excuse to get involved," Bailey said.

"And why not? Every citizen should be willing to contribute to public safety."

Steve snorted. "Is that what you were doing when you were almost arrested last summer?"

"A mere misstep."

"Hah," Steve said. "I bet the reason they didn't promote Peter to the new unit was to keep you from poking your nose in their investigations."

Bailey's eyes went wide. "Goddess, Lia. Do you think we ruined Peter's chance at a promotion?"

"I don't see how. Brent would never rat you out. If anyone killed his promotion it was me."

LIA STOOD on a portable scaffold in the Hopewell recital hall, adding green tendrils to morning glory vines when Hannah approached.

"Care for a break? I just made a pot of chai ... I've got biscotti," Hannah wheedled, waving the pastry in a tempting manner.

Honey roused from her nap and met Lia at the base of the scaffold. She leaned against Lia, beating the back of Lia's legs with her wagging tail while looking up at her with an I'm-such-a-good-girl-I-know-you-want-to-share look. Chewy trotted up to Hannah and sat, confident a gourmet duck treat would jump from one of her copious pockets and into his mouth.

The recently renovated hall had newly upholstered seats, new carpet, and a state-of-the-art, computerized lighting system. Lia's frieze, a narrow painting of morning glory and trumpet vines circling the hall, was the icing on the cake. Geoff Lawrence had arranged the commission after she'd painted the Fur Boys, a gift from Constance.

"Join me in the office?" Hannah asked. "There's no one to man the phones except me."

The Fur Boys left their tapestried pillows under Hannah's desk as soon as she opened the door to the office, gathering at her feet like sycophants of the highest order while she pet each in turn and doled out duck treats.

Toll paid, Hannah poured chai from a Bodum coffee press into a pair of hand-painted mugs decorated with peonies. She set out the biscotti, then broke off bits from the end of one to feed the dogs now crowded on her lap.

Lia handed a bit of biscotti to Honey, who gobbled it down before proceeding to lick the crumbs off Lia's hand. "Thank you for letting me bring the dogs."

"They're no trouble at all, and we're used to it."

Dasher, the most outgoing of the Fur Boys, head bumped Hannah's hand for a treat. Chewy, insulted that Dasher was using his signature move, head bumped Hannah's other hand, causing her latte to slop over the rim. Reflexes honed by Chewy's habit of unfortunate timing, Lia grabbed a napkin and blotted Hannah's skirt.

"Sorry about that. ... This place is deserted. Where is everybody?"

"Classes are cancelled for the rest of the week out of respect for Geoff, but people are still calling in to find out what's going to happen with him gone. It's a disaster. He was in charge of half of the school and had his hands in everything. His students—they auditioned to work with him and he got the cream of the crop. Our other teachers are booked solid."

"There's no way we can come up with a stellar voice coach, now that the semester is half over. That means our rising stars are out on their collective asses in the cold unless we can come up with a miracle. These students expect the best. They paid for the best."

"Is it that important who their teacher is?"

Hannah rolled her eyes. "It's like fraternities—no, more like the bloodlines of royal dynasties. Who you studied with means everything."

"I had no idea. Art isn't like that. A well-connected teacher can introduce you to the right people, but it's not life or death."

"Artists can work alone. Performers need people unless they're buskers or street corner mimes. You add people, you get politics. There are lots of galleries but few big performance spaces. The competition for parts is blood thirsty."

"You think someone killed Professor Lawrence over a part?"

"No, I don't. Killing Geoff also killed *Faust*. It's not like we have someone waiting in the wings to take over for him, never mind someone who would cast the show differently. Someone might poison their competition, but they wouldn't scuttle the show. That defeats the purpose. And *Faust* is the only production Geoff had in the works worth killing for."

"Do they do that? Poison each other?"

"There are rumors. Nasty tricks to ensure less competition when there's an opening in someone's studio. We know it goes on from time to time but it's impossible to prove. It's also impossible to ignore when a talented newcomer is hospitalized with food poisoning hours before their audition."

Hannah looked out the office window. "It's ironic, someone sending Geoff to purgatory on All Souls Day. It was hell to put that concert together on such short notice."

"I thought Dr. Lawrence put it together."

Hannah spewed out her chai. "Where did you get that idea?"

"Well ... I just assumed."

"He selects the music, the performers, and conducts the pieces. The rest—arranging the venue and making sure we have everything we need, all the communication, the advertising, even designing the posters—is dumped on me."

"I had no idea. Why such short notice?"

"Toby's father wanted it. You remember him."

"How could I forget?"

"He commissioned the performance and promised to fund *Faust*. He even promised to get Music Hall for it. Geoff likes Fauré's *Requiem,* but *Faust* was his baby. Music Hall sent him over the moon."

Hannah put on her best high tea accent and crooked a pinky. "Tobias Grant is a veddy impawtawnt personage," She rolled her eyes, resuming her normal voice. "And he makes sure we *all* know it."

"Toby said he was supposed to be the soloist at Wednesday's concert. Whose decision was that?"

"It was Geoff's, but he's—he was—very aware of which side his bread was buttered on."

"And the lead for *Faust?* Was that pre-ordained?"

"I'm sure Toby was in the running, but Geoff would never make a choice that would damage his own reputation. He would have waited to see how Toby did last night. *Faust* would be a huge step and Toby doesn't have the chops that Geoff normally expected from a lead, not for a production the size of *Faust.* He might have hired a pro instead of casting a student."

"Like who?"

"Leander, maybe. It would be like him to toss Leander a plum role to keep him mollified, and Leander would be terrific."

"I've been here for weeks," Lia said. "Why are you so chatty all of a sudden?"

"We went through the fire last night." Hannah clinked mugs with Lia. "We're sisters in arms now."

Someone rapped "Shave and a Haircut" on the door-jamb, interrupting their conversation.

Hodgkins and Jarvis strolled into the office, still wearing the suits they'd had on the night before. Lia wondered if they'd been to bed. Jarvis's eyes widened in an aborted double take when he saw Lia.

"Hanging out where you don't belong again, Ms. Thinks-She's-a-Detective?"

Lia caught Hannah giving her a confused look out of the corner of her eye, but stayed focused on the men. "Detective Jarvis means me. … I'm not snooping. I'm painting a frieze for the school. Hannah and I were taking a break." She dusted off her hands and stood up. Honey and Chewy popped to their feet, ready to follow. "But it's time for me to get back to work."

"Hold on, Missy. Why didn't your boyfriend tell us you worked here?"

"I have no idea. You might ask him."

"Please stay," Hannah asked. Rory shivered in Hannah's lap, staring at the strange men with his slanted, buggy eyes. Dasher and Buddy jumped down and crowded around her feet, growling. Hannah bent over to reassure the dogs. "Shhh. It's all right. You don't need to be afraid."

"I suspect the detectives would prefer to speak to you alone," Lia said.

"Don't go too far. We need to talk to you, too," Hodgkins said.

HECKLE AND JECKLE joined her twenty minutes later. Lia called down from her scaffold, "Sorry, my paint's drying. I can't stop now." She didn't bother to tell them that the oils would be viable for several hours.

Hodgkins yelled at her back. "Take a message back to your boyfriend. He isn't part of this investigation. You are not his spy and …"

Lia let the rant go in one ear and out the other. When

she was sure they were gone, she wiped her brushes and scrambled to the floor. She found Hannah at her desk, chai in hand, a vertical line pinched above her nose.

"I see you survived," Lia said.

"Barely. Morons. What was that business about Peter?"

"Peter says it was hate at first sight between him and Hodgkins, and Jarvis goes along with anything Hodgkins wants. Peter and Brent call them Heckle and Jeckle. They cut Peter out every chance they get."

"Why isn't it Peter's case? He was there first."

"Murder cases go to the homicide unit. The unit can use local detectives or not, but it's their show. As long as those two are in charge, Peter is persona non grata."

"That stinks. I liked Peter. I felt a lot of confidence in him."

PETER WATCHED as Captain Ann Parker stood at the entrance of the narrow room District Five laughingly called the bull pen, searching the jumble of desks crammed along the walls. She hadn't been with District Five long enough to know where all her detectives sat. Peter suspected she was looking for him.

She was a tall woman of military carriage and handsome, androgynous features. Despite being in her forties, she continued to qualify for SWAT every year though her responsibilities kept her from participating in call-outs. She told anyone who asked that she expected to go through the door like any of her men when the need arose. No-nonsense did not begin to describe her.

Captain Parker had taken over command of District Five

a few weeks earlier. Peter wasn't sure what to expect when she leveled her direct gaze at him, though her expression said she would tolerate no less than full and immediate compliance.

She extended one hand toward Peter and Brent and twitched her index finger in a "come here" gesture. She pivoted and strode out of the room, as if certain the men would follow her. They always did. She could kick their asses and they all knew it.

Peter and Brent put their computers to sleep and went, giving each other uh-oh looks.

"We knew this was coming," Brent said, voice low. Peter knew Brent feared super hearing was one of Parker's powers. They passed through a gauntlet of speculative looks and snickers from the other detectives as they exited the bullpen. "Assholes," Brent said as they stepped into the hall.

Peter shook his head. "Damned if you do, damned if you don't. No way around it once H and J were brought in."

They caught up with Parker in her inner sanctum. She was already seated at her desk, an inquiring expression on her face. Peter and Brent took the pair of visitor's chairs in front of the desk and waited for her to speak.

"Tell me about last night." Parker's face was impassive, giving away nothing she knew, felt, or concluded about their involvement with the Lawrence case. *That woman has the best damned cop face of anyone I know.*

"Where do you want us to start?" Peter asked.

"The beginning is often a fine place."

"My girlfriend, Lia, you've met her—she had tickets to a choral concert at Norman Chapel …"

Peter relayed events with Brent fleshing out details as needed.

"So you came upon a crime scene; you contained it; you called for backup; you culled out witnesses and got rid of anyone who did not need to be interviewed immediately; and you kept a panic from destroying the scene. You made sure wits talked to each other as little as possible and you started taking statements, all before the assigned detectives arrived. Sounds very efficient to me."

"Thank you, sir," Peter said.

"I'm sure you realize there has been grumbling from downtown," she said.

"We did consider that possibility," Brent said.

"Still you acted to the full extent of your abilities."

"Yes, ma'am—sir."

"Is it true you were interviewing one witness in front of another witness when Hodgkins and Jarvis arrived?"

"Porter was on the premises at the time of the murder," Brent said. "We needed to be sure the killer wasn't nearby. We didn't take time for niceties."

"He doesn't sound like much of a witness."

"That was our assessment, sir."

"Hodgkins and Jarvis transferred to Homicide before I took over here. But I can read between the lines in the old case reports. The Willis case, there was some conflict there?"

"Yes, sir."

"And Lia was involved?"

"Not by choice, sir."

"They'll say you overstepped your authority last night. Did you?"

"We provided leadership until the assigned detectives arrived, then we turned over command," Peter said, sitting as tall as he could in the squishy visitor's chair. He wondered if she chose those chairs for the purpose of putting subordinates at a disadvantage. She seemed too straightforward to resort to that kind of manipulation, but you couldn't discount the effect.

"I can't fault you. Procedures for the centralized units to interact with the districts have yet to be established. I won't be surprised if there's a pissing contest brewing. I'll do my best to deal with it, but we may have to have a meet and sing Kumbaya."

"One more thing, sir," Peter said.

"Yes?"

"Lia has a mural commission at Hopewell. That's how she got the tickets. Last night the admin drove her home since I was working the scene."

Parker shrugged. "Understandable."

"They went to Lawrence's house."

"Why did they do that?"

Peter was struck by the difference between Parker and his former captain. Roller would have erupted in a cacophony of profanity if Peter made that report to him.

"Ms. Kleemeyer was concerned about Lawrence's dogs. One of them is epileptic. She removed them from the house."

"You released two witnesses and they went straight to the home of the deceased, before the assigned detectives were able to search it?"

"Yes, sir."

"Did you know they were going to do this?"

"No sir. Hannah didn't tell Lia until they were at her car."

Parker drummed her fingers on the desk, the sound like rapid hoofbeats. Peter waited, off balance by his inability to read her. He noted that her nails were trimmed down to the quick, clean and bare. *A lot like the woman.*

Parker sighed. "Did Lia keep Ms. Kleemeyer in sight while they were on the property?"

"Yes, sir. They took the dogs and some food, bedding, that sort of thing. Lia said they went into the living room and kitchen, nowhere else."

"And took nothing else? She wasn't using this as an excuse to search for something?"

"Lia said she went directly to the cupboard where the dogs' things were kept and nowhere else. There was no searching."

"Looks like you already asked the important questions. Nothing to be done about it. It would have been better if they'd asked for a police escort."

"Yes, sir."

"Expect bellyaching."

"Yes, sir."

"Dourson, you were offered a position in Homicide. Your actions last night suggest you're well qualified for it. Why are you still here?"

"The occasional murder is interesting and challenging, but all death, all the time is not my ideal career path."

"Some people would call that lazy."

"I like being part of a community, sir. The homicide unit has no connection with the people they serve."

Parker waved a dismissive hand in the air. "Get those reports uploaded, and make sure there is no cause for complaint in them. Davis, the reports you filed under Roller had a tendency to slide into innuendo. Do not do this, no matter how richly warranted. Capiche?"

"Yes, sir," Peter and Brent said simultaneously.

Brent steered Peter outside. He paced the lot, running a hand through his hair, sending the expensive cut into disorder. "After that I need a little fresh air. I felt my balls shriveling, despite the fact she's backing us up. I hope I never make her angry."

"The guys in SWAT call her The Rock."

"I don't doubt it."

"She's tough, but I think she'll be fair. Roller was a knee jerk commander. When the shit started flying you never knew where it would land," Peter said.

"Roller would have fried our asses at the first complaint out of Homicide before asking us what happened."

Peter stared into the woods behind District Five, thinking. "Why do you suppose she didn't have Cynth in there with us?"

"I bet they know each other from SWAT qualifications. Right now, they're laughing their asses off at us."

## 3

# FRIDAY, NOVEMBER 4

LIA STROKED A PRUSSIAN BLUE GLAZE ON THE UNDERSIDE OF A trumpet flower. She stepped back the two steps allowed on her scaffold to consider the effect when a voice drifted up from the floor of the recital hall.

"Hello. Can you take a break?"

Lia looked down to see Constance's hesitant and hopeful expression. Despite her recent loss, the woman's appearance was faultless, her dark hair in a gleaming French twist, her face a porcelain perfection hovering over an understated black dress. Lia reached back to touch the messy knot she'd secured with a paintbrush and only remembered when it was too late that she still had a wet brush in her hand. *Dammit, I would be using oils.*

"Give me a minute." Lia gave one more swipe of paint to the flower, then wiped her brush and snugged it between the coils of a spring-like rack that held dirty brushes suspended in mineral spirits. She cleaned her hands with a baby wipe, then climbed down the end of the scaffold.

Constance sat in the first row of seats, petting Honey and Chewy. "Don't you get nervous, up high like that? I would."

"I'm okay as long as I have a good platform to stand on. This one is very solid. What can I do for you?"

"Come sit down." Constance patted the seat on her right. The one on her left held a carryout tray containing two Styrofoam cups and a white paper bag that smelled like Heaven.

"Hannah says you don't drink coffee or black tea. I hope a green tea latte is okay?"

"That's very thoughtful of you. What smells so wonderful?"

"Chocolate croissants."

"Really? What did I do to deserve this?"

"I just want to say thank you for being so kind Wednesday night."

Lia mentally kicked herself for her uncharitable thoughts. *Maybe it's like the momentary insanity parents experience when their baby has a screaming fit and I didn't really mean it.* "I'm sure anyone else would have done the same."

"I don't think so. You had your hands full between me and Toby. I would have run screaming if it had been me."

"I'll say you're welcome if that will get me one of those croissants."

Constance produced the pastry with a flourish like a magician pulling a rabbit out of his hat and added a napkin. Lia took a bite of the still-warm croissant. The dark chocolate filling melted against her tongue, a pleasure just short of sex. Lia decided she liked Constance after all.

"This is wonderful. How are you holding up?"

Constance kept her eyes on the napkin she was

unfolding on her lap. "Conflicted. Geoff was a difficult man to live with. He didn't stop being difficult when we divorced. Part of me is relieved that he can't play around with my life anymore, and part of me remembers that he was everything to me for a very long time. I will miss his brilliance."

Lia considered Constance over the rim of her latte. She barely knew the woman. Prior experience taught Lia that she could not always trust her instincts. Still, some kind of connection had been born Wednesday night. *Some bonding experience, discovering a corpse.*

Lia scratched Chewy behind the ears while she decided what to say. The woman needed to talk, but how much would she be ready to hear?

"I felt so guilty after Luthor was murdered. It happened right after I split with him, and it was staged to look like suicide. I was torn up for weeks. I know how it feels to miss someone who was toxic to you, while hating yourself because in a small place deep in your heart, you're relieved it's over."

"How did you ever resolve it?"

"I wish I could say it helped when I found out it wasn't suicide, but it didn't, not much. Peter made the difference. He's such a good guy. He has his faults but he loves me in a way that Luthor never could. Letting myself love Peter allowed me to see my relationship with Luthor for what it was, how he manipulated me and how I let him."

"Peter? The nice detective at the chapel?"

"Yes. I met him while he was investigating Luthor's death."

Constance tipped one corner of her mouth up in a sad smile. "How is it that we don't see controlling men for who they are? That we allow them to make us settle for less than a whole relationship?"

"I don't know your story. I've been terrified of relationships all my life. It was easier for me to be with a hot guy who was all about himself, someone who wanted an audience, than to be with someone who expected intimacy."

"That's very deep, and sadly cynical."

"It's a form of abuse when a relationship is all about one person, but sometimes you're the one abusing yourself. Luthor was selfish and amoral but I can't say he was ever malicious. I had my own reasons for choosing him, and I've been in therapy working that out. I colluded because his narcissism kept him from really seeing me. It enabled me to keep the core of myself safe and private."

"You sound very self-aware."

"I have an excellent therapist."

"Are you still terrified?"

"I'm learning to manage it."

Constance brushed the nonexistent crumbs from her fingers onto the napkin covering her lap, then balled up the napkin and dropped it in the bag. Lia suspected Constance tidied up to give herself time to think.

"I met Geoffrey in college. He was so handsome." Constance's face went soft and wistful. "I was swept away by his talent, and by the way he looked at me. He made me feel like I was the only person in the room, the building, even on the planet. It was years before I realized that some people become skilled in making others feel special because they feed on seeing their own reflection in your eyes. It was even longer before I saw the malice in him. I used to take everything he said as gospel, and his criticisms as meant to improve me when they were really his way to kill my confidence and keep me dependent on him. I thought, 'This amazing, brilliant man wants to take plain, ordinary me along on his trip to the stars.'"

"You were crazy about him."

"Yes, I was. Then middle age came along and I woke up married to an over-rated diva with a penchant for stomping on ant-hills."

"Yet you continued your connection to him."

"To an extent. Geoff is one of those people it's safer to keep close to you so they can't sneak up on you in the dark."

"Do you think you'll ever marry again?"

"I didn't dare think of it as long as Geoff was alive. Anyone marrying me would be taking him on as well. Geoff might stand for an amicable dissolution of our marriage—he had to. He wouldn't risk the effect my testimony might have on his reputation if we went to court. But by the same token I could not be free of him. While he could accept me leaving him, he would not stand for me replacing him. He would have made any happiness I tried to create with another man impossible."

"Where do you go from here?"

Constance shook her head. Her laugh was quiet and mirthless. "I hardly know. I'm fully on my own for the first time in my life. A lot depends on his will. Geoff promised he would always take care of me, but he never would say exactly what that meant."

**Ask Sandy Wilson how she lost her job. Then ask where she was Wednesday night.**

PETER STARED at the email on his computer. "What the hell is this?"

Brent rolled his chair over and peered at the screen. "Who is Sandy Wilson and why do we care?"

"Wednesday night. ... Has to be about Lawrence."

"Who's it from?"

"SomeoneWhoCares." Peter clicked "reply" then typed in, "Who are you?" He sent it off. "Five gets you ten it bounces and the account is deleted.

Peter's computer dinged. The email read: "Someone who cares."

"Well, duh." Peter typed in "Meet me" and clicked send.

Brent left the bullpen to brew a pot of coffee. Peter was still staring at an empty inbox when he returned with a fresh cup.

"Why send it to you? How do you suppose they got your email address?"

"I announced my name at the scene. Anyone who wanted to send me a message could have gone to the department website and checked out the contact emails. They'd see we all use first name dot last name. It's not rocket science."

"It has to be someone who was at the chapel."

"Most likely. They could have talked to someone who was there, but chances are they were on scene.

"We could have Cynth trace it," Brent said.

"I may do that, though I don't expect much. It will come back from a public hotspot. If they sent it from the library, they probably sat in their car and never walked inside. If we find the place, we might learn something from security footage, but I'd be surprised if someone who went to this much trouble didn't avoid cameras."

"What are you going to do with it? It doesn't mention Lawrence. H and J will toss it as a crank tip. Or they'll throw it back at you and tell you to check it out after you finish emptying the bedpans."

"If we hand it to Cynth, we're creating a record of active participation in a case that's not ours. I'd rather find out if it's anything before I open up a stink pot—no pun intended." He took out his cell phone and tapped Lia's smiling face.

LIA SIGHED, irritated when the theme from *The Good, the Bad, and the Ugly* sounded from her pocket. That it was Peter's ringtone made the interruption slightly less annoying. She set her palette on the inverted milk crate she used as a makeshift work table and fished out her phone.

"What's up, Kentucky Boy?"

"Where are you?"

"Twelve feet in the air. Where did you expect me to be?"

"Are you up for a little social engineering?"

"I seem to recall someone wanting me to butt out of his cases."

"That's another conversation. I got an anonymous tip and I need to know if it's anything or nothing. You said Hannah knows everyone.

"At Hopewell? Sure."

Peter told her about the email. "Can you work this Sandy into the conversation next time you talk?"

Lia rolled her eyes. "Why don't I just ask her?"

"I don't want her to know it's part of an investigation— especially one I'm not supposed to be doing."

"I'll figure a way around it." She looked at her phone. Time to take the dogs for a pee break. She could swing by the office on her way back.

Hannah was crooning over the Fur Boys and feeding them tidbits when Lia entered the office. She gave Dasher a last pet and poured Lia a cup of chai. Lia took a few sips and exchanged pleasantries, choosing her moment.

"Tell me about Sandy Wilson."

Hannah's eyebrows popped up. "Why are you asking about Sandy?"

Lia shrugged. "I heard her name in the hall. I thought it might have something to do with Professor Lawrence."

"I doubt it. It's been more than five years."

"Who was she? A student?"

Hannah shook her head. "She was the admin before me."

"How did she get along with Dr. Lawrence?"

"From what I heard, she got along fine with everyone."

"Was there anything unusual about the way she left?"

"Why do you want to know? It's very left field."

Lia paused, wondering if she could trust Hannah. "Can I tell you something in confidence? As in stick-a-needle-in-your-eye, pinky-swear confidence?"

Hannah ruffled Dasher's ears. "What do you think, precious? This sounds ominous. Do I want to know?"

The apricot poodle panted up at Hannah.

"Dasher says you can tell me as long as it won't interfere with his supper."

"Dasher's dinner is safe. Peter got an anonymous tip. It didn't say anything except to look at Sandy. He doesn't want to dig into it unless he knows it's relevant."

"Everything I know is gossip. I heard they made her quit. I don't know why. There's a picture of her, from some event. She's cute, like a chipmunk. Same color hair. She doesn't look like a person who could bludgeon someone to death, but I never knew her."

Lia thought about Luthor. She hadn't believed any of her friends were capable of murder, and it almost got her killed. "People can hide who they are."

Hannah shook her head, disagreeing. "I only knew Sandy from the notes in her files, but she was just a secretary. She took messages, she passed them along. My impression of her was of a simple soul who went home at night and watched *Mike & Molly* reruns. She didn't secretly run things."

"You mean like you?"

Hannah laughed. "I openly run things. I just don't get credit."

"It was probably nothing then."

"Probably."

"What's going to happen Monday when you open up again?"

"I don't know. Michael and Suki have been shut up in the conference room all day hashing out a solution. They may have found a stand-in for Geoff, at least for the rest of the semester. Odd thing, she's only available because Geoff made it impossible for her to get more than adjunct work. Ironic, don't you think?"

PETER GRUNTED over his plate of—he didn't know what to call it—chicken with pesto served on bean thread instead of pasta. The texture was different, but it wasn't bad.

Dinner at Lia's was always an adventure. She was

obsessed with healthy food, and what constituted "healthy" changed from month to month. Despite her willingness to experiment with his stomach, she held the line at bacon. It didn't matter how many restaurants and food blogs were dedicated to the stuff, it would never pass his lips in Lia's kitchen.

"How did it go?" Lia asked, taking the seat across from him with a plate of her own. Streaky hair too vivid to be called "brown" slipped out of its usual knot, trailing along her neck. A smudge of blue paint remained on one high cheekbone like a beauty mark, calling attention to eyes that were both warm and green and reminded him of moss. Those eyes now searched his face.

Peter slipped a sliver of chicken under the table to Viola. "Go?"

"Sandy Wilson. Will Hodgkins and Jarvis do anything with the email?"

"Doubtful. Last I heard they were hammering at the furnace guy." He looked at his watch. "I bet they're still at it."

"But this is important."

Peter shrugged. "Most anonymous tipsters don't know anything. They're just trying to get someone in trouble."

"Sandy is connected to Hopewell. That's legit."

Peter set down his fork and took Lia's hand. "She was connected five years ago. I wrote the report and shot it over to Homicide. Someone at Homicide will burn it on a CD with ninety-nine other reports and put it in the murder book with forty-nine other CDs and no one will ever look at it. That wouldn't be my call, but I can't do anything about it. Leave it alone."

## 4

## SATURDAY, NOVEMBER 5

Lᴵᴬ ᴘʟᴀᴄᴇᴅ ᴀ ᴄᴜᴘ ᴏꜰ ᴄᴏꜰꜰᴇᴇ ɪɴ ꜰʀᴏɴᴛ ᴏꜰ Pᴇᴛᴇʀ. Hᴇ ꜱᴀᴛ ᴀᴛ her kitchen table, rubbing his hands over a face creased from six hours in his sleeping bag on that damn air-bed. Viola curled around his ankles with her head on his feet, making up for lost time, no doubt. Peter said she hated the way the bed shifted under her and refused to sleep on it.

"I wish you didn't have to sleep in the basement. It's getting colder. I'm afraid you'll get sick."

"That's where the copper thieves will go, so that's where I need to be."

"Let's get a bigger air-bed. Then I can spend most nights with you."

"There's no reason for both of us to suffer."

"Maybe I should sleep in the basement so you can stay home and get some rest."

"What good would you be against guys who rip out other people's walls for a living?"

"I'll have the dogs. You'd only be two houses away."

Peter looked at Honey and Chewy. Lia knew what he was thinking. Both dogs were likely to walk right up to an intruder and demand a pet. He looked at Lia over the top of his mug and snorted.

"I'd call you if I heard anything," she said.

"By the time I got there, your visitors would have cracked your head open with the sledgehammer they brought with them. Your only chance would be if they decided to have their fun with you first. Did you forget what happened when you did those shooting scenarios at the academy? You don't have the skills, babe."

Lia's foray with the laser pistol had been a spectacular failure. She did well with the target practice, killing tin cans and knocking down targets on the huge screen. Then she'd teamed with Peter to investigate a break in at a hospital pharmacy.

The pharmacy was a labyrinth of labs and storerooms with aisles of tall shelving. They finally pinned down a man in one of the aisles. He was down on his knees, still holding an armful of pill bottles when another man popped out from behind the end of the shelves and raised a gun.

Her heart pounded as the second man rounded his sniveling partner and ran at her. Lia pulled the trigger six times before he went down. When the light came on and the trainer put her shots on the screen, none of them had hit her attacker. She'd forgotten to aim. Peter's third shot had taken him down.

She killed a meter reader in the next scenario. During the third scene, she hesitated long enough for a bank robber to hide behind a gaggle of school children. Then he shot her.

It had been an eye opening experience. She couldn't

imagine having to make those split second decisions and aiming on the run with a real person coming at her. Then there was the kick of a real gun to consider.

"Don't call me 'babe.'"

"Okay, Sugar Lips."

"That's not much better."

"What's wrong with 'babe'? It's a classic endearment."

"Did you ever call Susan 'babe'?"

Peter gave her a wary look. "Where are you going with this?"

"Do you really think I want you calling me the same thing you've called every other woman in your life? You call Brent 'Grasshopper.' That says something about your relationship. Guys call women 'babe' when they can't remember their names. Babe says nothing about us, nothing about how you see me or who we are together."

"I could call you what my cousin Dave calls his girlfriends," Peter said.

"What's that?"

"Piece."

It took a moment for his meaning to sink in. When it did, her mouth fell open and worked for several soundless seconds. She gathered herself and decided to disregard the provocation. "You are the only Kentucky Boy in my life. When I call you that, I'm talking about you and nobody else. It's about recognition and respect."

"Ah, like Native American naming traditions. So I should call you, ummmm Nit Picky Woman With Paintbrush Stuck In Head?"

"I guess that's not too bad for six a.m." Lia brushed the bangs out of his eyes. "It's going to be months before the house is ready to move in. I can't stand that you're sacrificing your sleep for me."

Peter pulled her onto his lap. The move dislodged Viola, who slunk away in a jealous snit. "It's what couples do, Kemosabe. They take care of each other. Sometimes one person gives more than the other, but it balances out."

Lia settled back against his chest, leaning her head against his shoulder. She toyed with a button on his flannel shirt. "What if we finish the second floor so you can move in and then we'll do the first floor? That would cut our time in half before the house is occupied."

"Let's do the ground floor first. Fumes rise. If we do the second floor first, I'll have to breathe in all the stink from the first floor when you paint it."

"Good point. But how is that different from me staying overnight now?"

"The house will be occupied, and you won't be sleeping alone. We can do something else to speed things up."

"What's that?"

"We can have a painting party."

Lia had a vision of splotchy paint jobs and indiscriminate splatter. She gave Peter a dubious look.

"I'm just talking ceilings and walls. If there are a few patchy places, you can hit them with a second coat the next day. No one will notice after the furniture is in, anyway. You can fuss over the trim to your heart's content."

Lia continued to look at Peter with suspicion. "That's walnut trim. I'm not doing anything with it."

"It'll be fun. If we get three people on each room, we can have the place knocked out in an afternoon."

"We'd have to feed them," Lia said.

"And we'd have to give them beer. It's expected. We can

do it at my place. It'll be cramped, but what's a party if it's not cramped?"

"I suppose they'll want pizza. That's going to cost a fortune."

"Get a couple of crock pots and make chili. I bet Alma would let us have everyone at her house. It will be practice for Thanksgiving."

"Like Alma needs practice. You've been thinking about this," Lia said.

"You artists always have to do everything with your own hands. Allowing friends to be part of making a new home is a good thing."

LIA WOKE in darkness and reached across the sheets, finding them cool and vacant. The illuminated clock beside her bed read 1:27 a.m. *Damn Peter and his obsession with those stupid copper thieves.*

After breakfast, they'd spent an hour at the park where her friends deluged Peter with questions about the Lawrence murder that he couldn't answer. After that he'd gone into District Five to catch up on paperwork, then home to catch up on sleep before he went back on sentry duty. Tomorrow—no, today—he would catch up on more sleep before heading over to Brent's for guys' night.

Lia slid into her slippers and padded through the murky shadows. Honey and Chewy trailed behind like silent wraiths. They entered the kitchen and she groped the kitchen wall, flicking on the light over the sink.

The dogs sat in front of the wire shelving unit that housed Lia's supply of dog treats, feigning indifference. In the canine universe, Lia could have no other reason to come into the kitchen except to feed them. Drool seeped out of the corners of their muzzles but they were too dignified to beg.

"Okay, you two." She grabbed a giant biscuit, broke it in half, and handed each a piece. "I've paid the toll, can I work now?" Honey and Chewy were too busy licking crumbs off the floor to respond.

She considered the steps she would take as she boiled water for chamomile tea. Finding Sandy Wilson was more Tree's territory, but it was also too simple to bother Bailey's hacker boyfriend with.

Peter wouldn't help her. He didn't want her involved. She wished she hadn't seen the frustration in his eyes when they'd talked over dinner Friday night. She wished she wasn't still seeing it on his face whenever he thought she wasn't looking. *If only it had been anyone but Heckle and Jeckle. Damn them for assigning those smug, incompetent thugs to the case.* To be fair, Hodgkins and Jarvis had their uses. Peter said they excelled when brute intimidation could quickly close a heat of passion killing. It was finesse they lacked, and a mind for complex situations.

Peter couldn't act, but she could, and maybe she would find something that would ease the concerns he wouldn't admit to.

She carried a steaming mug to the table and booted her laptop. *How hard can it be?* If she Googled Sandy Wilson, she'd wind up wading through click-bait sites that wanted her to pay for background checks. She'd save that for a last resort. Social media was a better choice.

Lia signed into her Facebook account. Six women named Sandy Wilson popped up in Cincinnati. She scanned their profile pictures, looking for chipmunk cuteness. Fourth from the top, Sandy Wilson Alich's long, reddish hair fell in loose curls around a softly-rounded face with an exceptional smile. Cute, just like Hannah said. *No, you don't look like you'd bludgeon someone to death, but that only means it would be easy for you to pull the wool over their eyes.*

Sandy was married to Joe Alich and had a daughter. She worked at Frisch's and was a Hopewell alumna. *Bingo.* The photo albums featured many shots of Sandy in an orange and black Bengals team jersey. Others were of a dark-haired man with a lazy smile holding a toddler in a ruffled pink dress. According to the interior shots, Sandy's taste leaned to homey and crafty, with a personal touch.

Sandy's public posts focused exclusively on family and homemaking. *What happened to you, Sandy? Why is there no mention of music on your page? Did parenthood change your priorities or did Hopewell sour you on pursuing a creative life? Don't you miss it?*

# 5

# SUNDAY, NOVEMBER 6

Lᴵᴬ ᴀɴᴅ Bᴀɪʟᴇʏ ᴇɴᴛᴇʀᴇᴅ Fʀɪsᴄʜ's Bɪɢ Bᴏʏ, ᴘᴀssɪɴɢ ʙʏ ᴛʜᴇ
coat rack and a cluster of high chairs outfitted with activity
placemats and boxes of crayons. They waited at the hostess
stand, using the opportunity to scan the dining room. Bailey
spotted Sandy first. She alerted Lia, nodding at a short
woman with a cloud of untamable reddish hair wiping
down the coffee station.

"Chipmunk hair at ten o'clock."

"I never should have told you about that," Lia said.

"The guys will be pissed we left them out," Bailey said.

"Right. All five of us ganging up on one poor waitress.
That will work."

"You know how they are. If the game is afoot, they want
to be afooting."

"We'll say we're saving them for surveillance."

Bailey raised an elegant eyebrow. "Will there be
surveillance?"

"Of course not. But they don't know that."

"Terry bought lock picks. He found them online."

"No! Peter will have fits."

"Don't tell him. He also has a slim jim and a magnetic GPS tracker."

The hostess joined them at the podium, interrupting Lia's groan.

"Two please," Lia said. "Can we sit in Sandy's station?"

"This way. Booth or table?"

"Booth," Lia and Bailey said in unison.

They sat, examining their menus. "Do we really want to eat here? Bailey asked. "I always think of these places as having plastic food."

"We are going to eat and we are going to leave a very big tip so Sandy will be happy to talk to us."

"My body is a temple."

"Every temple needs a bit of desecration once in a while. Hush up, here she comes."

Sandy stopped by their table, the expression on her face quizzical. "Donna said you asked for my station. Do I know you?"

"Not exactly," Lia said. "I'm Lia and this is Bailey. I'm hoping you'll talk to us about Hopewell."

Sandy's polite expression turned stony. "If you aren't here to eat, please don't take up one of my tables."

"I'm sorry, we didn't mean to upset you." Lia gave Bailey a hard look. "We're having dinner."

Bailey plastered on a grin. "I'd like the veggie wrap with ice tea, please."

"Cranberry pecan chicken salad, and water with lemon," Lia said.

Sandy gave them a curt "thank you" before walking away on stand-on-your-feet-for-twelve-hours nursing shoes.

"That went well," Bailey said.

"So we back off. She may soften up if we let her know we won't bite."

"Even if she doesn't talk to us, it hasn't been a total loss."

"How's that?"

"I caught a bit of her aura. She had a pink haze around her when she walked up. The minute you mentioned the conservatory it turned dark gray, like flipping a switch. Something must have happened at Hopewell. Whatever it is, she doesn't want to talk about it."

"Like I couldn't tell that by the cold shoulder she gave us," Lia said dryly. "Be useful and tell me when her aura clears up so we can try again."

"I can't do it at will. But I'll signal you if I see anything."

"Oh, what's the high sign?"

"You won't be able to miss it. I'll kick you."

Lia watched Sandy take orders and serve meals, chatting with customers as she cleared their tables, laughing at jokes and demonstrating an enviable efficiency. She moved around Lia and Bailey as if they weren't there.

Sandy returned with their food, her demeanor brittle. She set the plates down with an audible snap and one eyebrow raised in challenge. "Anything else?" she asked.

Lia shook her head, wondering how they were going to salvage the situation. Despite obvious attempts to pretend they were not there, Lia caught Sandy watching them as they ate, with an expression that grew increasingly darker.

Sandy hesitated by their table when she dropped off the check, fighting an internal battle and losing. "Why do you want to talk about Hopewell?"

"Have you heard about Dr. Lawrence?" Lia asked.

Sandy averted her eyes as she cleared their dishes. "What about him?"

"He's dead," Bailey said.

Sandy froze, then appeared to do a mental shrug. "I hadn't heard. When was this?"

"Wednesday night. He was murdered in Norman Chapel, before a concert."

Sandy stared at Lia, making eye contact for the first time since Lia explained why they were there. "That's down the street. Do they know who did it?"

"No."

"Too bad, I'd like to throw them a parade," Sandy said. "What does this have to do with me?"

"Awkward," Bailey said.

"There was gossip that the police should look into why you left."

Sandy set the stack of dirty dishes down with a thump. "What for?" Light dawned in her eyes. "Me? You think I killed him?"

"Did you have a reason to kill him?"

"Every third person at that school had a reason." She glanced around. "Look, I'll talk to you, but not here."

"Where?"

"The Old Timber Inn, down Spring Grove. I get off in thirty minutes."

"The fish log place?" Lia asked.

"CREEPY," Bailey said of the Victorian monstrosity sitting opposite the far end of Spring Grove Cemetery.

Bailey's assessment wasn't quite fair. While the fire

escape and roof showed signs of neglect, the former train station had been repainted a few years earlier and featured a nice mural on one side. A portable marquee sat in the gravel parking lot, proclaiming "Fish Logs" and "Reuben Sandwiches." The only illumination came from a pair of beer signs in the tiny windows and a neon sign that said "Open." One other car, a white truck, sat in the lot.

"I have a repellent fascination with this place," Lia said. "I never see anyone walking in or out and there's never more than one or two cars in the lot. I'm curious enough to want to go in, but fear of food poisoning holds me back."

"Do you suppose Sandy sent us here knowing we wouldn't be willing to go inside? Maybe she's hoping we'll just go away instead."

"Maybe she wants to know how badly we want to talk to her, or maybe she wanted to meet where she wouldn't be seen talking to us."

"Probably all of the above." Bailey said.

"Let's wait for her in the car. I can keep the engine running so we don't freeze."

Thirty minutes later Lia spotted Sandy walking down the sidewalk, one hand firmly on her shoulder bag and the other fisted with keys poking out between her fingers.

"Girlfriend is the cautious sort," Bailey said.

Sandy walked up to Lia's Volvo. Lia rolled the window down.

"Would you like to talk out here?" Lia asked.

"Oh, for Heaven's sake. Pull on your big girl panties," Sandy turned and headed for the door without another word.

Lia and Bailey followed, passing through a tiny vestibule.

Ahead of them a hall led to a darkened dining room, now closed off. Sandy turned into the lounge.

A friendly, white-haired man stood behind the bar, setting crispy fish fillets the size of bricks in front of a pair of men in flannel shirts. The fish was surrounded by fries that golden color you see on menus and nowhere else. The men said nothing, continuing to stare at a news program on the television overhead as they picked up their forks.

A mounted swordfish hung on the wall while a miniature disco ball dangled over the liquor bottles. Several ball caps with military patches shared the shelves with bottles of booze, one proclaiming the owner to be a Korean War veteran. Instead of the decades of grime and despair she'd expected, Lia found the little bar homey and clean.

"Hey, Elmer," Sandy said, waving at the man behind the bar. "Too bad you already ate. Elmer has the best home cooking in Cincinnati."

"Does he run this place by himself?" Lia asked.

"Mostly."

Elmer patted the bar. "I got seats for you and your friends right here," he said.

"Thanks, but I think we'll take a table instead. I'd like a coke and a slice of cheesecake." Sandy turned to Lia and Bailey. "Get the cheesecake. I don't want you drooling on mine."

"Two more slices of cheesecake," Lia said. "We'll take water to drink."

"Coming right up," Elmer said.

Sandy pointed Lia and Bailey to a Formica table topped with a bud vase and artificial flowers. She joined them minutes later with towering slices of cheesecake marbled with raspberry.

"Oh," Bailey said.

"You're buying," Sandy said.

Lia forked up a bite of Heaven and wondered how she could have lived in Northside for so many years not knowing about Elmer's cooking. She slid her eyes over to Sandy. *Get a grip, Anderson. This isn't a coffee klatch.*

Sandy leaned forward, her eyes narrowed. "If the police were tipped about me, why aren't they here?" she demanded.

"I don't know if anyone spoke to the police," Lia lied. "I'm working at Hopewell right now. I overheard someone talking while I was in the office."

"Who?"

"I didn't know them."

Sandy sat back, folding her arms. She gave Lia a hard look. "That bastard set me up to lose my job. Why is it any of your business?"

Lia fumbled for a plausible answer. "I date a detective. I should tell him, but I didn't want to say anything until I talked to you."

Sandy snorted. "Mighty thoughtful of you."

"How did Dr. Lawrence get you fired?" Bailey asked. "The current admin says you resigned."

"The director gave me a choice. Quit or be fired. I quit to save my work record, but somehow Lawrence made sure people knew the circumstances were questionable. He was against me having the job at Hopewell and I went through hell finding another job after I left. Now, instead of a nice admin job, I'm waiting tables at Frisch's. No one will ever trust me in a job with responsibility again." Sandy's face crumpled as if her hard ass act had run out of gas and folded its tent.

"Why didn't Dr. Lawrence want you to have the job?" Lia asked.

Sandy sniffed, then fumbled for a paper napkin in the dispenser. "I used to be his student. He never liked me after I corrected him about a historical reference."

"What happened with your job?" Lia asked softly.

Sandy pressed her lips together. Her eyes dropped. "I handled paperwork for department purchases. Purchase orders had to be signed off by a department head or the director before they were given to me. I'd order whatever it was. I kept the purchase orders and invoices in a file in my desk. Some of the purchase orders Lawrence brought me were strange."

"How so?" Lia asked.

"He'd order a sterling silver necklace for a costume piece, something that cost ten times what anyone else would spend for a prop. Or he'd order something that had nothing to do with music or putting on a production, and he'd mark the purpose as 'gift.' I asked Dr. Wingler, he's the director—at least he was then. I don't know if he still is—and he said to pass them through and not worry about it."

Sandy paused to take a drink of water.

"One day Lawrence got into my desk and took the file with the funny purchase orders. He took them to Dr. Wingler when he knew a member of the board of trustees would be there. He told them he saw the folder sitting open on my desk and his signature popped out at him. He said he didn't recognize the paperwork. Then he pulled out all the funny purchase orders and claimed he never signed them."

"What happened?" Bailey asked, breathless.

"The director called me into his office after the VIP was gone and asked me about it in front of Lawrence. I looked him in the eye. I told him I remembered him handing me every one of those purchase orders. He put on this innocent face and had the nerve to say—" Sandy sat up straight and put on a pompous voice. "'Would I order an expensive piece of jewelry the size of a dime for a stage piece? It's ridiculous, and you, young lady, should be ashamed of yourself for suggesting it.'

"That bastard made those orders and then he went digging through my desk. If I'd been so stupid as to steal from Hopewell, I sure wouldn't leave the proof on my desk for anyone to see!"

"How long did he pass you the funny purchase orders before he pulled the rug out from under you?" Lia asked.

"Most of the school year. I think he ordered those things because he wanted them but later decided he could get extra mileage by using them to get rid of me. I'm sure he did it just as much to screw with Dr. Wingler, because Dr. Wingler hired me and we got along really well. Lawrence made sure one of the VIPs was there so Dr. Wingler couldn't sweep it under the rug."

"Why didn't you fight it?" Lia asked. "Surely a handwriting specialist could have exonerated you."

"Lawrence had friends on the board. They would always pick him over me. If I managed to keep my job, my life would have been hell as long as I was there."

"I don't blame you for leaving," Bailey said. "You were in an awful position. Being the target of someone's hate can drag you down."

"Everyone is nice to me at Frisch's, but I miss Hopewell. I didn't just lose a job. I lost a home. ... Doesn't matter now. I have a husband and a daughter. They're my world. But it nearly killed me when it happened."

"Were you working the night Dr. Lawrence was killed?" Lia asked.

"I got off at seven, same as tonight."

"You walked down here. You don't drive?"

"Joe gets the car. I take the bus."

"Which bus stop?" Lia asked.

"It's right across from Frisch's."

"Wow," Bailey said. "You would have been getting off work when the performers were taking their break before the concert. Did you see any of them?"

"They were all dressed in black," Lia added.

Sandy pursed her lips. "When did they take their break?"

"Seven-fifteen," Lia said.

"I was gone by then."

"But you were across the street. How long before the bus came?" Bailey asked.

Sandy looked directly into Lia's eyes and made an apologetic half-smile. "Not that long." She looked at her watch. "I have to go if I'm going to catch the next bus. What are you going to tell your boyfriend?"

"What do you want me to tell him?"

"You can tell him to leave me the hell alone."

A PAIR of hand-blown wine glasses sat in the dish drainer— a wedding present from Sandy's maid of honor. Sandy pressed her lips into a hard line and shut her eyes against the sight, praying for something, she wasn't sure what.

She called into the living room. "Who came over?"

Joe strolled into the kitchen and dropped a kiss on the

side of her neck, breathing beer on her skin. She heard the refrigerator door open.

"Dave was by."

Sandy turned around, leaned against the counter. She gave Joe a placating smile. "How is Dave these days?"

Joe shut the refrigerator and popped the top of his beer can. He shrugged, giving her a long look as he took a pull from the can. "He's Dave. What more can you say?"

The smile on Sandy's face felt like it could crumble into dust and blow away. *Since when does Dave drink wine, Asshole?* "Nothing I guess. Chelsey give you any trouble tonight?"

"Nah. She's an angel. Went right to sleep." Joe grinned his charming, bad-boy grin.

"I think I'll go look in on her."

Sandy climbed the stairs, thanking God Cheryl hadn't had the wine glasses monogrammed. They were so lovely. She wouldn't want to keep them after a divorce if they'd had Joe's initial on them. He sure as hell couldn't appreciate them. Would she want them now that he'd let some slut put her lips on them? *Such pretty glasses. Maybe I'll throw them at his head when I finally get up the nerve to toss him out. If he doesn't leave first.*

Sandy stroked the head of her sleeping angel. At nearly two years old, Chelsey still had that baby scent and hair so fine it slipped out of all attempts to restrain it, like Houdini performing a magic trick. This disappointed Sandy, who wanted to put ribbons and bows in Chelsey's hair and dress her up like an Anne Geddes greeting card.

She wished she'd been home in time to give Chelsey her bath. She didn't like working evenings, but that meant Joe could stay with Chelsey when he got home from work and they saved on babysitting.

At least for now. It was about time for another job to blow up. Then Joe would stay home while she worked double shifts at a job that earned a fraction as much as he could make if he'd just accept that life isn't always the way you want it.

Joe meant well, but he didn't quite understand responsibility. He didn't understand that sometimes you had to bite the bullet in life and take it just to keep things going.

Sandy worried his restlessness signaled more than the end of his current job. He had a six-year-old daughter from a previous marriage. He'd left when that child was two, and he never saw her. She didn't want that for Chelsey.

Joe was married when Sandy met him. He and Amy had never been compatible. He said she was a royal bitch and he'd only married her because she was pregnant.

Sandy walked on eggshells, not wanting to be a bitch like Amy. Being a pleasant wife was hard when Joe was so irregular about feeding the family coffers. Now she was beginning to believe Amy's bitchiness was a result of Joe's lack of focus, and that Joe left Amy because she expected him to be an adult. Now she was wondering if what went around would now come back around and bite her in the ass.

Sometimes Sandy felt the burden of being Joe's wife more heavily than others. But Joe gave her Chelsey, and for Chelsey she would do anything—including the thing that occurred to her when she found out that bastard Lawrence was dead.

She'd thought they had a deal. Lawrence would keep his mouth shut about her forging his signature for that darling little necklace, and she wouldn't question his purchases. One lousy time! One little necklace that didn't cost hardly anything and that bastard made it look like she was robbing the department blind.

Worse, when Dr. Wingler showed her those purchase orders, she could see there was something off about Lawrence's signature on the dicey ones. It wasn't his usual scrawl. Lawrence set her up, one invoice at a time, just so he could pull the rug out from under her whenever he wanted. And she'd been too dumb to notice.

Sandy wasn't going to cry about his murder. If only it had happened before she lost her job and all her benefits. But Lawrence's death might be an opportunity for her to provide a little cushion, a little security for her and Chelsey.

It wouldn't do to tell Joe about it. Joe would want to buy a boat or a TV the size of Montana, and they'd be just as broke as before. It would be her nest egg, something to make things easier when Joe decided he didn't like this family any more than the last one.

Could she pull it off? Did she dare? The bastard deserved what he got and she didn't want to hurt anyone. But didn't she deserve a little consideration for keeping her mouth shut about what she'd seen? That wasn't a bad thing, was it?

Sandy wished she'd watched more mysteries on television so she might have a better idea how to go about it. She experienced a momentary shiver of fear. It might not be the smartest thing to blackmail a killer, but this killer had more to lose than she did. She wouldn't ask for much. It would hardly be missed.

# 6

## MONDAY NOVEMBER 7

PETER SMELLED COFFEE AND GRILLED ONIONS WHEN HE arrived at Lia's Monday morning. She'd ditched her morning smoothies and now made him breakfast, a side benefit of his decision to sleep in her new basement.

*Sometimes guilt is a wonderful thing. Who knew she had such a rare hand with fried potatoes? Better than Granny's, though I'd never tell Mom that—not that I'd tell Mom any woman is cooking breakfast for me—It almost makes up for sleeping on that damn air bed.* Reminded of the bed, Peter stretched his back to ease one of the twinges he woke to these days.

Lia stood over the stove, her hair piled in a messy bun with tendrils falling about her face, the elegant line of her neck rising from one of the ancient T-shirts she liked to wear when she painted. Peter slid a hand under her shirt till it met the warm flesh of her stomach, making her jolt.

"Cold hands, Kentucky Boy."

He pulled her back against him and placed a kiss where

her chin met her ear. "Good morning, Woman of Fire and Onions. Keep this up and I'll never eat another Pop Tart."

"If only. Enjoy it while you can. This is temporary."

He kept his arms where they were and leaned over her shoulder to view the spinach wilting in her sauté pan. "Omelets? What did I do to deserve this?"

She slid the spinach into a bowl and turned in his arms. "You're you." She kissed him lightly, then patted his chest. "Out of my way."

He grabbed a mug of coffee and sat at the kitchen table. He preferred Pepsi, but it seemed sacrilegious to drink Pepsi with a home-cooked breakfast, especially when she only brewed it for him. She'd abandoned coffee for a variety of herbal concoctions that were slightly less scary than her swamp water smoothies.

Honey and Chewy lay on the floor by Peter's feet. The three of them were staring at the stove with equal anticipation. The realization made him shake his head. "Viola's going to be sorry she missed this."

"She loves spending time with Alma more than she likes being with me. Bribing her with eggs won't change that." She popped two slices of the Ezekiel bread she liked into the toaster.

"You may be right."

Lia dropped a spoonful of ghee into the sauté pan and turned the heat back up. She cracked two eggs on the rim of her blender, poured in a dollop of almond milk, and turned it on. The blender roared at a decibel level slightly below that of a Cessna Skyhawk. Lia pulled the blender off the base before it finished spinning and poured the eggs into sizzling butter.

Peter enjoyed watching her tease the edges of the omelet

as he drank his coffee. He soaked in the homey domesticity of her graceful movement around the kitchen, the sizzle as she turned the potatoes, and the rich scent of coffee, which he had to admit was a pleasure he'd never get from Pepsi. These things were both balm and anchor, something that would carry him through the inevitable frustrations of his day.

Lia stepped back, lifting the pan off the stove and shaking it to loosen the eggs. A quick jerk sent the omelet up in the air and over before it landed neatly in the pan. She set it back on the stove and dumped a handful of grated cheese and half the spinach on it before sliding the finished omelet onto a plate, folding it in half as she did so.

"My granny could never do that."

Lia added a healthy portion of crispy potatoes to the plate and set it in front of him. Peter nearly wept. *God, I'm going to miss this. Maybe I can talk her into cooking on weekends. Maybe she'll cook omelets for dinner if I ask.* "This looks great. Are you sure you won't marry me?"

Peter felt the brush of Lia's lips on the top of his head. "Silly man. Why buy the cow? You're getting the milk for free. Dig in before it gets cold." She set a plate of toast by him and nudged a small bowl of ghee in his direction.

It was the same old argument, softened by ritual. He couldn't deny the logic of Lia's point of view—not when you considered her upbringing—and they were moving in together, no matter what she wanted to call it. Still, he mourned for the stability of marriage, even if statistics proved the promise of forever to be an illusion.

Lia scrambled eggs for the dogs while he dug into the omelet, then joined him at the table. "How was the *Fast and Furious* marathon at Brent's last night?"

Peter swallowed a mouthful of potatoes. "We drank beer, ate pizza, and everything went boom. What did you and Bailey wind up doing?"

She hesitated, biting her lip. It was a bad sign. He cocked an eyebrow at her and waited.

"We went to see Sandy Wilson."

Peter sat back and shut his eyes. While he often found a loud expletive relieving, Lia reacted poorly to verbal aggression. When he was upset around her, he relied on a trick he'd learned to keep his composure as a cop, to swear inside his head when he needed to blow off steam in a situation where shouting wouldn't help. He took a moment to trot out his most colorful mental profanities.

"Tell me about it." He listened as she talked, breaking off bits of toast and sneaking them under the table for the dogs. They didn't mind that the grain was sprouted.

"I thought I could find out enough for you to cross her off your list and stop worrying about her, but there was something off about her."

"What list? I don't have a list. It's not my case."

"Maybe not on paper, but it's in your head. It's been bugging you since Friday. I knew you couldn't talk to her, so I did. She was nearby when Dr. Lawrence died."

"And now she knows she's on our radar."

"I didn't say I would tell you."

"You didn't say you wouldn't."

"Does it matter? You said Heckle and Jeckle won't follow up."

"The problem is, it looks like something that needs to be investigated, but I shouldn't have anything to do with it. It looks like I had my girlfriend do an end run for me." He found himself tapping the table, the rapid beat signaling that he was not nearly as calm as he wanted to be. It reminded him of his meeting with Parker. *This is why I never want to be Captain.*

"What are you going to do?"

"There's only one thing I can do. I'll dump it on Parker and let her decide. That's what she gets paid for."

"Will you be in trouble?"

"I don't know. Maybe it will be enough to push them into acting on it. I just wind up looking like the class tattle-tale."

Lia said nothing but the expression on her face was enough to turn the breakfast he'd just eaten into lead in his stomach.

"It's not your fault. I never should have involved you in the first place."

PETER DROPPED into his desk chair with an audible thump and scowled at his computer as he booted it up. Brent looked up from his desk, raising an eyebrow at Peter's foul mood.

"Lia burn your toast today?"

"My toast was fine. She and Bailey decided to interview Sandy Wilson while we were watching Vin Diesel."

"The Scooby Gang strikes again. Why am I not surprised?"

"Thing is, they may have run into something. Now I have to figure out how to tell Parker." Peter turned on his computer and sat back.

"Way to impress the new captain. I'm ever so glad it's you and not me."

Peter spotted the email from SomeoneWhoCares as soon as his computer came on line.

**Kari Bennett is one of Geoff Lawrence's victims. She was at the chapel that night. Why haven't you talked to her?**

"Damn. I got another one," Peter said.

Brent swiveled in his chair. "Who did your secret admirer finger this time?"

"Someone named Kari Bennett. Any idea who she is?"

"I saw her name on the list of people Cynth and Hannah sent home. I don't know anything about her. Gonna tap Lia for this one too?"

"That'll happen. Looks like I talk to Parker sooner than later." Peter clicked "print" at the top of the email and got out of his chair.

PETER STOOD in front of Captain Parker's desk as she read the email. He watched her eyes scan the document twice before she looked up.

"We'll pass this along, like the other one. Send your stalker a reply and suggest she contact Heckle—I mean Hodgkins—with any future tips."

Peter continued to stand in front of Parker's desk. She waited.

"Respectfully, Captain, I doubt Hodgkins will do anything with this. They didn't do anything with the last one."

"And you know this how?"

"A conjecture based on experience, sir."

"Do you want to pursue it?"

"It seems a waste to let it go. My tipster seems to know a lot about the players."

"Oh?"

"I asked Lia to run Sandy Wilson by their administrative assistant. Wilson has history with Lawrence."

"The centralized homicide unit is new and they have yet to work out the protocols for interfacing with the districts. It's touchy territory and it's frustrating, but we need to respect those boundaries." She gave Peter a pointed look. "Send the email. If you get another one, I'll address the situation with Hodgkins's captain. I don't want you going near it."

"It's too late for that, sir."

"Why is that?"

Peter sighed. "Lia took it upon herself to find Sandy and talk to her."

TOBY BURST INTO THE OFFICE, surprising Lia and Hannah with their morning biscotti at mid dunk.

"*That man* is in this conservatory! I won't stand for it!"

The Fur Boys raced out from under Hannah's desk, barking at Toby's ankles. Honey lifted her head up, then lay it back down on her paws, turning her muzzle to the side as if to say, "Oh, *please*."

"Get the vermin *off* me!"

"Rory! Buddy! Dasher! Bed!" The dogs halted. They turned to Hannah, giving her hurt looks, then emitted low mutters as they returned to their den away from home.

"What man are you talking about?" Hannah asked, obviously used to high drama.

"*Leander*. Geoff's *murderer*. He says he is my teacher now. My father will not allow it!"

"Leander is a member of this faculty. While your father is a highly respected and appreciated donor, he does not run this school. Nor do you."

"Replacing Geoff with Leander! It's *appalling*."

"Geoff was very fond of Leander, no matter what you may think."

"But he killed Geoff! I saw him!"

"Did you see Leander beat his head in?"

"I saw them arguing! He was the last person with Geoff. It had to be him."

"It did not have to be him because I was still in the chapel and we left together."

"I didn't see you."

"No, I imagine you were focused on other things. Be careful what you say, Toby. Gossip takes on a life of its own. Leander is welcome here. You are too, as long as you are not creating a hostile atmosphere for others."

"Are you *threatening* me?"

"I'm just reminding you of school policy."

Toby dropped into the vacant visitor's chair. The dogs peeked out from under Hannah's desk. Toby patted his leg. "Come here, darlings. Uncle Toby is sorry, he was just upset." The dogs retreated to the dim recess. Toby fished a handful of tiny dog biscuits from a jar on Hannah's desk and dangled one close to the floor, making kissy noises. "What am I supposed to do? I can't study with Leander!"

"I don't suppose you can, can you? There's Kari."

"She's not competent. Geoff said so. I can't believe she's

the only other option." Dasher, Fur Boy most susceptible to bribery, came out of hiding. Toby picked up the apricot poodle and settled him on his lap, playing with Dasher's ears while the dog gorged on treats.

Lia caught the glint of steel in Hannah's hazel eyes.

"Geoff was a brilliant voice teacher, but his opinions of others were often skewed, which you would have noticed if you weren't so busy being his fanboy toady."

"I beg your pardon!"

"If you don't want Leander or Kari, you can ask another teacher if they'll take you on."

"You said everyone was full up," he accused.

"They are. You're welcome to ask. But don't ask while you're screaming accusations about Leander, or I guarantee no one will take pity on you. You are not their problem."

Toby mulled Hannah's suggestion over, though he maintained a mulish expression. Hannah lifted her cup. She looked over the rim at Toby, her unrelenting gaze making clear she would not pet on him or give in to him. Toby looked away first.

*Score one for Hannah.*

Toby stared silently out the window, then stood, dumping Dasher on the floor. He left without a word.

"That was interesting," Lia said.

"You have to be firm with divas."

"Is that what he is? A diva?"

"That's what he wants to be. He hasn't earned it yet."

"Looks to me like a case of the tenor doth protest too much. What do you think about Toby? Could he have done it?"

"Only if he wanted to slit his own throat. He's genuinely panicked about changing teachers, and he has reason. Now he'll only be a footnote in Geoff's dynasty. This is worse than those vacations where they send you to a hotel they say is comparable to a Hyatt Regency and you wind up in a poor cousin of Motel Six. He has every reason to be upset, but there's nothing we can do about it."

"Will one of those other teachers take him on?"

"Doubtful. I only suggested it to get him out of the office. Let him spread his misery elsewhere."

"You told me once that Toby's mother was the Grace Kelly of opera. Was she that good?"

"I saw a video of her in Aida. She was phenomenal. Opera buffs the world over mourned when she retired."

"Poor Toby, having that to live up to."

"It's sad. Toby doesn't have her range, her presence, or her nuanced delivery. Some people command presence just by standing on stage. Emmylou Harris is like that. Maria Callas was like that. Toby might learn nuance, but you can't fake presence. You either have it or you don't. You can grow your range, but if he had her potential we would see it in him by now."

"That doesn't seem fair."

"It's not. I sometimes think painters and writers have it easier than performers. They can create in private and let it stand on its own. Performers have to be the art. If they achieve any fame at all, they have to be that person the minute someone recognizes them. If they don't they risk alienating fans."

Lia munched her biscotti. "Is it truly a risk?"

"I was with the Renaissance Festival for years. People would recognize me at McDonald's and be disappointed I wasn't wearing brocade and eating my Big Mac with a dagger."

# 7

# TUESDAY, NOVEMBER 8

"Have you ever noticed the clock tower over the old cemetery office?" Toby asked, handing Lia a paper plate bearing a gorgeous slice of flourless chocolate torte to go with her yerba mate latte, another gift.

He and Lia were sitting in the front row of the recital hall, Toby having arrived bearing treats much as Constance had the week before. *Gratitude or loneliness?* In a tiny, cynical corner of her heart she wondered if the latte was a bribe meant to repair her impression of him after his meltdown of the day before.

"They have a clock? I never noticed."

Toby's grin was shy and sly. "There isn't one. It's a clock-less tower because time doesn't matter to the residents. Isn't that perfect? A place with no time."

"How do you know so much about the cemetery?"

"Grandpa started taking me to visit grandma at the family mausoleum when I was six. Have you seen our mausoleum? It's like a cross between a Greek temple and a very conservative bank—but with a Tiffany window and Art Nouveau metalwork."

"It sounds beautiful."

"Grandpa knew all the groundskeepers. He bribed one of them to give him a key to the old office so we could climb in the tower. It's not very high, not compared to the old growth trees, but nobody knows you're there except the pigeons.

"I used to imagine I entered a magic kingdom when I went through the trap door, like the wardrobe and Narnia. I would look out over the grounds and make up adventures. The badgers would have wars with the foxes among the monuments."

"Do we have badgers in Ohio?"

"Some, but they're very secretive. They like open grassy areas, so they would do well in a cemetery and they burrow. They've got crazy sharp claws for digging."

"They must keep the groundskeepers busy. Whose side were you on?"

"Oh, the badgers. The foxes were all girls. They were the enemy." Toby gave her a mischievous look. He'd dropped his usual affectation of jaded ennui and Lia found him charming. "What do you expect? I was eight."

Lia laughed.

"After Grandpa died I found the key and started going there alone. By that time I was too old for badgers. I decided the people walking around the cemetery were zombie revenants of the Civil War soldiers buried there. I would imagine I was the last human, like Will Smith in *I am Legend*. I'd hide in my barricaded tower and pick them off. Mentally, you understand."

Lia found Toby's offhand sharing of his macabre fantasy

a disturbing segue. "Do you like video games?"

He gave her a cynical smirk. "You mean, have I been training myself to commit mass slaughter a là Columbine? Nothing so bourgeois. The old man's nod to bonding with me was years of trap shooting. I excelled at sporting clays." He noticed Lia's confused expression. "It's like golf with a gun. I love watching clay pigeons explode. They're not made of clay. They don't look like pigeons, either."

PETER'S politely worded email to SomeoneWhoCares received the following response:

> **Detective Hodgkins is a gorilla with a badge. I will not talk to him. The reading of the will is tomorrow night. Will you be there?**

He took the message to Captain Parker, who scanned it and sighed.

THE CONFERENCE ROOM at Homicide was far superior to the cramped meeting room Peter was used to, having chairs that matched around a table large enough to accommodate all participants and their nearest and dearest. Hodgkins sat across from Peter, arms folded, shuttered eyes concealing what Peter didn't doubt was seething resentment. Jarvis sat next to Hodgkins, mirroring his position. *The feeling is mutual, assholes.*

Captains Parker and Arseneault conferred privately at

the far end of the room. Arseneault was a tall man with a face like a well-loved Barcalounger. He had tired eyes and a tall forehead made taller by a receding hairline that he offset with a Van Dyke beard. Peter's impression of him was of a methodical man. Peter had interviewed with him when the spot in Homicide was on the table. He liked the captain, though he didn't want the job. He hoped there were no hard feelings.

Hodgkins jerked his chin at Peter. "We've been chasing wits 24/7 for a damn week. What makes you think you can waltz in here after your cozy weekend off with your girl-friend and muscle in?"

"I don't want your case. You can lose the attitude."

"Sure, Hillbilly. Like you'd rather chase your copper-thieving cousins," Jarvis jeered.

"No, it's the punks stealing UPS deliveries off porches he aspires to," Hodgkins said.

The pair sneered and bumped fists.

Peter opened his mouth to respond, then shut it when the captains approached.

Captain Arseneault sat, steepled his fingers and leaned forward. He looked each of the three men in the eye, reminding them this was his turf and he was in charge. "Parker and I discussed this matter and are in agreement."

"Sir," Hodgkins interrupted. "Jarvis and I have our man. It's just a matter of time before we prove our case. This email business is just some crank. It's not worth pursuing."

"It's been a week and you have yet to tie Porter to the victim."

Jarvis opened his mouth to protest, but Arsenault waved him off. "Continue to pursue your case. Meanwhile, we're opening up a second line of inquiry."

"That's just going to muddy the waters, sir," Hodgkins said, hotly.

"Or stir the pot. Parker has agreed to extend her resources to us. We propose that Dourson pursue this informant and follow up on any leads generated."

Hodgkins and Jarvis glowered like a pair of malevolent Buddhas.

Arsenault held up a finger. "We also have a backlog of license plates and background checks to run on the bystanders at the scene."

Hodgkins's and Jarvis's jaws dropped simultaneously.

"Sir," Hodgkins said, "we ran the principals. Running the rest would bog down our investigation. Porter could go free if we don't nail him down."

Arseneault waved a hand. "I know, I know. But we want to ensure nothing falls through the cracks. That's why we're tapping Detective Davis at District Five for this assignment."

The malevolent Buddhas turned to each other and snickered.

Brent exited Parker's office, jerking his head in the direction of the parking lot. Peter followed, philosophically chalking up the coming bitch session as the price of friendship.

District Five's station house was built fifty years earlier to serve thirty officers. More than a hundred and twenty now clocked in every day, making privacy hard to come by.

The only way to have a private conversation inside the station house was by text. It was either that, or shut yourself into the tiny brick closet that was the interview room. Peter and Brent preferred to hold their confabs outside, no matter the weather. At least there you could see if anyone was listening.

The door had barely settled back into its jamb when Brent gave an explosive huff and stalked across the gravel. He stopped at the edge of the woods bordering the lot, then turned on Peter, his breath harsh with rage. Fog issued from his mouth in the chill air, making Peter think of fire-breathing dragons. *And he's just about that angry.*

Brent shoved tense fingers through his hair, disordering his usually perfect do as he started pacing. "How did I get tapped for this? I wasn't even at your bleeping meeting! Two hundred wits and half as many license plates. Did I volunteer for this? No, I did not."

Peter waited for Brent to wind down. It was a rare and fascinating event, seeing Brent without his usual veneer of Southern cool. "Are you really so attached to your pawn shop lists?"

"That's not the point."

"Grasshopper, you're missing a prime opportunity here."

Spittle flew as Brent tossed out his response. "Oh, and what's that?"

"It would be natural to tag our IT specialist for this, in the spirit of cooperation with our newly-formed homicide unit. I'm surprised you didn't suggest it when you met with Parker."

Brent paused mid-step. His eyes lit up like high beams at a monster truck rally. "What wasn't I thinking? I imagine she'll spit fire about it."

"You like her like that. Admit it."

Brent slapped Peter on the shoulder and turned to head back into the building. "I'm a sick man."

"I WAS one of his victims? Someone knows way more than I do." Kari Bennett continued shelving books in her new office while she talked to Peter. Several pieces of framed art —the real thing, not prints, leaned against chairs and walls. The tiny room was piled with cardboard boxes that made Peter wonder how much stuff a person needed to teach someone to sing. He'd learned in choir. All they'd ever had was an upright piano and hymnals.

Nesting, he supposed. Lia was like that, needed her things around her to feel at home and couldn't function in an ugly space. His own apartment was a place to sleep or watch sports. As long as the refrigerator worked, the cable bill was paid up, and the sofa was comfy, he was fine.

Kari finished unloading the carton and stood. She was a slim woman with a sleek build and dark, shoulder-length hair waving sexily around her face. *That's not a salon job. I bet other women hate her for it.* She had plump pink lips that Peter thought were also natural.

The slacks and long, batik vest she wore were professional while being loose and comfortable, the stuff Hyde Park matrons dressed in for lunch and woo-woo seminars. He thought about asking her about the vest. Lia would love to have something like it.

He wondered if Lawrence ever pursued her sexually. The man had once been married, he hadn't been a stranger to sex with women. *Then again, you never know what does or does not go on in a marriage.*

Kari tossed the empty carton in the corner and pulled a box off a visitor's chair. She looked around for a place to put it, then gave up and set it on the floor.

"Take a load off." She dropped down in the other visitor's chair, shoved her hair out of her eyes and smiled. "Sorry about the mess. I wasn't expecting company." She stroked a jade carving of a cat sitting on her desk, as if she were petting the real thing.

*Nerves?* "Hannah said you agreed to pick up some of Dr. Lawrence's students. Is today your first day?"

"That was Monday. I wasn't quite sure what to expect, so I waited until now to move my stuff in."

"What weren't you sure about?"

"I'm a former student of Geoff's. He paved the way for me to get my doctorate at Carnegie Mellon and he was very enthusiastic about hiring me when I was finished. They told me it was a tenure track position to lure me back to Cincinnati. I gave up other opportunities to be here. A week before Easter vacation I was told my contract would not be renewed. It was a shock. I'm still in town because my other opportunities dried up and I haven't been able to find a decent position."

"What have you been doing since then?"

"Constance—Geoff's ex—got me an adjunct gig at CCM —University of Cincinnati College Conservatory of Music." She made a face. "It's music history, not voice, but it was the best she could do. That and waitressing. Anyway, after being let go like that I wanted to be sure nobody was going to pull the rug out from under me again."

"I understand you're splitting Dr. Lawrence's students with Leander Marshall. Why didn't you take the full load?"

"I still have obligations at CCM. I won't make a full

commitment to Hopewell after the way Wingler dumped me last spring, not until I have the lay of the land."

"Why do you think someone said you were one of Geoffrey Lawrence's victims?"

"I honestly don't know. We always got along well. I adored him as my teacher and I was thrilled to come back. I suppose this person believes he had something to do with my contract not being renewed."

"What do you think?"

She patted the jade cat absently. "I always assumed it was someone on the board of trustees. I figured their nepotism trumped Geoff's nepotism. Geoff was very apologetic and offered to write me a letter of recommendation when it happened."

Peter wondered what that recommendation looked like.

"What was your relationship like?"

Kari shrugged. "Friendly, supportive, paternal."

"Did he ever hit on you?"

Kari smiled. "Geoff wasn't into women. It made things easier, really, having a gay teacher. I always assumed Constance was a beard."

"When you were here last year, did you have any conflicts with Dr. Lawrence?"

Kari shook her head, uncomprehending. "Not that I can think of. What kind of conflict?"

"How about differences of opinion about programming or teaching styles?"

Kari pursed her mouth, blinking as she thought. "At one point I asked him to look at some research material, new ideas about the effect of certain types of training on the health and longevity of a performer's voice."

"Tell me about this."

"Vocal cords are like any muscle, but more vulnerable in many ways. If you push them the wrong way, you might get the effect you want today, but five or ten years from now, your voice is ruined."

"Why did you want him to look at it?"

"Geoff's secret sauce is training that maximizes a performer's ability to hit the high notes with power. The study suggested such techniques could pave the way for long-term damage."

"Did you agree with it?"

"I didn't know what to think. I wanted his opinion."

"How did he react?"

"He said he'd look at it. Later he said the study used a very small sample and it would be best not to confuse the students. I prefer making students aware of different schools of thought so they can make informed decisions, but I let it drop."

"Do you always question authority? I had the impression Hopewell was mired in tradition."

"I didn't know enough to question anything while I was here. If I get the opportunity to stay and have an impact on the department, I'd like to institute a wider approach."

"Who do you think will run the department now that Professor Lawrence is gone?"

Kari paused, considering. "Geneva is a follower. I don't think she has the personality or the ambition to run a department. Mark and Leander only have master's degrees and I don't have enough experience. I suspect they'll bring in someone. I'm sure they'd prefer a big name, someone who can be a rainmaker with the donors. Geoff could charm the socks off the little old ladies. Especially the ones who didn't realize he was batting for the other team."

"What do you think about the nepotism angle now that you're back?"

"I don't know what to think." One finger tickled the chin of the stone cat. "They hired Leander to replace me. He's another student of Geoff's. He's qualified. I don't know if he has connections with the board."

"How much do you know about Leander?"

"Not much. He was behind me. We didn't run together." She rubbed the cat's ear, thinking. "Oh, I know the rumors about him and Geoff. I guess they're true, if Toby can be relied upon."

"Toby thinks Leander killed Geoff. What do you think?"

"Toby." Kari gave a gentle snort and shook her head. "I'm out of the loop but Toby was our most outrageous gossip when I was teaching last year. They tell me Geoff's head was smashed in. I don't think Leander has the stomach for that kind of violence."

"Someone said you were in the audience Wednesday night. You didn't see the body?"

"No. I never made it into the building."

"How do you feel about being back?"

"Everyone is being so nice and helpful. Not that they weren't last year—until they let me go. I'm reserving judgment. It's possible last year was just a false start. I'll consider coming back full time, but this time they'll have to step up to the plate with a multi-year contract and tenure track spelled out. I won't make the same mistake twice."

Peter left with the opinion that Kari Bennett would be running the department in five years, if not sooner. *Motive? Possibly.*

# 8

# WEDNESDAY, NOVEMBER 9

THE YOUNG WOMAN WHO USHERED PETER INTO THE GIANT mausoleum Lawrence called home was carefully groomed to walk the precarious line between sexy and professional. Everything about her, from the subtle twitch of her hips to the very expensive and conservative cut of her hair whispered, "I am so too-rich-for-your-blood, you and five of your best friends couldn't pony up to buy my bubblegum." This was not the kind of high maintenance woman to be mollified with jewelry and cars after a snit, but one for whom nothing but money aged through generations would do. *Lawrence's lawyer must have a hell of a practice to afford her.*

It occurred to Peter that she was one more suitable decoration in the catalogue of old wealth in the spacious hall: marble floors, check; Asian rugs, check; an antique sideboard featuring intricate carving from the days when Cincinnati was known as the Paris of the West, check; a grandfather clock that probably came over shortly after the

Mayflower, bonus points; old art in fussy gilt frames, check, check, check; and lastly, the girl: a servant whose blood is bluer than yours will ever be.

The palatial interior was a disturbing contrast to the prison-yard ambiance outside. He calculated the market price of the land and house at an easy four million if the property were broken into smaller lots. *I bet the cash value of the antiques would more than double that. Lawrence didn't pay for this on a teacher's salary. Has to be family money. Family money, family connections. Which might explain Lawrence's influence. Someone is going to rake it in tonight.*

Joel Girgenti stood at the end of the hall. The lawyer was short and stocky with thick fingers and a receding hairline, a combination calling Danny DeVito to mind. *Too bad Brent's not here. He could tell me where that suit came from. He's going to be pissed he missed this.* Peter was surprised when the man opened his mouth and Michigan, not Jersey, came out.

"Welcome, Detective Dourson. I've never had a detective at the reading of a will before."

"I don't imagine you have many clients who were murdered."

"There is that. I've spoken to Constance and the other heirs and they don't object. We're all anxious for you to find out who killed Geoff."

"Thank you for having me. I don't want to intrude. I'll keep a low profile."

The house was chilly. Peter bet the thermostat was set below sixty-five degrees. *A house this size would cost the gross national product of a small country to keep comfortable. A rational person would have space heaters for rooms that are used a lot, electric blankets at night. Was Lawrence the frugal one?*

*Probably not. I bet the executor doesn't want to watch the estate go up in gas bills while it's being settled.*

Girgenti ushered Peter into a room that must be what they called a drawing room. *No TV. This room is meant for high-minded cultural discussion by witty people who read The New Yorker, not screaming sports fanatics yelling obscenities at bad calls and spilling beer.* Fire danced in a massive hearth, bringing the room up to a tolerable temperature. Light from the fire reflected on a gleaming grand piano. A discrete mahogany bar sat in the back. A painting of three dogs hung over the bar. *Lia's work.*

In the center of the room, people sat in a circle on possibly real Chippendale side chairs that Peter imagined came from an equally elegant dining room. Displaced sofas, stuffed chairs, and low tables were pushed to the sides.

He entered the group, nodding to Michael Wingler and Suki Thomas, the director and dean stifling bright-eyed avarice behind appropriately somber expressions. *Personal bequests, or for Hopewell? Has to be the school. Had they known?*

Hannah sat a few chairs away, her head bent in commiseration with the young man next to her. A fluffy white dog from the painting cuddled in Hannah's lap while a bug-eyed Chihuahua and another dog—this one looking like a cross between a young Peter Frampton and Rowlf from *Sesame Street*—guarded her feet, the pair of them looking like living bunny slippers.

The young man was no one Peter knew. He scrolled through his mental cast of characters, looking for a major player who wasn't at the chapel. *Must be Leander Marshall.*

Leander was tall and attractive, someone you expected to be the center of a party. Tonight he was the fish out of water, gasping for air. He may have been Lawrence's lover, but he had never belonged.

Constance's smile was strained as she patted the empty chair beside her. "I only agreed to this because you and Lia were so kind to me the night Geoff died. I would have said no if those other detectives wanted to come. They were at the funeral, giving everyone nasty looks. Geoff deserved more respect."

Peter nodded, wondering why she sat alone instead of sandwiched between Wingler and Thomas. *Persona non grata? Opposing interests?* "Thank you for having me."

Constance, though no longer mistress of the house, must have still felt the need to act as hostess. "You know the director and dean and Hannah. This young man is—was— Geoff's good friend, Leander. We're also expecting three more of Geoff's friends."

*Is she being euphemistic, or doesn't she know her ex-husband was bi-sexual?*

Three more people arrived and settled themselves into chairs before Girgenti took the last seat, leaving his assistant standing like the loser in a game of musical chairs. Peter's eyes drifted around the group as Joel Girgenti read the preliminaries, studying faces that displayed properly subdued attitudes—*except for those greedy eyes.* Constance worried a lacy handkerchief in her lap. *Haven't seen one of those in decades.*

Joel Girgenti reached the bequests, starting with the gift of a small Duveneck painting to a couple, two of the three latecomers. They beamed in happy appreciation. "We always loved that painting," the woman cooed. "It was just like Geoff to remember."

The other latecomer received another priceless knick-knack, a huge and hideous Rookwood era vase which reminded Peter of the old joke, "The food was terrible, but there was a lot of it."

The trio left, glowing with pleasure over their prizes and planning to continue their evening over drinks.

"... To Leander Marshall, I leave the watercolor we bought along the banks of the Seine in the hope that you will remember me fondly when you look at it. To Constance—"

Leander leaned forward and cleared his throat. Peter saw shock in the young man's eyes.

"Excuse me, Mr. Girgenti, was that all? The watercolor?"

*The drama begins. Expecting more, Leander?*

"That is the extent of the bequest." Joel Girgenti pushed his half-rim reading glasses up on his nose and returned to the document.

Leander's lips pressed tightly against each other as if to prevent him from saying the things that were bursting to get out. His free hand, the one not holding Hannah's, clenched and flexed in his lap, the knuckles white. *He can't decide whether to storm out, or stay to find out who Lawrence really loved.*

Leander slumped back in his seat. When he lifted his head, his face reeked of despair born of grief and betrayal.

"... To Constance I leave the memories of our time together and the appalling candelabra her mother gave us and that she so thoughtfully left behind when she moved out. Darling, if you wanted more from me you should not have left me."

Constance stiffened, then closed her eyes for a moment,

relaxing as if by force of will. "Seriously, Joel?" She crumpled the handkerchief in her hand and sighed. "I don't know why I expected anything different."

Girgenti beetled his Danny DeVito eyebrows, looking unhappy. "I'm sorry, Constance. I have to read the will as it is written."

"So many years ..." Her voice trailed off. She looked down and blinked at the hand now gripping Peter's arm as if she just realized it was hers. She let go, smiling apologetically. Peter suspected apologetic smiles were her default.

Girgenti nudged his glasses up and took a deep breath, as if steeling himself for the next bit. Wingler and Thomas sat up straighter. "My home and all my remaining assets and possessions are to be placed in trust, the proceeds of which are designated for the care of my beloved dogs, Dashiell Hammett, Bud Spencer, and Prince Rurik, who are to remain in their home for the rest of their natural lives. At the end of this time, the entirety of this trust will be given to Hopewell Music Conservatory for the construction of a 1,000 seat concert hall, provided Hopewell complies with the following provisions:

1. No item of any kind may be removed from the premises except as designated previously in this will. All else will remain as is to ensure Dashiell, Bud and Rurik live out their days in a secure and familiar environment.

2. All of the dogs will live out their natural lifespan. Euthanasia of any of the dogs makes this arrangement null and void, as does any death resulting from negligence, such as automotive accident, withholding medical care, or poisoning.

3. The concert hall will be named the Geoffrey Lawrence Memorial Hall.

4. Construction of the Geoffrey Lawrence Memorial Hall will begin no more than one year following the death of the last surviving dog.

5. Following the death of the last surviving dog, monies from the trust may only be used in the construction of the Geoffrey Lawrence Memorial Hall and in staging an inaugural production of *Lucia di Lammermoor* along with a suitable reception. Any monies—"

"Oh, God," Wingler moaned. "Where will we find a Soprano who can sing Lucia?"

"We can find a Lucia," Thomas bit out. "If we need to, we can train one. The glass harmonica is another matter."

Girgenti cleared his throat before continuing. "Any monies remaining will revert to the State of Ohio."

6. Hannah Kleemeyer will move into the house within thirty days of the reading of this will. She will be responsible for the care of Bud, Dashiell and Rurik until their deaths. She will keep the dogs with her at all times when she is at the conservatory."

Hannah jerked to attention. "I have my own home, and I like it very much, thank you."

"That's certainly up to you," Girgenti said. "If you don't take up residence, then the bequest is null and void."

"That's ridiculous." Hannah jumped out of her chair and threw her arms up. "You can't make Hopewell's bequest contingent on where I live."

Wingler stood, looking as if he wanted to pat Hannah's shoulder but couldn't get past her wildly waving arms. He settled for clasping his hands, giving them a vigorous shake.

Girgenti spoke gently, as if to a traumatized child. "Ms. Kleemeyer, these are Geoffrey Lawrence's wishes. A testator can make bequests contingent on anything they like."

"Surely there is another way to satisfy the provisions of the will beyond Hannah sacrificing her life for the next several years?" Wingler asked hopefully.

"I'm sorry," Girgenti said. "The provisions are the provisions. You can refuse the bequest, in which case the trust will revert to the state after the dogs pass on. If Hannah does accept the provisions of the will, there are additional conditions detailed in a separate document."

Thomas spoke. "Does the trust compensate Hannah if she is willing to make this sacrifice?"

"The will is very specific about this matter. Mr. Lawrence said if you felt Ms. Kleemeyer needed compensation, it would be up to you to provide it. It will not be provided out of any funds from the trust. Those monies are earmarked for the care of his dogs and construction of the concert hall."

"I don't believe this," Hannah dropped into her chair and glared at Wingler. "That bastard screwed me from the grave. What did I ever do to him?"

"You can certainly refuse," Girgenti said.

"And my career is over and my name is mud." She made a disgusted sound.

Suki Thomas scooted over to the seat next to Hannah and patted her hand. Suki's eyes darted around the room with calculation, as if she were attempting to put a valuation on the estate but was too cagey to ask. *It would damage Hopewell's bargaining position to point out to Hannah how much money is at stake.*

"You have every right to be upset," Thomas said. "But let's have a conversation about your options after we all sleep on it."

PETER SAT on the floor with his back against Lia's couch, swigging a Pete's Wicked Pale Ale while Lia rubbed his shoulders. Viola lay beside him with her head in his lap.

"It's not such a bad deal," Peter said. "She can rent her house and I bet the school will be willing to double her salary for her to dog sit. The trust will pay for housekeeping. She can even have a cook if she wants one."

"What if she doesn't want to stay at Hopewell? What if she wants to leave Cincinnati? Rory is only three years old. He could live another fifteen years, even longer." Lia's fingers dug into Peter's shoulders, making him wince. "Trigger spot? Sorry."

Lia lightened her touch. "But how would you like to have your life decided without your say-so? She's not even forty. She should be free to spend a summer in Europe if she wants instead of being chained to dogs that aren't hers. It's blackmail. Think how the board and administrators are going to react if she puts the kibosh on that much money for them."

"He was a bastard, no doubt about it. You know more about him than I do. Why do you think he tied Hannah to the dogs without compensating her?"

Lia's hands stilled on his shoulders. After a moment she spoke. "Those dogs adore Hannah. I suspect they love her more than they loved Dr. Lawrence. This would be a way to get even with her for stealing their affection, a way to destroy her love by making her resent them."

"Hell of a deal."

"The ruling powers at Hopewell will have her walking

on eggshells to make sure nothing happens to those dogs. Nobody can live that way for so many years."

"That's some revenge," Peter said. "Why do you think he stiffed Constance and Leander?"

"No matter how good your relationship, there are going to be times when your partner doesn't live up to your expectations. Someone like Dr. Lawrence would pile it all up, save it for a payoff. The longer he waits, the bigger the payoff. I think he decided to get even for every little slight he ever felt from Constance and Leander, real or not. And he rubbed it in by erecting a shining edifice to his own memory instead of taking care of them."

Peter huffed. "They say you find out who a person really loves when they die. Looks like the person Geoff Lawrence loved most was himself." He climbed on the sofa and pulled Lia's feet into his lap. She leaned back on the opposite arm while he pulled off her socks and pressed his thumbs into an instep.

Lia, who'd spent too many hours on her scaffold that day, groaned in pleasure and relief. "How much do you think the estate is worth?"

"Joel Girgenti hemmed and hawed but I pinned him down. He said ten million easily. That's with current property values."

"Where do you think he got it?"

"Family money, for sure. The place is full of Cincinnati antiques. I'll bet they built that house."

"And he's the last of them. Poor Constance. She said Geoff promised he would always take care of her."

"I guess he did take care of her, in his own sick, sadistic way."

"If I were Hannah," Lia said, "I'd demand one percent a year of the current valuation of the trust as long as she maintains the provisions of the trust. Over ten years, that would equal a grant writer's fee. They get ten percent of everything they raise."

"Hell of a lot of money to come up with up front."

"And it's a fraction of what's at stake. If she's going to give up her life for this, it ought to be worth it. They can finagle one of their other trusts to make it work. They can even make it non-taxable."

Peter considered the complexities and took a moment to be grateful he never went to law school. "Neat trick."

"Why do you suppose your secret admirer sent you there?"

"The usual reason is to see who benefits and how they react when they find out what they did or didn't get."

"And?"

"Constance and Leander were shocked. Wingler and Suki Thomas had to repress the urge to do an end zone dance. Hannah was livid."

"Constance expected to be in his will. Could she have faked her hysterics at the chapel?"

Peter considered the sobbing heap that was Constance the night Lawrence died. "I don't know. It would have been safer for her not to be front and center when the body was discovered."

"Don't some killers get a thrill from that?"

"She doesn't strike me as the type. Does she have acting in her background?"

"I think she's strictly a musician. How does this affect your impression of them as suspects?"

Peter rubbed his chin. "An inheritance might be a side

benefit, but Lawrence was killed in a fit of rage. The motive is going to be something primal."

"Primal? As in?"

Peter released Lia's feet and crawled over to her. He nuzzled her neck. "Forget Lawrence. Forget this whole damned case. Let me show you primal."

# 9

# THURSDAY, NOVEMBER 10

TOBY SAT IN ONE OF THE VISITOR'S CHAIRS IN HANNAH'S office with Dasher on his lap. He played with the apricot poodle's long, floppy ears.

"You're my silly little man, aren't you? You're such a little love." Dasher smiled his red-carpet smile, soaking up the attention as if it was his God-given right, while Rory gave Toby the stink eye and Buddy curled in a disgruntled ball at Hannah's feet.

"I wish Geoff had put me in his will. I'd live in that big house and take care of you, cutie pie, yes I would," he crooned, adding an extra syllable to "would."

Lia and Hannah exchanged eye-rolls.

"Let me move in with you," he begged, turning wide, dark eyes on Hannah. "I can be the au pair."

Hannah leaned down to the pups on the floor. "Would you like Unca Toby to be your nanny?" Buddy and Rory looked at her, snorted, and laid their heads on their paws.

"Do you miss your daddy as much as I do?" Toby stage-whispered in Dasher's ear. He turned to Hannah. "It's not fair. Geoff loved me and I can't show my grief because Leander works here. Everyone feels sorry for *him*. Nobody cares how I feel."

"I'm sure that's not true," Lia said.

"It is. No one takes my pain seriously, but Geoff *loved* me. I didn't just lose the most amazing man I'll ever have in my life, I lost my entire career. He was grooming me, you know. It was all laid out. Now he's gone and I've lost his guidance and his connections. I've lost everything. I'll never have another opportunity like it. I may as well quit."

Lia knew they were expected to soothe, but she didn't have the patience for it. "If your success depends on having one specific teacher, it doesn't say much for you, does it?"

Toby's eyes shot up, shocked, his mouth gaping.

"Cream rises to the top on its own. As much as we like to think someone powerful will lift us out of obscurity, it's your peers who are with you for the long haul. Those are the relationships you need to foster. They are the people who will return your kindnesses years later and who will remember you, for better or worse, when it counts.

"You'd do much better to be a good friend to the other students than to continue prancing around like you're the special snowflake. There are plenty of people with enough talent. You've got to be someone people want to work with or they will choose someone else."

"People are just jealous, aren't they, sweet boy?" Toby muttered into Dasher's ear. Dasher panted, his opinion a mystery.

"People want their lives to run smoothly," Lia continued. "If you're difficult and demanding, they'll choose someone less talented who makes life easier. If they know you'll make them look good, they'll want you around. It's that simple.

"The world isn't going to bow down because you have talent. You still have to earn your place at the table."

Toby carefully placed Dasher on the floor and stood up. "I've been earning my place at this table my entire life." He squared his shoulders and left. Robbed of adulation, Dasher stared at the door.

"A little harsh, weren't you?" Hannah asked.

"Some people need a reality check. Daddy's checkbook won't pave the way forever. Don't you get tired of his drivel?"

"I'm used to it. You get a lot of artistic temperament around here."

"Was I wrong to say what I did?"

"No, but better you than me. I have to live here. Offending the heir of a big donor is not a career enhancing move."

"He'll either learn or he won't," Lia said.

"Isn't that the truth."

"What's Toby's story? Are you and he such good friends? He hangs out here a lot."

"He hangs out here because I'm nice to him. It's part of the job description."

"Don't you like him?"

"I feel for him because it's really not his fault."

"I thought likability was always your own fault," Lia said.

"He's the poor little crown prince of opera. Toby's mother raised him on stories of her past glory and visions of future curtain calls at the Met. He's had private coaching since he was four. According to him, his coaches said he was a prodigy."

"Seriously?"

"I don't think Toby lied. I think they wanted to keep his mom happy. He started here when he was in high school, but we tend to coddle our youngsters. Then he started the degree program and was reduced to being one newcomer in a highly competitive, often vicious herd. He never adjusted."

"Ouch. I take it he lacks social skills?"

"He's okay as long as talk doesn't steer in any direction that would reveal his innate sense of privilege. Unfortunately, those conversations are rare in this environment."

"I imagine the kids who had to claw their way here are not kind."

Hannah traced a finger around the rim of her cup. "Nope. Then the mom who doted on him died. I'm not too clear on the rest of it, but I have the sense that Toby is not the rich man's scion that the elder Grant wanted. There's speculation he'll marry a convenient trophy wife so he can have a shot at another son."

"So Toby is expected to perform like a trick dog while having no one who loves him unreservedly."

"Pretty much," Hannah said. "He may have friends among the servants, but it's not like being accepted by your own kind. If he had his mother's talent ... but he doesn't."

Lia thought of people she knew in college who had money to spend semesters in Paris and Florence, but lacked the eye to benefit from the experience. "They resent the hell out of him, don't they?"

"Not everyone, but plenty do. Then Geoff singled him out, and Toby thought it meant he really was destined for greatness."

"What do you think?"

"I'm sure Geoff found Toby attractive, and the connection sealed the deal."

"Poor Toby," Lia said.

"Poor Toby," Hannah agreed.

"Peter told me about the bequest. I hope you don't mind."

Hannah shrugged. "Everyone else knows, why not you?"

"What are you going to do about it?"

Hannah leaned over and petted her new wards. "I haven't decided. I'm happy to take the dogs but I won't be chained to the trust without compensation, and they know it. Michael and Suki are already making kissy noises."

BRENT WAS BREATHING chili when he leaned over Peter's shoulder to read the newest email.

**Hannah Kleemeyer had her own reasons for hating Geoffrey Lawrence.**

"This tells us one thing," Brent said.

"What's that?"

"Your admirer doesn't know much about the investigation, or she'd know Lia and Hannah have been thick as thieves. Everyone at Hopewell has to know that Lia is your girlfriend."

"Maybe there's something Hannah hasn't told us," Peter said. "Why do you say 'she'?"

"What guy is going to call himself 'SomeoneWhoCares'?"

"We're talking about the arts. Traditional gender roles don't apply."

"It still feels female to me."

Peter shoved his chair back and folded his arms. "A woman who was at the chapel, who knows the players, but isn't at Hopewell? Who does that leave?"

"No one." Brent frowned. "It leaves no one, unless there's more to the furnace guy than anyone knows."

SANDY SAT in her car with the heater running. She'd backed into a parking space at the secluded picnic pavilion so she could see approaching headlights. That would be the only thing she could see. The miles of road inside Mount Airy Forest were pitch black at night.

She'd been right about Joe. One of the neighbors saw him say goodbye to his "cousin" yesterday. She suspected the woman knew Joe didn't have any cousins by the sneer in her eyes. *Looking for a reaction, the bitch. ... Damn Joe.* A tear made its way down her cheek. She would allow herself that for her crumbling marriage. *At least Chelsey loves me.*

She groped for her phone on the passenger seat and woke it so she could see Chelsey in the pitiful light it gave off. Chelsey's little head drooped to one side as she slept in her baby seat, a bit of drool puddling at the corner of her mouth. She still clutched a limp, stuffed giraffe. She'd been dragging it around for months. Her baby wouldn't go anywhere without it.

It would have been better to leave Chelsey with Joe, but he asked questions if she wanted him to babysit, and she didn't have any good answers. Instead she told him she was taking Chelsey to the store. If she brought back plenty of groceries it would never occur to him that she'd been anywhere else. She just had to find a way to sneak the money into the house.

Sandy was nervous enough without worrying about a fussy baby and had given Chelsey cough syrup to keep her asleep during the payoff. Had she given her too much? The baby gave a soft sigh and murmured in her sleep. Reassured that Chelsey would be okay, Sandy turned back around.

Her phone said it was 9:25. Five minutes and it would be too late to back out. Ten minutes, and the last four terrifying days would be over.

Her life had been a tightrope since she decided to do this thing. Each step she'd taken left her breathless that she was still moving forward: finding the unlisted number in the old Hopewell directory she'd neglected to toss out; remembering the phone booth—it had to be the last fully-enclosed phone booth in Cincinnati; the library volunteer offering to take Chelsey to story hour when she needed to use a computer to write her blackmail script. Every success was a sign telling her she was on the right path. And every action she took ratcheted the tension up one more notch.

Making the call had been the worst of it. She'd thought about email or a letter, but those would be too easy to ignore and the limbo of waiting for a response would have been unbearable.

Two nights before she'd bundled Chelsey up and driven to that old hotel downtown, the one with the phone booth. She settled Chelsey on the floor of the booth with a box of animal crackers and shut her eyes for a moment before she picked up the handset.

In the movies blackmailers put scarves over telephone receivers to disguise their voice. The only thing she had was a gauzy, floral infinity scarf Sherry had given her. It was a good thing no one could see inside the old booth because if anyone did see the scarf bunched on the handset they'd know she was doing something illegal.

Her finger shook as she punched the number in, her heart pounding so loud she was sure it would be heard over the line. The phone rang. Once, twice—*What am I doing?* Before she could hang up, the phone clicked.

"Hello?"

It was the right voice. She took a deep breath and fumbled her paper. The words swam in front of her eyes, difficult to read.

"Hello?" The voice was now annoyed.

"Don't say anything, just listen." She did her best to sound harsh, fighting her natural instinct to appease.

"Who is this?"

"I know you murdered Geoffrey Lawrence." That was better, nastier.

Silence.

"I don't care that you murdered him. I'm glad the son of a bitch is dead." *Did that sound apologetic? Why didn't I rehearse this? Be firm!*

"Why are you calling me? What do you want?" The voice was now angry.

"I don't want to tell anyone what I saw, but people are asking questions. I hope you understand the risk I'm taking."

"I repeat, what do you want?"

"A little consideration."

"How much? You obviously want to be bought off, so what do you think it's worth to me?" The voice was calmer. Sandy's heart slowed. It was going to happen. Now it was just a matter of business.

A faint glow in the darkness pulled Sandy out of the memory. She strained her eyes. Yes, those were headlights flickering faintly through the trees. *Still a ways off.* She patted her right pocket, reassuring herself that the travel-sized hairspray was still there. It was the best weapon she could come up with on short notice, and less than a dollar at Walgreens. She popped the cap off.

The car pulled in, blinding her with LED high beams before parking twenty feet away. She couldn't see what kind of car it was except that it was long and dark, a black on black blur lurking in the darkness like the shadow of a shark in the water. *What if it's someone else? Stop it, Sandy, you're making stuff up. Why would anybody else be here?*

The car sat, its windows dark. Waiting for her. Her apprehension increased, as if she were about to poke a sleeping bear.

The overhead light flashed on when she opened the door. She reached up and turned it off, cursing herself silently as she checked Chelsey one more time. *Still asleep.* The sound of a car door shutting would wake Chelsey. She left it ajar, barely open so the cold wouldn't make her baby sick.

*Keep your eyes up. You're just as good as anyone. You deserve this. This is for Chelsey. Remember that.* She gripped the can in her pocket as she approached the other car, her heart thudding. The driver side window lowered.

"Get in."

*Good, it's the right voice. Dammit, I wish I could see!*

"Just give it to me and I'm gone."

"We need to come to an understanding. Get in or forget it."

The light didn't come on when she opened the passenger

door. Geoffrey's killer obviously knew more about this sort of thing than she did. She faced the inky silhouette blur head on, as if it were daylight and they were having a friendly conversation.

"What's to understand? You pay me and I don't tell anyone I saw you come out of the chapel after you killed Geoff Lawrence. I'm not asking very much."

"That's a matter of perspective. I didn't murder Geoff."

*That can't be true! What do I do now? Brazen it out!*

"If you didn't, why did you show up tonight?"

"I wanted to talk to you."

*What do I do? What do I do? Get tough, Wilson!*

"If you aren't going to pay me, we have nothing to talk about." Sandy kept her eyes on the dark shape in front of her while she popped the door handle. She hesitated, waiting for a reaction that didn't come, then shoved the door open and turned to exit the car.

The slide of a gun racked behind her.

Sandy froze.

The sound of Chelsey crying broke the silence.

"You brought a baby?"

Sandy barely had time to register the amazement in the voice. Somehow she whipped the hairspray out of her pocket and sprayed it into the faceless blur, shoving herself out of the car. She fell out on the pavement as the gun fired.

## FRIDAY, NOVEMBER 11

HONEY AND CHEWY RACED FROM THE KITCHEN BEFORE THE person on the other side of Lia's front door had a chance to ring the bell. Lia waded through a cacophony of fur and barking to peek through the blinds. Hannah stood on the porch, Fur Boys at her feet, the crease between her eyes signaling distress. She didn't wait for Lia to ask what she wanted.

"I'm sorry to bother you so early. I need to talk to Peter. Is he here?"

"Come on in," Lia said, opening the screen door and waving Hannah to the Mission style sofa with its colorful embroidered pillows, replacements for those destroyed by an intruder the year before.

"Peter," Lia yelled. Honey and Chewy circled the Fur Boys, sniffing rapidly the way dogs do when something doesn't make sense. Hannah sat, knees together, hands twisting in her lap, eyes darting about like birds desperate for a place to land.

Peter shuffled in and sat, coffee in hand and eyes at half-mast. Still in the preverbal stage of his day, he raised his eyebrows and sipped.

Hannah took a deep breath. Words tumbled out when she exhaled. "Leander texted me an hour ago. He said he couldn't stand it anymore and he was going to see Detective Hodgkins to confess. I'm sure you want to know why I lied."

Peter took another sip and nodded slowly. "We should do this downtown, with the detectives."

Hannah shook her head and held a hand up in a "stop" gesture. "I don't want to talk to Hodgkins and his nasty sidekick. I just want to tell my story in my own way without them hounding and harassing me. Please let me do it here. You can record it and they can give me the third degree later."

She turned to Lia, her eyes pleading. Lia sat beside Hannah and squeezed her hand, amazed at Peter's casual attitude. *Maybe he's not awake yet.*

Peter dragged his phone out of his pocket, started the recording with the necessary data, and laid it on the coffee table. "Go ahead," he said. "It's your show."

Hannah paused as if uncertain how to proceed. Rory whined, now quivering with nerves he'd no doubt picked up from her. She settled the Chihuahua onto her lap and soothed him for a moment before she spoke.

"I need to go back a few years. Geoff started seducing male students when he arrived at Hopewell. It was an open secret. No one would ever provide the evidence so he could be fired—afraid of retaliation, I'm sure. Shortly after I was hired on, one of the students came to my office and told me Geoff was kissing and fondling Leander in one of the practice rooms. I was new, so I didn't know how ready Michael —Dr. Wingler—was to fire him.

"I was afraid it would be my word against Geoff's, that I'd lose my job and not find another one as good. I dithered for ten minutes until my conscience got the better of me. I didn't know what I was going to do, but I had to do something. By that time they were gone. If I'd gotten him fired, he would have had no hold over Leander, and Leander would not have been pushed to the point where he was driven to kill Geoff."

"That's why you lied the night of the concert?" Peter asked.

"Yes. I know I'm not responsible, but if I had acted then, none of this would have happened. I couldn't stand to think that Leander's entire life would be ruined because Geoff twisted him up to the point of no return."

"What happened the night Dr. Lawrence was killed?"

"I missed most of Geoff's tirade. The minute he started screaming about the heat—"

"What about the heat?" Peter asked.

"The furnace was on the fritz that night, you know, you spoke to Nigel. Body heat would have warmed the chapel up soon enough, but Geoff wasn't having it. He was furious it hadn't been fixed. But that wasn't what the tirade was about, it was just more fuel on the fire."

"What was he upset about?"

"It was the same before every performance." Hannah huffed in frustration, one hand erupting from her lap like a startled bird. Rory started at the unexpected movement, turning one buggy eye on Hannah before settling down again. "The choir is going to singlehandedly bring about the end of music with their horrible performance, and he should shoot them all now before they destroy all that is worthwhile in human endeavor."

"Did he threaten to shoot them?"

"Oh, I don't know. He has before. I knew what was coming. I wasn't performing, so I didn't have to stand there and take it like the students do.

"I was already a wreck from making arrangements for the concert on short notice. Wednesday we had the cold snap and the furnace hadn't been turned on for the season, and I had to deal with that. Geoff's impossible—always shoving a size eleven foot into a size four shoe like Cinderella's sisters, always a pre-concert explosion of epic proportions because the laws of physics won't bend to his will.

"I slipped out the door off the utility room and walked around to the magnolia trees. You've seen them, they have multiple trunks that lean out and run sideways so you can sit on them. With the branches hanging down it's like the inside of a tent.

"I was hiding in one so I could have a little quiet before everyone started arriving. The singing stopped. Within a minute everyone was pouring out the door from the family chamber—you can see it from where I was sitting. They all walked right by me, rushing to their cars so they could grab a quick bite at one of the fast food places down the road, or just to sit for a bit. A few minutes later, Toby came out, looking very satisfied."

"Which way did he go? Toward the cars?" Peter asked.

Hannah shook her head. "The other way, into the grounds."

"Okay, please continue."

"Leander came out. I could see he was upset, so I called

to him. He was babbling and I couldn't understand what he was saying. I made him sit down and gave him a drink from my water bottle."

"What was he saying?"

"He kept saying, 'I didn't mean it, I didn't mean it, I didn't mean it,' over and over."

"I said, 'didn't mean what?' and he said, 'Oh my God, I killed him. I can't believe I killed him.'"

"I asked him what happened and he told me that he found Geoff kissing Toby and he started screaming at Geoff, so Geoff smacked Toby on the ass and told him to leave, as if it was no big deal. Toby left and the argument escalated. Leander said he didn't remember half of it, he just saw red and grabbed that huge candle stand and swung it at Geoff's head like a baseball bat."

"What did you think when he said that?"

"I thought Geoff was hurt and might need to go to the hospital."

"You didn't think he was dead?"

"Not then. I thought Leander was being overly dramatic."

"What did you do?"

"I told him to stay where he was, and I would go see. I went into the chapel—"

"Which door?"

"The closest door, the one through the family chamber. I found Geoff on the ground with blood around his head and that candlestick on top of him. I knew he was dead but I checked his pulse."

"Wrist or neck?" Peter asked.

"Wrist. I didn't want to step in the blood."

"Then what did you do?"

"I wiped the candlestick to get rid of Leander's fingerprints—"

Peter interrupted. "What did you wipe it with?"

"A glove. I had gloves in my pocket. I went back to Leander and told him we needed to go for a walk."

"Which way?"

"We walked across the grounds to the waterfall. We sat there and watched the water. I told Leander Geoff was dead but I would not let him go to prison for it. I told him the story we told you before and made him repeat it to me so he had it straight. I said if we stuck together, nobody could prove differently. I couldn't let him go to jail. … I hope you understand that."

"What happened to the glove? Did Leander know about it?"

"I showed it to him and dropped it in the water."

"Go on,"

"We walked back to the chapel. By that time it was after eight o'clock. The doors were supposed to be open at eight, so people were already there."

"What happened to the door shims?"

"Sorry, I forgot that part. I kicked them out before I went back to Leander. I didn't want a student to find Geoff like that."

"Who was supposed to unlock the doors at eight?"

"Geoff or Constance. Really, anyone who was inside at eight o'clock."

"When we saw you at the door, Leander wasn't with you. Where was he?"

"I felt it best if he were not the one to discover Geoff. I told him to hang back and just be part of the crowd, and nobody would think anything about it. I guess he lost his nerve, because he left."

Hannah took a sip from a glass of water Lia had snuck onto the table. "I miscalculated. I forgot Toby saw Leander, and that everyone else would think Toby was the last to see Geoff. Of course Toby started screaming about Leander as soon as he saw Geoff."

Hannah dropped her head into her hands, her auburn hair falling around her face. No one said anything. Dasher and Buddy jumped on the couch and wormed onto Hannah's lap. Rory lifted his muzzle and sniffed her nose. Hannah's voice trembled behind the curtain of her hair. "What happens now?"

Peter rubbed the back of his neck. "That will be up to the district attorney's office, whether they want to press charges against you for accessory after the fact. For now, we need to take you downtown so you can make a formal statement."

"Didn't I just do that?"

"We need to get this typed up so you can sign it."

Hannah sighed. "I suppose I'll have to talk to those despicable detectives."

"You'll survive. We took away their rubber hoses."

She put a resolute expression on her face, gently removing the dogs from her lap before she stood. They gave her pleading looks, not understanding.

Hannah looked at Lia. "You'll watch them for me, while I'm downtown?"

"Sure I will," Lia said. "We can all ride down together, can't we Peter?"

LEANDER STARED at the walls of the interview room. That's what they called this cold, depressing space. Such a benign name for a place that reeked of guilt, of incrimination and betrayal. A camera hovered in the corner of the ceiling like the all-seeing eye of Sauron.

Would this be his life from now on? Concrete and security cameras and gang rape in the showers? *Coming here was a mistake.*

He stared at his hands, nails bitten to the quick and bleeding. They twisted on the table in front of him as if they had a life of their own. He couldn't take one more night of horrible dreams about Geoff, dreams of Geoff and Toby leering at him. Geoff, who abandoned him in death and was now reaching from beyond the grave to destroy his life. Toby who had felt entitled to that which wasn't his. *It doesn't matter. It's all ruined. I thought he loved me and I meant nothing to him.*

The door opened and two detectives walked in, the ones who looked like they should play mafia guys on television. The taller of the two dropped a fat file on the table. The sound made Leander jump. The other detective set a glass of water down and nudged it toward him.

"Mr. Marshall," the tall man leered. "I understand you want to talk to us."

Leander swallowed hard and closed his eyes, pulling himself together before he responded. This was no worse than opening night of a bad play. *Except they'll lock me up and I won't get out for a very long time. Why didn't I have one last latte at Sidewinder? Why didn't I have a quick fling in Barbados?*

"Yes sir. I've come to confess."

"Have you now?" the shorter of the pair said.

"I killed Dr. Lawrence—God, I'm so sorry." He covered his face with his hands and sobbed.

"We're going to read you your rights. Then we'll take your statement."

*You little prick.*

The last was unspoken, but Leander heard it in the detective's voice. He had no doubt that when he lifted his face he would see contempt in their eyes: contempt because he was gay; contempt because he was weak; contempt because he caved in and was whimpering to unload his guilt; contempt because he was himself, a contemptible human not good enough for Geoff to love. *A cheesy water-color by a no-name street artist. Is that all I meant to Geoff?*

He drew a deep breath and steadied himself while Jarvis —was that his name? Why didn't detectives wear name tags like officers did?—read him the Miranda rights.

The taller of the two introduced himself as Hodgkins and pressed the button on the recorder, the click bouncing off the ceramic tile walls, marking the beginning of the end of his life.

"Now, Mr. Marshall, what do you have to tell us?"

Leander drew himself up and looked straight ahead, through the detectives as if they weren't there. He would tell his story as if he were playing a part, a soliloquy in this play that was his life. Then he would be able to get through it. "I killed Geoffrey Lawrence. I didn't mean to, it was an acci-dent. I was so angry I couldn't think. Then the candlestick was in my hands and it was swinging through the air, and it smashed his head before I could stop it."

Leander glanced over to see the detectives exchange evil, smarmy grins, like snakes.

"Why don't you tell us what happened, from the beginning," the taller detective, Hodgkins, said.

Leander took a sip from the glass, his hand shaking. Water splashed onto the table.

"I'm sorry, I'm sorry." He looked around and saw nothing but a box of tissues with which to mop it up. He reached for the tissues. Jarvis blocked his hand.

"Leave it. Get on with your story."

Leander took another deep breath. "Everyone was leaving for the break before the concert and I went to the bathroom. There was a line, so it was a while before I got in and out."

"How long?"

"I don't know. It was all guys, so it wasn't that long."

"Who was in front of you?"

"Does it matter?" he looked at the pair of stone faces and sighed. "Eric and Tom were standing outside the restroom door, and Joe came out right after I walked up." He struggled to pick up his narrative.

"I took a little time while I was in there."

"Was anyone in line after you?"

"No."

"Not Hannah Kleemeyer?"

"No."

"So you lied about that."

"Yes, yes. I lied. May I please continue?" He glared at the detectives. *I'm handing you my head on a platter, assholes. Why don't you let me?*

"Be our guest," Hodgkins said, unfolding his arms to wave a hand in invitation.

"I took my time so everyone else would be gone when I came out. I wanted to catch Geoff alone."

"Why is that?" Jarvis asked.

"We were lovers. Do I need another reason?"

"It would set the stage. You understand that as a performer, don't you?" Hodgkins said.

"Toby Grant had been dropping little remarks at the last few rehearsals. Not to me, but in earshot. I'm sure it was deliberate. I think he wanted me to know he was screwing Geoff."

Leander examined their faces. Were they shocked? Disgusted? If there was ever a pair of latents likely to act out homophobic behavior, it was these two.

"You were going to confront him about cheating on you." Jarvis said this as a statement of fact, not a question.

"I was going to ask him about it. Nothing more. You don't confront Geoff, it never ends well. I just wanted to put him on alert that his latest pet was bragging about doing him."

"You wanted to jam Grant up, so to speak," Hodgkins said.

"Geoff does not like his toys talking out of school."

"What happened?" Jarvis asked.

Leander felt like a ping pong ball. Really, the way these two were bouncing back and forth was very disconcerting. "When I went into the nave, they were alone. Geoff was sitting on the end of the organ bench and Toby was strad-dling his lap and they were kissing. I lost it. I screamed at them."

"What did you scream?"

"Something like, 'Must you do that in front of me?'"

"Then what happened?"

"Toby got off Geoff's lap and he turned around and said something snotty like, 'Oh, there you are. I was just keeping

Geoff warm for you.' Geoff patted him on the ass and told him to run along like a good boy and he'd talk to him later. I waited until Toby left and started screaming at him again."

"What did Lawrence do?"

"He waited until I ran down and he had this little smile on his face, the superior one when I know he's going to treat me like a child up past bedtime. Finally he said, 'Oh, Leander, Toby is nothing for you to worry about. I'm just keeping him happy so his father will fund *Faust.*'"

"What's Fowst?" Jarvis asked.

*Seriously?* "It's an opera. It's very famous."

"How did you respond to that?"

"I said something like, 'the only way you can keep him happy is to give that little slut the lead.' And Geoff said something like, 'Don't you worry, You've still got *Faust.* It doesn't matter that he can suck like a vacuum cleaner. He'll never be good enough for *Faust* and I won't damage my reputation by giving it to him, no matter how many pots of money his father has.'"

"And?"

Leander stared down at the glass of water, rotating it between his hands.

"This next bit is hard."

"As hard as killing someone?" Hodgkins asked.

"Then he said, 'So you'll just continue to do what I tell you, and it doesn't matter how many fanboy sluts I take on. From now on, you'll keep your mouth shut.' It was so ugly and he said it in such a reasonable voice, like we were discussing what to have for dinner. I just lost it. And I hit him with the candlestick before I even knew what I was doing."

"How many times did you hit him?" Hodgkins asked.

"Just once."

"You're lying," Jarvis said.

"I'm not lying! That's what happened. I hit him so hard he fell off the bench. He wasn't moving. It happened just like I said."

Jarvis sneered. "Said today, or in the statement you made a week ago?"

"You already confessed to killing him," Hodgkins said. "Why lie about how many times you hit him?"

"I told you, I only hit him once!"

Hodgkins removed a photo from the file folder and dropped it on top of the puddle of water. It was a closeup of Geoff Lawrence's head in a pool of blood, his skull crushed.

Leander lurched back, toppling his chair. He fell, rolling onto all fours, vomiting violently until his dry heaves devolved into keening wails.

"I didn't do that. I swear I didn't do that. I couldn't do that." Jarvis righted the chair while Hodgkins dragged Leander up by the collar. He dropped Leander onto the chair and shoved his face inches from the photo.

"Does that look like you hit him once, asshole? You lost it. Maybe you didn't realize how many times you hit him, like you didn't realize you were swinging that candlestick in time to stop yourself."

"No, no, no, no," Leander moaned. "Take it away, take it away."

Leander didn't understand what he was seeing. It hadn't been like that. Not even in his nightmares had it been like that. Hodgkins's sweaty hand forced Leander's nose into the photo, sending him into a flashback of having his head shoved into a toilet by jocks in high school.

His stomach convulsed at the memory. Then the anger

147

grew and cleared his head. *Think, think, think!* He shoved away from the table and looked Hodgkins in the eye. "I recant my confession."

"What the hell?" Jarvis said.

"When I left Geoff, he was lying on the floor, but there was no blood. I only hit him once, like I told you. Someone else did that. I couldn't have killed him because if I had, there would have been no reason for anyone to crack his head open. If you want to talk to me again, it will be with a lawyer. I'm leaving now."

"Hold on, even if we believe you, just because someone else beat his head in doesn't mean you didn't kill him first," Hodgkins said.

"Yes, it does. If I'd killed him first, his heart would have stopped and there would be no pool of blood."

Leander stood up, dry-eyed. He wiped traces of vomit from his chin with the back of his hand, then shot his cuffs. "Gentlemen, good day to you." He turned and walked out the door.

LIA SAT in the rear seat of the Blazer as Peter took the long way downtown. Hannah sat in front, cuddling the Fur Boys in her lap as he drove. Lia supposed Peter chose the tree-lined drive down Central Parkway to give Hannah a chance to gather herself before she faced Hodgkins and Jarvis. He could be kind like that.

The interview should take about an hour, time enough to walk the Fur Boys over to the chi-chi canine water feature at Washington Park. Peter didn't anticipate an arrest. While Hannah had tampered with evidence, Heckle and Jeckle would be too busy with Leander to sort out what charges to file against her. That would come later, if the D.A. wanted to file charges at all.

Lia remembered the betrayed looks Honey and Chewy gave her when she left without them and tamped down the guilt she felt. Handling five dogs would be too much, even with dogs as well behaved as these. She kept her fingers crossed that Hannah would not be detained. If that happened, she would wind up taking the Fur Boys back home. Honey and Chewy were tolerant of most dogs, but the Fur Boys were attention hogs and her own four-footed children could be jealous on their own turf.

The drive took them over the Ludlow Viaduct, a steep bridge that climbed up from Northside, over I-75 to Clifton. Tall, arching walls of hurricane fencing encased the viaduct on both sides to keep vandals from throwing bricks on the cars below. As they drove through the chain-link tunnel, Lia wondered if Hannah was experiencing the sensation of being caged in as an omen. She placed a hand on Hannah's shoulder and gave it a gentle squeeze.

Hannah turned around in her seat and reached out to Lia. "Thank you for coming with me. I need all the moral support I can get."

Lia took her hand. "I'm your friend in this. There isn't much I can do, but I can be here for you."

They were silent for the rest of the drive. Peter pulled his Blazer into the parking lot behind District One, a looming edifice of yellow brick many times the size of District Five and taking up most of a city block.

"Walk with us to the door?" Hannah asked Lia. "That way I can spend a few more minutes with my guys."

"Certainly," Lia said. She felt a niggle of impatience with

Hannah. *It's an uncomfortable interview, not hard labor in Siberia. ... Be nice, Anderson. She was trying to do the right thing. Now she's facing charges and she doesn't know what to expect. A police interview room is horrible, even when you're innocent and everyone knows it.*

The group made a solemn parade as they rounded the building, halting when the sidewalk opened onto the busy concrete plaza fronting the building. Hannah squared her shoulders, mutely handing the leashes to Lia.

One of the quartet of glass doors into the building caught the sun as it flung open, flashing in their eyes. Leander stormed out. He stopped, stunned, when he saw Hannah. "You bitch!" he screamed. "You killed Geoff and made me think I did it!"

Activity halted as civilians and officers stared at the pair now facing off like gunslingers in an old western. Leander flew down the steps and launched himself at Hannah. Hannah ducked behind Lia. The three of them went down in a clumsy tangle of legs, dogs, and leashes. The dogs snapped and howled. Leander roared as Rory bit him, then rolled on top of Lia, trying to get an open shot at Hannah, while Hannah shoved at Lia ineffectually from the bottom of the pile and yelled over the din for the dogs to chill out.

"Buddy!" Hannah shrieked.

The little dog stood, frozen and glassy-eyed, then fell onto his side, foaming at the mouth and paddling his legs as if he were swimming.

"Buddy," Hannah shrieked again, redoubling her efforts to push Lia aside. "Let me go, he's seizing!"

Leander's crushing weight disappeared as he was plucked away by Peter. Hannah gave Lia a brutal shove. Lia tumbled over, her eyes landing on Leander as Peter forced him face-down on the concrete. Behind her, Hannah crooned," It's all right, it's going to be all right," while Buddy's fur sibs continued to howl.

Lia sat up as Peter wrenched Leander's arms behind his back and held him immobile. A uniformed officer stood over Peter, handing him a pair of cuffs.

"Thanks, man," Peter said.

Lia glanced over at Hannah. The admin stroked Buddy with one hand and stared at the phone in her other hand, speaking soft nonsense while Buddy's legs continued to paddle. "Such a good little love, it's going to be all right, it's just a little spell, you'll be better in a minute, just relax." It dawned on Lia that Hannah was timing the seizure.

Leander lay and moaned, his face red, tears streaming down his cheeks. "She killed him, she killed him. Oh, Geoff, oh, God, Geoff."

"Are you finished?" Peter asked.

Leander lifted his head, bits of debris stuck to his scraped, tear-streaked cheeks. He nodded. Peter grabbed his collar and pulled him into a sitting position. They were now surrounded by officers.

"What's going on here?" a sergeant asked, his hands on his duty belt, ready to reach for his Taser if needed.

"I don't know. Leander, would you like to explain why you attacked Hannah and Lia?"

"I didn't mean to hurt Lia. She was in the way. ... All this time ... I thought I killed Geoff. Hannah told me I killed him—and it wasn't true! I never did that to Geoff! I hit him, but I didn't beat his head in! They showed me the picture. I would never do that to Geoff. I wouldn't do that to a dog!" He glared at Hannah, who sat on the concrete, stroking Buddy. Buddy lifted his head and whimpered while Dasher sniffed at him. Rory stood, quivering, his buggy eyes leveled accusingly at Leander.

"She saw Geoff last!" Leander insisted. "She killed him!"

"Leander, no! Geoff was dead when I found him." Hannah turned to Peter, "Everything I told you is the absolute truth!" She turned back to the traumatized dogs, gathering them to her.

Peter bent down to Lia. "Are you okay?"

"A bruise or two, nothing serious."

He handed her his keys. "Take the Blazer. I'm going to be here a while."

"No, I don't know when your mommy is coming to get you. Maybe never. I'm sorry. You lost your dad. Now, maybe you don't have Hannah anymore, and I don't know what's going to happen. Did your mommy kill your daddy? How would you know? You weren't there."

The Fur Boys huddled at Lia's feet, Buddy's head resting on her instep. Four freaking hours full of worry. *Damn Peter, he could have called. He should have called.* She wanted to get up, needed to stretch, but Buddy's head pinned her foot to the floor and she couldn't bear the idea of disrupting his life any more than it already was, even in such a little matter. *Poor little guys. They haven't a clue what's happening. And neither do I.*

Hannah had given her hurried assurances that Buddy would be fine now that his seizure was over and all she needed to do was keep him quiet. Lia looked up canine epilepsy on the internet just in case. She knew Buddy was already taking medication. According to the website, his seizure was most likely a reaction to extreme stress. *Taking the dogs down with Hannah wasn't such a good idea after all.*

Alerted by some silent signal, the Fur Boys popped their heads up and dashed for the door, barking maniacally. *Thank God. That has to be Hannah.* Honey crossed her paws over her muzzle. Chewy joined in the chorus, for once his voice not the highest pitched of the pack. Viola padded to the door and shoved the other dogs aside, her lip curled.

A car door slammed. Lia could barely hear Peter's faint "Thanks," through the canine din. A hand, Peter's hand, smacked the roof of a car as if he were slapping the flank of a horse.

Lia opened the door as the patrol car pulled away. The dogs dashed out, jumping on Hannah. She sat on the steps and gathered them in, her head bowed.

Lia exchanged a look with Peter. *Later,* he mouthed. "Can you drive Hannah home in her car? I'll follow in the Blazer."

"I'll get my jacket. Will you bring the dogs along? We've all got cabin fever."

Hannah handed her keys to Lia and stood up. She opened the back door of her Hyundai. The Fur Boys jumped in but continued to stare at Hannah as if worried she would disappear again. Lia got in the driver's side. Hannah sat in the passenger seat, silently looking out the side window.

*Okay, if you don't want to talk, that's your business.*

The minutes ticked away as Lia drove, winding up Hamilton Avenue to College Hill and through the business district.

"It's okay if you don't want to talk, but I don't know where you live," Lia said.

"Sorry. Belleair Place. Left on North Bend, two blocks down on the left.

Hannah pointed through the windshield a few minutes later. "That's it. Halfway down the street, the brown brick with the porch swing." Lia pulled into the drive and turned off the engine. It was a neighborhood of big yards, old trees, and covered porches that ran the width of every house. Lia could understand not wanting to trade this quiet street for Dr. Lawrence's mansion.

"I didn't do it," Hannah said quietly. "No one believes me, but I found Geoff just like I said. I thought I was protecting Leander. Now I don't know." Peter pulled in behind them. The women got out of the car, Hannah trailed by her furry escort.

Lia gave Hannah a hug. "It will work out. I'm sure of it."

Hannah sniffed and gave her a sad smile. "I hope so."

Peter retrieved something from the back of his Blazer that turned out to be a brown paper bag. He followed Hannah to her doorstep. "I'll just be a minute." He told Lia.

Lia hopped into the Blazer. She dropped her head against the headrest and closed her eyes. Honey's muzzle snuffled at her ear. Lia reached back and scratched her ears. Chewy squirmed between the seats and climbed into her lap. "It's okay, guys. The alien invaders are gone. You can have your mommy back."

She heard Peter pop the rear hatch and slam it shut.

"What happened?" Lia asked when he joined her in the car.

"A lot of he said, she said. They let both of them go for now because they don't know who to charge. Heckle and Jeckle expressed their displeasure that I took Hannah's statement."

"Assholes."

"Your mouth, God's ear."

"What happens next?"

"Hannah gave me the clothes she wore that night. She already washed them, but there should be traces of blood spatter if she killed Lawrence. Leander has also been asked to provide clothes. H and J will try to decide who's lying and dig up evidence to support a charge."

## 11

## SATURDAY, NOVEMBER 12

Lᴵᴬ ᴄᴏɴᴛᴇᴍᴘʟᴀᴛᴇᴅ ᴛʜᴇ ꜱᴛᴀᴄᴋ ᴏꜰ ᴘᴀɪɴᴛ ᴄᴀɴꜱ ꜱɪᴛᴛɪɴɢ ᴏɴ the kitchen floor of her new home. She'd gone for easy neutrals in all her previous apartments. In her first true home after a lifetime in rentals, she would let color live. She wondered what that said about her.

For the living room, she'd selected a faded salmon color that reminded her of fallen leaves on the forest floor, when the light hit them just right. Turmeric yellow would warm up the kitchen. She went with taupe in the studio, a neutral with a hint of warmth that would not distort colors while she was painting. It had been murder to match at the paint store.

She'd been nervous about the inevitably blotchy, amateur paint job she expected until she'd seen the opportunity this situation presented. Any flat color eventually felt dead to her, and it was always impossible to get exactly the shade she wanted. So she bought three cans of paint for each room, a gallon of a base color and quarts of two hues a half tick away in opposite directions.

Today they'd slop paint on the walls. Tomorrow she'd come back and play with sponges and rags to add texture and depth with the extra colors, and it would actually help if the base coat was a bit uneven. After that, the guy she'd hired would refinish the floors. Everyone would be happy. She could move in after Thanksgiving, and Peter could stop sleeping in the basement.

Peter popped in the back door, jacket-less in the unseasonably warm weather and carrying a cup of coffee. Lia recognized the misshapen mug as one Alma made in a ceramics class. He wrapped an arm around her shoulder and pulled her to him as he surveyed the pyramid of cans.

"Good morning, Woman of Many Colors. The kids are settled with Aunt Alma." He nodded at the paint. "When do you want to get started?"

BAILEY AND CYNTH were first to arrive. No stranger to physical labor, Bailey came ready to work in disreputable painter's pants, her swing of red hair restrained with an ancient bandana. Cynth had stuffed her waist-length braid under a knit cap in a lumpy tower that Lia was certain would not survive the day.

Lia started them in the space Lia designated for her office. Cynth began rolling paint while Bailey masked the woodwork. Lia took a brush to the corners, cutting in edges the roller wouldn't reach.

"I'll be back after I get the rest of the baseboards," Bailey said, leaving with an arm loaded with rolls of masking tape like so many gypsy bangles.

It was after one when Bailey popped back in, munching an apple. "Nice job."

"Thanks." Lia set her roller down and put her hands on her waist, stretching until her back popped. "We should be finished here in another—ten minutes, you think?"

"If that," Cynth said.

"Good," Bailey said. "Then we can eat lunch together."

"What's on the menu?" Cynth asked.

"Taco Bell," Lia said. "We're eating light so we don't fall into a food coma afterwards. Who's picking it up?"

"Brent and Peter left fifteen minutes ago. They should be back any time."

"Since you're here, I have a question for you," Lia said.

"Shoot."

"Does John have a pet name for you?" Lia asked. John was Trees's real name, and the only name Bailey used for her hacker boyfriend except around a very few, trusted friends.

Bailey held a finger in the air while she swallowed her bite of apple. "Wow, that's out of the blue. John likes to change it up. My favorites are 'my goddess' and 'my swan.' Why do you ask?"

"Peter always calls me 'babe.'"

"Oh. I'm so sorry."

"What's wrong with that?" Cynth asked. "All guys call their women babe."

Lia shuddered. "That's just it. It makes us all interchangeable. It's part of the McRomance #1 package at the drive through: surf and turf, roses, champagne, a box of

Godiva chocolates, and you get your choice of 'babe' or 'baby.'"

"Add a white limo and caviar, and you've got an episode of *The Bachelor*," Bailey said.

"If he's an alpha-male billionaire, it has to be a helicopter ride," Lia said.

"I like roses and champagne," Cynth said.

"I like Cristal and Dom Perignon," Lia said, "but the cheap stuff never did it for me and the good stuff is so expensive I can't enjoy it. I keep thinking about the utility bills one bottle could pay for."

"I think roses are sad," Bailey said.

"Why is that?" Cynth asked.

"It's the aroma that gets your glands going. For romance, give me ylang-ylang or freesia. Domestic hybridizers have bred roses for longer lasting blooms and lost the scent in the process. They feel sterile to me."

Cynth pouted. "You're tromping all over tradition. These things are tradition because they're the best of everything."

"According to who?" Bailey asked. "I bet all the guys got together one day and picked out the most expensive stuff they could find so they'd never have to think about romance again," Bailey said.

Lia looked away from her half-painted corner. "Romance should be unpredictable. It's when someone surprises you with a gift unique to you, something they see that reminds them of you and no one else. When you get it, you realize that they really know you and want to please you. … Or when they give you a piece of themselves that no one else has." She touched the lump under her shirt, a pendant Peter had made from an opal he found as a boy. *I should feel guilty for nitpicking.*

"Sometimes John gives me something I want, something I never told him about. That blows me away," Bailey said.

"It shouldn't," Lia said. "He's psychic."

"I'm just happy when a date bothers with more than pepperoni pizza and their favorite beer," Cynth said.

Lia scraped the paint off her roller and into the can. "To me, roses and champagne are pizza and beer. They just cost more."

"There's something obligatory about roses and champagne," Bailey said.

"Exactly," Lia said.

"You guys are ruining any love life I ever hope to have," Cynth grumbled.

"Don't you deserve better than ordinary?" Lia asked.

Cynth was silent, making Lia wonder if she'd gone too far.

"Excuse me, ladies." Brent stood in the doorway looking uncharacteristically disreputable in paint-splattered jeans and a tee shirt so faded Lia couldn't read it.

"Brent, if you want to make a woman feel special, what do you bring her?" Bailey asked.

Brent eyed Bailey suspiciously. "Roses and champagne. Why?"

Lia and Bailey looked at each other, snickering.

"What's wrong with that?" Brent asked.

"Why roses and champagne?" Bailey asked.

"Why not? It works."

Bailey snorted.

Lia folded her arms. "That's not romance. That's manipulation."

"How is it special if you give the same thing to everyone?" Bailey asked.

Cynth continued to roll paint on her wall, saying nothing.

"You're serious." Brent said.

"As a heart attack," Bailey replied cheerfully.

"It's expected. If I bring daisies I'm cheap. It's too easy to get wine wrong. A woman understands roses and champagne. Look, I just came to tell you lunch is here. I'm leaving."

Lia caught Bailey looking at Cynth, who was stubbornly facing the wall and rolling so much paint on one section it was about to start dripping. She had a split second to form a mental protest. *Oh, no, don't—*

"Cynth likes champagne and roses." Bailey tossed this bit of intel casually at Brent's retreating back. Cynth jerked her head from her task to give Bailey a murderous glare.

"She wouldn't if I brought them," Brent muttered.

LIA LEANED out the bedroom window and peered down the swath of grass that separated her house from Alma's, looking toward the street. She could see the rear of Peter's SUV through the narrow slice between the buildings. Peter and Brent had their heads in the back of Peter's Blazer, unloading bags of ice destined for Alma's. *Because nothing ruins a party like warm beer.*

Bailey hovered above Lia on a ladder, her elegant hands manipulating the blue painter's tape around the window frame with an assured touch.

Lia leaned against the sill and eyed her quarry. Across the room, Cynth knelt on the tarp and cautiously dipped a wooden stirrer in a new can of paint, a cross between jade and moss carefully selected by Lia after much deliberation. The rest of the guys were tackling the kitchen. *Time to lance the boil.*

"What's the story with you and Brent, Cynth?"

Bailey looked down from her perch, her Marty Feldman eyes bright. "I like stories."

Cynth kept her focus on the paint, stirring slowly as if worried she might not do it right.

*Stubborn, much?* "Brent started mooning over Cynth before I met him and she won't give him the time of day."

"Brent?" Bailey asked. "He's so pretty, how can you resist?"

Cynth scoffed, her eyes still on the paint. "Looks aren't everything."

"No," Bailey agreed, "but they sure are something. Especially his."

"Is it true what Peter told me about the District Five Christmas party three years ago?" Lia asked.

Cynth smirked. "That I gave him an Amazon Dash button? Best four dollars and ninety-nine cents I ever spent."

"Isn't that a thing you stick on the wall so you'll never run out of your favorite product?" Bailey asked. "What's the big deal about that?"

Lia watched Cynth for signs of cracking. So far it wasn't happening. "It was a Trojan Dash button, so he can have condoms on his doorstep whenever he needs them. It was the hit of the party," Lia explained.

Cynth looked up from her paint and grinned. "He thought it was funny until he found out I was the one who gave it to him. Poor baby went around looking wounded the rest of the night. The badge bunny he came with finally gave up on him and started hitting on the other guys."

"You never miss an opportunity to give him a hard time," Lia said. "What's up with that?"

Cynth sat back on her sneakers and looked at Lia and Bailey. Lia knew their faces must be as avid as baby birds under a dangling nightcrawler. "You really want to know?" She exhaled audibly. "Of course you do."

"It's obvious there's history between you," Lia said.

"You can't repeat this. Not even Peter knows."

Bailey and Lia nodded in sober, wide-eyed agreement and waited.

"I was still a patrol officer when I met Brent and I'd just started at District Five. We were at McKie Rec Center. District Five is too small to have a gym, and McKie gives a special deal to cops."

"You met him when he was hot and sweaty? Be still my heart," Bailey said, patting hers.

"I was the sweaty one. I was halfway through a 30 minute run on the treadmill when he walked in."

"Love at first sight," Bailey sighed.

"Get real. Lust maybe. I noticed him, that was all."

"And?" Lia asked.

"He hopped on the treadmill next to me and we started talking. He said he was an accountant from Atlanta, working on a project for Proctor and Gamble."

"That's not right," Lia said. "Brent was on the force in Atlanta before he came here."

"Exactly. He was here on loan, working undercover. There was a rumor that cops in District Five were working with the Taliband, that Northside gang operating back then. The rumor was they hooked up at McKie. Trouble is, lots of cops hang out at McKie and the brass downtown didn't know who to trust. The chief was friends with the chief in Atlanta, so they sent Brent up."

"I'm fascinated. What happened?" Bailey asked.

"He slept with me because he thought I was in on it."

"Oh, wow." Bailey said.

"He played me like a fish, met my folks, went to ball games with my brother. I thought we were in a relationship. He was looking for a collar."

"Oh, Cynth," Lia said, her heart brimming. "I'm so sorry."

Cynth looked up, a steely smile defying the wet glitter in her eyes. "That's the story. If you repeat it, I'll rip your eyeballs out and eat them."

She returned to her stirring. "I think that's good enough. Do you want me to pour it in the pans now?"

Lia nodded. "Sure, go ahead."

Bailey bit off a strip of tape. "What I want to know, is why you never went for Peter? You knew him before Lia. It was an open field."

Cynth glanced at Lia, assessing. "Besides him not being my type?"

"Peter's the kind of guy that grows on you," Lia said. "Why didn't he grow on you?"

"Too laid back. That, and he's the only guy I never caught staring at my boobs with drool leaking from the corner of his mouth. He was the only guy who took me seriously when I started at District Five and I wasn't about to risk that. Now he's like a brother. If he hadn't been a cop I might have looked in his direction, but it wouldn't have mattered."

"Why not?" Lia asked, riveted.

"He was looking for a woman he could take care of."

"How the hell did he wind up with me?" Lia asked.

Cynth smirked. "You were traumatized from finding Luthor's body when he first laid eyes on you. You imprinted on him, just like a baby duckling. By the time he realized that wasn't who you are, it was too late."

"I think he's still working that one out," Lia said dryly.

"It's good for him," Cynth said. "That family of his is too traditional. Have you met them yet?"

"No, they live too far away."

"They came up once to make sure the big city wasn't corrupting him and he brought them by the station. They're nice, but they thought I should be teaching kindergarten."

Lia decided to take advantage of Cynth's uncharacteristic chattiness. "Peter seems frustrated lately. Are Heckle and Jeckle giving him a hard time?"

"No more than usual. I don't think it's them, or not just them. I think it grinds his ass that he turned down the promotion to Homicide and wound up under their thumbs because of it. Add that to the way they're bungling Lawrence's case and ..." Cynth gave Lia a curious look. "You didn't know."

"No." Lia's attempt at a smile turned into a rictus. "I didn't. He said they passed him over."

"Idiot," Bailey said.

"Open mouth," Cynth said, "insert foot. I'm sorry. I can't believe he didn't tell you."

"Neither," ground out Lia, "can I."

PETER SIPPED his properly chilled beer and inhaled the steam coming off his chili spaghetti. *Is there anything better*

*than chili and beer? Chili, beer and a ball game, maybe.* He could see Lia through the doorway to the kitchen, laughing with Alma while she fed biscuits to a milling horde of dogs. He hadn't had a chance to talk to her all day.

Terry set his plate next to Peter's, then proceeded to twirl his fork in the spaghetti, loading it up with impressive skill. "This murder case, it's quite the cock-up, isn't it?" Light glinted off the lenses of Terry's Teddy Roosevelt glasses as he shoveled the monster forkful of Alma's chili spaghetti into his mouth.

"I can't talk about cases," Peter said.

"Bosh," Terry said around his food. He chewed, then swallowed. "You'll talk to Lia and eventually she'll ask for our help. I'm just cutting out the middleman, or in this case, the middlewoman."

"That's one way to look at it," Brent said. He sat at the other end of Alma's ancient dining table. With all four leaves added, the table took up the entire room, pinning Brent against the wall. "But I suspect we should maintain a pretense that we aren't leaking confidential information to civilians. Peter needs plausible deniability to soothe his conscience."

"It's not my case," Peter stared at his plate and wished violently for their friends to be gone, for Lia, a soft bed and an empty room.

Terry waved his fork in the air. "Though why there's such an uproar about a dead—"

Alma, in the process of setting a bowl of freshly spiral-ized zucchini noodles next to Bailey, jabbed a wooden spoon in Terry's face. "Stop right there. I heard about you, Terry Dunn. You're welcome in my house, but if you make slurs against my gay friends I will have Peter toss you out."

Terry backed away from the spoon, eyes fixed on it as if it were a poisonous snake ready to strike.

"That means no pie," Steve said conversationally. "In case you're wondering, I hear it's apple."

Terry looked down at his now threatened dinner plate.

Peter suppressed a chuckle. *Weighing his principles against Alma's excellent chili.*

Terry raised his head. "Ma'am, I respect your delightful hospitality and shall avoid demographic commentary for the duration."

Alma nodded. "See that you do."

"We might as well bring everyone in," Cynth said. "H and J screwed the pooch on this one. It's going to be anyone's game before you know it."

Conversation halted as Lia and Alma set large bowls of salad on both ends of the table. Lia looked around, apparently wondering why all eyes were trained on her. "What?"

"The Scooby Gang wants in on the Lawrence case," Peter said.

"Don't ask me," Lia said. "It's your case."

"Technically, it isn't Peter's case," Brent said. "We're just foot soldiers, assigned tedious and tiresome tasks at the whims of Hodgkins and Jarvis."

"Then you're free to gossip at will," Terry said.

"I can leave the room," Alma said.

"Don't be silly," Lia said. The look she gave Peter spoke volumes. *Volumes in Swahili.* "This is your home. Peter trusts you as much as I do."

Peter caved. "How much does everyone know?"

"Beside your main suspect recanting his confession, then implicating the woman who gave him an alibi?" Steve asked, stroking his Van Dyke beard.

Peter winced.

"Don't look at me," Lia said. "It was all over the news and social media this morning."

"What's the status of the investigation?" Jim asked.

Peter looked at his beer, the beer he'd hoped to sit back and enjoy after a hard day's work. "Heckle," he caught himself and began again. "Hodgkins and Jarvis were focused on the furnace guy until that scene at District One yesterday. Now they believe Hannah and Leander were both in on it and they're still colluding—only now their strategy is to screw up the case with mutual accusations."

"What would the point be to that?" Jim asked.

"The DA has to prove which one of them did it and how it was done. You can't present a jury with multiple possibilities. The mutual accusations create so much confusion, the DA won't be able to get beyond a reasonable doubt in a trial, no matter who they charge or what scenario they present—not without physical evidence that nails one of them, and we don't have that."

"Heckle and Jeckle came up with that?" Cynth asked. "They're not usually that smart."

Brent waved his fork. "Hot and Shi—" He cast a glance at Alma. "—Shinola's brain cells don't have the ability to accommodate theories of such sophistication. It was an ADA. I do know one thing. It was never the furnace guy."

"He looked good after I turned up that lawsuit Lawrence filed against him," Cynth insisted. "Porter is one of the few guys around who works on antique heating systems. He did a job for Lawrence years ago. Lawrence refused to pay the bill and topped that off with a bogus lawsuit. It cost Porter tens of thousands of dollars."

"What makes you say Nigel Porter is innocent?" Lia asked Brent.

"Porter was working on the furnace before the final rehearsal. The ladder that leads up to the trap door is painted white and it was clean when I went up. If he'd left the attic after he started on the furnace there would have been smudges all over that ladder. He left plenty of grease on it going down, with unfortunate results for my favorite suit."

Peter made a "huh" sound. "Did you pass that observation along?"

Brent swallowed a mouthful of chili. "They told us to butt out. I butted out. No skin off my nose if they run around in circles chasing the wrong guy."

"Poor Nigel," Lia said. "What about him?"

"He's a feisty guy," Brent said. "I have a feeling he likes the idea that people think he offed Lawrence."

"Who do you think did it?" Bailey asked Peter.

"That scuffle at District One had me wondering if they were both telling the truth."

"How is that possible?" Alma asked.

"You think someone slipped in after Leander left and finished him off before Hannah went back?" Steve said. "Who? And why?"

Terry jabbed a finger in the air. "As the first detective said, 'Once you eliminate the impossible, whatever remains, no matter how improbable, must be the truth.'"

"Sherlock Holmes wasn't a detective. He was a fictional character," Steve said. "He wasn't even the first fictional detective. That was Auguste Dupin in *Murders in the Rue Morgue.*"

"Mon Dieu," Terry said, eyes to the ceiling.

"The first real detective was François Vidocq," Jim said, "years before Poe."

"Who has a motive?" Bailey asked.

"It's a mistake to focus on motive," Peter said.

"Why?" Bailey asked.

"Motive can steer you in the wrong direction. People sometimes kill for reasons that make no sense."

"Still, it would be instructive to know the involved parties and the circumstances that drive them," Terry said.

Peter waved his hand in a Vanna White flourish at Lia. "You know the players. Be my guest."

It took Lia more than ten minutes to share her knowledge of the people around Lawrence.

"It's the Director of the school, obviously," Terry said. "And the Dean is in on it."

"Why do you say that?" Cynth asked.

"Cui bono? Who benefits? The money leads straight to them."

"I don't know that either of them would kill someone over a bequest they might never get." Lia said. "The money depends on the dogs living out their natural lifespan. If someone wanted to kill the bequest, all they'd have to do is sneak into Hannah's office when she's in the ladies' room and give one of the dogs a poisoned liver treat."

"But who would want to do that?" Jim said. "Then nobody gets the money. If the dogs die prema ... prema ... early, it goes to the state."

"The governor," Terry said.

Bailey rolled her eyes. "Like a few million is enough to make a difference in the state budget."

"I dunno," Steve said. "State finances aren't in such great shape right now. Ten million might not be enough to make the governor murder a person, but I bet he wouldn't hesitate to poison a few dogs."

Lia dumped a handful of cheese on top of her chili. "This bequest is like the Tar Baby. Hopewell has to build the concert hall according to specifications in the will to get the money. Who's to say how much building costs will go up in the next ten years? They could get in over their head with no way to pull out."

"Property values could skyrocket and double the value of the estate," Brent said.

"Or they could tank," Cynth rebutted.

"It's Clifton. The only way property values will tank is if it gets hit by an asteroid," Bailey said.

"Maybe Hannah's bosses knew about the bequest but not the conditions," Jim said.

"I had my eyes on everyone at the reading of the will," Peter said. "Girgenti was the only one who knew."

"In that case," Jim said, "the conditions are super-super-"

"Superfluous?" Lia said.

"Immaterial," Jim said.

"Do you think the dogs will live ten more years?" Cynth asked.

Lia shook her head. "Longer. Rory is only three. I've known Chihuahuas who lived to be twenty."

"I can't believe anyone would expect so much from Hannah—or anyone else—without giving her anything," Bailey said.

"He wanted it all to go into his concert hall," Steve said. "He knows the school will pony up to keep Hannah happy."

"Appalling and presumptuous," Brent agreed. "But I think you're looking in the wrong direction. I have my eye on the sweet young thing."

"Toby?" Bailey asked. "He's out of it. He left the chapel while Leander was there. He has no motive."

"Think about it. You're a self-absorbed, spoiled brat in a hot and illicit affair. When the shit—" Brent turned to Alma. "Pardon my French, I don't know what I was thinking."

"If you think that was French, I'm cutting off your beer. Keep going," Alma said.

"Ah … When the cow manure strikes the oscillating wind machine—"

Cynth snorted.

"—you're banished from ground zero. How could he resist sneaking back to hear what they said about him?"

"He was supposed to solo that night," Lia said. "You saw how upset he was. Do you really believe he would ruin his first chance to be center stage?"

"He might if it would preclude him from the suspect list," Brent said.

"You didn't spend half an hour with him right after it happened. I don't buy it."

"Young Toby is a performer," Brent said. "His behavior is so melodramatic, it would be difficult to tell the difference between an act and the real him."

"But that would go for everyone from Hopewell," Jim said. "They're all performers."

"I vote for the ex-wife," Steve said. "There's no one more vindictive than a woman scorned. Being left for a guy would amp that up a thousand percent."

"Did she know about the professor's gay lovers?" Alma asked.

Lia shook her head. "No one knows. Hannah says Constance has been very tight-lipped, and Hannah never had the nerve to ask her. Constance and I talked for a long time after Dr. Lawrence died and I couldn't say one way or the other."

"Suppose she didn't know and she overheard the argument," Alma said as she collected empty dishes. "Finding out you'd spent your life married to a man who cheated on you with other men, couldn't that send her over the edge? If he was my husband, I'd give him several good kicks if I found out I'd been treated that way. I might do worse."

"Excellent point," Lia said.

"Would you bash my head in if you found out about my gay lover?" Peter asked Lia. A momentary splinter of anger flashed in her eyes.

"I'll throw you an engagement party. That way I can be the first to toast your happiness."

"Ouch," Cynth said.

## 12

# SUNDAY, NOVEMBER 13

Lɪᴀ ᴘɪᴄᴋᴇᴅ ᴜᴘ ᴀ sᴘᴏɴɢᴇ ᴅᴀᴍᴘᴇᴅ ᴡɪᴛʜ ᴍᴏssʏ ɢʀᴇᴇɴ ᴘᴀɪɴᴛ and assessed the walls of her soon-to-be bedroom. There were the inevitable patchy areas, but those would only be noticeable to someone with a very critical eye and then only while they were looking at a blank wall. Peter was right. Add furniture and no one would notice. Even she would forget they were there.

But she hadn't been able to pass up the opportunity for more. Adding depth and texture to the color with sponges and rags made her feel like a kid with finger paints. It also provided a welcome diversion from the bombshell Cynth dropped the day before.

She found it necessary to walk away from anger and hurt, and terrifying to face it. Peter didn't like it when she withdrew. That was something she couldn't change, wouldn't change. After a lifetime of her mother's rages, Lia treated anger like a feral dog, to be approached with caution and safeguards, and only when you knew exactly what you were doing and why.

The party had run late the night before, until time for Peter to resume his vigil in the basement. This morning he'd gone straight to District Five instead of stopping by for breakfast. It had given her time to think. It had also given her time to stew. *Why didn't he tell me?*

The front lock rattled. Honey and Chewy, banished to the fume-free living room, barked excitedly. Peter's voice drifted down the hall. "Greetings, Woman Who Hides in Giant Cave."

"I'm in the bedroom," Lia called. *Okay, Anderson. It's clobbering time. How are you going to handle this?*

"I brought Dewey's. Where do you want to eat it?"

"Living room. I'll be right there."

She found Peter by the card table they'd set up, taking a plastic container of salad out of a brown bag and placing it next to an extra-large pizza box. He gave her a warm hello peck.

Lia shut her eyes. *Dammit, dammit, dammit. How do married people do this?*

Peter drew back and gave her an odd look. "I assume we eat the pizza while it's hot and the salad for dessert?"

Her answer was automatic. "You have to ask?"

They sat, drooling dogs scattered at their feet in strategic positions to protect the floor from marauding crusts. Peter passed Lia a paper plate.

"You drove this with lights and sirens going?"

"I used your Costco thermal bag to keep it warm."

Lia kept her eyes averted. It made it easier to make light conversation. "Ah. The man has brains as well as a nice set of glutes."

She selected a slice of pizza and set it on her plate, appetite warring with her desire to blast Peter with the news that had been smoldering in her since the day before. *Hangry is as hangry does. We'll have a more adult conversation if we're not starving.*

Peter stopped in the middle of his second slice and set it down. "Something's bothering you. What is it?"

Lia sighed. *Time to rip off the bandage.*

"Cynth let it slip yesterday that you turned down a promotion to Homicide."

Peter sat back and closed his eyes. "Do we need to talk about it right now?"

"You asked. We can finish the pizza first, since you went to so much trouble to get it here hot."

They continued the meal in silence. Lia kept her eyes on the salad as she dished portions onto paper plates. "I don't understand why you kept this from me."

Peter started to run a hand through his hair, then stopped to wipe grease off his fingers with a paper napkin. "I wasn't sure you'd understand why I turned it down."

"So you just kept it from me?"

"It seemed easier that way."

"How can we be life partners if you deliberately withhold something so important?"

"Married people don't tell each other everything. Dad doesn't tell mom everything, and they get along better that way."

"I'm not willing to have a relationship where partners share selectively to keep the peace and manipulate each other. Is that what you want?"

Peter shifted on his folding chair and took a bite of salad, chewing ruminatively. "I always thought of it differently. I figured Dad kept stuff from Mom so as not to worry her when telling her would get her upset over something that she couldn't do anything about."

"You mean he was using her as an excuse to engage in denial and try to handle everything himself. Maybe she couldn't have done anything about it, but maybe talking it out with her might have helped him work through problems or at least get something off his chest. Or was he keeping stuff from her that he knew she wouldn't like, like Blondie hiding her shopping sprees from Dagwood?"

"They have a good marriage."

"—Because that stuff leads to twenty years of quiet antagonism and no sex. Johnny Lee Miller was right about that. If you lose your job, are you going to head out the door every morning, pretending you're off to work while you drain the savings?"

"That's extreme, Lia."

"Where does it stop? You kept secrets from me about Desiree and the results went viral on YouTube. I'll never know what would have happened if we hadn't had that catfight. She might still be alive."

"You don't know that."

"No, I don't. I was too angry to call her back when she texted me. I'll never know what that was about. Protecting me from that uncomfortable truth didn't work out so well."

Peter pushed back from his salad, saying nothing. He walked to the window and stared out. "You couldn't have saved her. Her death had nothing to do with you."

"Can't you see that hiding things from me keeps us apart?"

Peter continued to stare out at the back yard. "I guess you think I'm a real jerk."

Lia walked to Peter and wrapped her arms around him from behind. "You turned down a promotion. I'm sure you had a good reason. Talk to me."

Peter turned in her arms and held her a long moment before he spoke.

"I don't want to work homicides all the time. I looked into homicide departments in other cities. Those guys never get any sleep. They're up for 36 hours straight and more sometimes. They don't have a life. Regular detective work is more nine to five and I get to know the people in the district. I like being part of a neighborhood. Homicide works all over the city and they never belong anywhere."

"That sounds reasonable to me. Why didn't you tell me they recruited you?"

"You're a career woman. You have your own business. Sometimes you work crazy hours to get projects done on time. I'm just not that ambitious. I like where I'm at and what I'm doing."

"So?"

"I figured you would be upset if I didn't take the promotion."

Lia pushed back in his arms, examining Peter's face. "I started my own business so I could do work I loved, the way I wanted to do it. Why would I want anything different for you? You haven't been fair to me."

Peter shrugged and looked away. "I wanted to tell you, but I got flashbacks of Susan screaming 'What kind of life will we have if you won't put yourself out there?'"

"You're going to lay this on Susan?"

"You don't get to be the only one with baggage."

"I guess not." Lia took Peter's face in her hands. "I'm not

Susan. I will never be Susan. If I turn into Susan, I will shoot myself. Do you have that straight?"

"Yes, ma'am."

"Your wallet and career do not reflect upon me as a person, and the life we lead will have a lot more to do with how we treat each other than how much money we have."

"It's only partly about Susan. That guy who went out the door pretending he was going to work, he did that because he needed his wife to be proud of him. It's what gets a guy like me up in the morning, knowing I'm taking care of my family, that my wife and kids are proud of me. You're my family. I need you to be proud of me."

Lia was dumbfounded. "Why wouldn't I be proud of you?"

"I was working a homicide when we met. It's a sexy gig for a cop."

"And?"

"I didn't even solve that one."

"You were the only one who believed it was a case. And you did solve it. You were just late to the party."

"You got there first."

"Not by choice."

"You have a bullet hole as a result."

"Peter, look at me." Lia took his face in both hands. "You spend your life helping people whose lives have been violated and torn apart. When you find answers for them, you help them feel safe again. That's big. And what makes Homicide the holy grail? Weren't you the one who said most murders can be solved in the first hour and the rest is proving it?"

"That may have been an exaggeration, but yeah. It's usually obvious who did it."

"You protect and serve, even when the people you're protecting and serving want to spit in your face. I will never have that kind of dedication. I will always be proud of you, and it's because of what's in here." She tapped his chest. "Not what title you have or how big your salary is."

She pulled his face down for a kiss.

"Trust is a two-way street, Kentucky Boy. You want me to rely on you more, I get that. But I won't have a relationship shored up with smoke and mirrors. I need you to trust that I will always support what you want in life. I need you to trust me enough to be honest with me about what's going on with you, no matter how unhappy you think it's going to make me."

## 13

# MONDAY, NOVEMBER 14

PETER STOOD IN THE TINY LOBBY OF DISTRICT FIVE WITH Hodgkins and Jarvis. The trio stared through the sidelights at Martha Culler's Volvo. She'd called a meeting for nine a.m. It was five till, but Martha still sat in her car, Leander Marshall beside her in the passenger seat. *Waiting for what?*

"Don't you have jaywalkers to cite, Dourson?" Hodgkins asked.

Jarvis snorted.

"You and your shadow don't live here anymore. Someone has to babysit while you're on the premises. I drew the short straw."

Martha Culler was the favored defense attorney of the well-to-do in Cincinnati. Her round, fresh-scrubbed face called to mind Sally Field. She was no nun, flying or otherwise. Martha's killer instinct had been honed gutting hogs on the family farm before she was tall enough to ride The Beast at King's Island. Rumor had it her efficiency with a knife was the reason her father never worried about her dates when she was in high school. Peter didn't know about her personal life, but he'd experienced her killer instinct in court.

Peter suspected Martha called the meeting at District Five for more than saving gas on a drive downtown. Saddled with a chair-less reception area only slightly larger than their excuse for an interview room, it was standard for officers at District Five to meet visitors out front. Martha had the perfect excuse to stage a public coup on the steps of the station.

A Channel 7 van topped with a satellite dish pulled into the gravel lot, confirming Peter's suspicions. The van driver circled the crowded lot, then parked in the lane, blocking cars.

"What are they up to?" Hodgkins growled. "She didn't say anything about reporters."

"I hope you don't mind if I go for popcorn," Peter said.

"Just as long as you go, hillbilly," Jarvis said.

Aubrey Morse, one of Channel 7's younger, hungrier reporters, jumped out of the van, leading with stoplight-red lipstick and a lack of concern for the fate of her pumps in the gravel. A cameraman handed her a mic as she strode toward the pair now emerging from the Volvo. The foursome walked to the base of the steps and stopped.

"They're setting up for a shoot. We'd better get out there," Hodgkins said. The big man smoothed his suit jacket and passed a hand over his hair.

"Have a care. That camera is pointed this way for a reason," Peter said, wondering why he bothered to warn them. *Maybe because I can count on them to do the exact opposite of anything I suggest.*

Hodgkins grunted at the reminder. He and Jarvis exited

the building at an unhurried pace calculated to communicate confidence. Peter waited for a count of three, then slipped out the door as if he was heading for a car. He leaned against a patrol car several feet behind the cameraman. *This should be good.*

Aubrey held her mic in front of Martha, whose face shone with the same zeal that won Sally Field an Oscar for *Norma Rae.* "Ms. Culler, Leander Marshall was last to see Geoffrey Lawrence alive. On Friday he admitted to striking Lawrence with the candle stand that was used to kill him. How can you say he's innocent?"

Martha held up a gym bag. "If Leander Marshall killed Professor Lawrence, he would have gotten blood on his clothes. These are the clothes he wore that night. You will find no blood on them. Leander Marshall assaulted Geoffrey Lawrence, but he did not kill him."

"How do we know these are the right clothes?" Jarvis asked. "They could be any clothes."

"Whose fault is that?" Culler demanded. "You would know you had the right clothes if you'd requested them when Toby Grant accused him. Where are Grant's clothes? Why didn't you line up all the performers and spray their clothes with luminol when you had them sequestered at the cemetery? Dr. Lawrence's murder would have been resolved before the night was out."

Aubrey's face was intent. "Ms. Culler, what is luminol and why should it have been used at the scene?"

"Everyone in Norman Chapel with Dr. Lawrence was wearing black. Blood doesn't show on black clothing. The killer could have easily walked off the scene with the full blessings of the investigating officers. If you spray an object with luminol, any blood stains will glow in the dark. There was plenty of dark at the cemetery. The failure of the investigating detectives to take this step has caused my client emotional trauma and put his freedom at risk."

"Leander Marshall left the scene," Hodgkins said.

Aubrey smiled as she moved the mic closer to Hodgkins. "And went home. I understand you made no attempt to find him that night. It's been twelve days since the brutal murder of Geoffrey Lawrence. How much longer did you plan to take before pursuing this avenue of investigation?"

"This investigation is ongoing and—"

Culler interrupted. "This investigation has been mishandled from the start, and my client is suffering from your incompetence."

Peter looked at his watch. Plenty of time for this to hit the noon news. Maybe he and Brent could scare up that popcorn.

PETER, Brent, and a contingent of uniformed officers from District Five followed Heckle and Jeckle into Hopewell's main hall. Peter caught sight of Lia having her mid-morning chai with Hannah as they passed the office. Lia's eyes widened. She opened her mouth to speak. Peter gave her a minute shake of his head and walked by.

Michael Wingler and Suki Thomas waited in the recital hall, the performers from Fauré's *Requiem* sprawled over the two rows closest to the stage in a sullen and disaffected horde. Lia's scaffold sat abandoned in the far aisle.

"We've gathered everyone here," Wingler began, "because the police need our help in their investigation into Dr. Lawrence's murder. I realize that as private citizens, you have the right to refuse your assistance until such time as a warrant is issued. As students of this school, your continued enrollment depends on your cooperation.

"The police have requested the clothing you wore the night Dr. Lawrence was murdered. As there are no identifying marks on your concert blacks, they will accompany each of you to your home and take all black clothing. You will be given a receipt. It will be returned to you as soon as possible, unless, of course, it contains evidence."

A young man with a skeletal build and shaggy, dyed-black hair jumped up. "That's my entire wardrobe! What am I supposed to wear, fig leaves?"

Suki Thomas pursed her lips. "Detective Hodgkins, black is a fashion statement for many of our students. Is there some way to limit this? Perhaps you don't need tee shirts or jeans? What about socks?"

Hodgkins rocked back on his heels. "We'll need socks and stockings. What would they have been wearing?"

"For performances we stipulate black slacks, vests, and dress shirts for the boys. The girls wear floor length dresses."

"We'll do that then."

"What about underwear? Do you want that too?" one of the girls asked, slyly.

"Gross! I don't want *them* sniffing my panties!" another girl said, pointing at Hodgkins and Jarvis.

Hodgkins rolled his eyes. "No underwear."

"You'll be transported home by one of these officers, who will collect your clothes and give you a receipt. You may choose to stay home or return to school."

"This is ridiculous! My father won't allow it!" Toby Grant shouted, folding his arms with a mulish expression.

Wingler's face remained admirably impassive. "You are welcome to pack your things and leave."

"I want a refund!" the skeletal boy complained.

"This is turning ugly," Brent whispered to Peter.

"Not our case," Peter whispered back.

"Whoever did Lawrence has gotten rid of their clothes by now, unless they're total idiots."

"Not all of these kids have money. If he was killed by a broke student, they may have kept the clothes."

Brent hissed in Peter's ear. "What a dog and pony show. We get to spend all day chasing down clothes and it won't prove a damn thing."

"You wouldn't be wrong. But if they don't do it, it'll leave a hole in the state's case and Culler will happily drive her Volvo through it."

Wingler raised his voice to be heard over the mutinous muttering. "While you are waiting, you need to turn in your phones and laptops, so you can't call anyone to remove the clothing from your premises."

The muttering turned into outrage.

The skeletal boy jumped up. "What are we supposed to do all day? Suck our thumbs?"

"May I suggest you study?"

BLACK CLOTHING DRIFTED down from the sky, piling around Peter until he couldn't move. A naked chorus sang Beethoven's Mass, the unified voices creating a wall of sound that beat down on him like cannon fire. The performers raised their faces and arms to the heavens at the crescendo. The sky opened up in response and a torrent of blood cascaded upon their bodies in red rivers. The chorus sang on, oblivious.

Something stroked Peter's back. It felt good, so he sighed and smiled in his sleep while the chorus sang. Geoffrey Lawrence whispered something too softly for him to hear. He wished Geoffrey would shut up because he wanted to enjoy the warm stroking. He reached out his hand and shoved Lawrence's face away. Lawrence bit his ear.

Peter shot up, shoving one hand under his pillow for his gun as he rose, the other arm sweeping around in an automatic defensive move as his eyes popped open.

"Whoa, Cowboy!"

Fully awake, Peter found himself staring into Lia's shocked face. It bobbed in the glow of her cell phone as they wobbled on the spongy inflatable bed.

"Not exactly the welcome I was expecting," Lia said.

Peter scrubbed his face with his hand. "You should know better than to sneak up on a man doing guard duty."

"Uh huh. And your strategy is to warn off the copper thieves with your snoring?"

"I wasn't snoring."

"Sure you weren't."

"You didn't have to bite me."

"I tried being nice. I rubbed your back for a good two minutes. When that didn't work, I whispered sweet nothings in your ear. I only bit you because you shoved me in the face."

"Sorry. I have no idea why I was sleeping so soundly."

"Copper thieves could have danced the Macarena on your head while they ripped my plumbing out."

"Viola would have sounded the alarm before it went that far."

Lia aimed her phone at the corner where Viola slept undisturbed. "Uh huh." She clicked the light off.

"She's used to you. She wouldn't sleep through a stranger. Not that I mind the company, but why are you here?"

Lia's disembodied hand stroked the hair off his forehead. "You didn't come for dinner and I missed you. I hated the way we left things yesterday. I'm horny. Take your pick."

"All of the above?"

"That, too."

Peter lay back down, tugging Lia with him. They sank into the uncertain surface.

"When did you last inflate this bed? It's treacherous."

"A couple days ago. I guess I could top it off, but I'm not getting up. What time is it?"

"It's after two. I couldn't sleep."

"Where are the children?"

"They're back at the apartment. They won't care where I am until it's time to go to the park. You were talking in your sleep. What were you dreaming?"

Peter reached for wispy images that slipped out of his mind like water through a sieve. He snagged one detail. "It was raining pants."

"Pants? Slacks or panties?"

"Slacks. And dresses and shirts. Leftover from rounding up all those clothes today. God, what a waste of time."

"The students were in such a foul mood over it I couldn't paint. That's why I left."

"A pointless exercise to make it look like we're taking strong, assertive action. All because Heckle and Jeckle didn't think to look for blood at the scene."

"I imagine it's hard to think of everything."

"Brent and I did everything but hand them the luminol. If they find blood on any of the clothes we collected today, I'll drink your swamp water smoothies for a month."

Lia stroked his face. "Shhhh. I didn't come here to raise your blood pressure. Not that way, anyway."

"Oh yeah?"

"I just wanted to connect."

"Is that so."

"Uh huh."

"And how did you plan to do that?"

Lia snuggled in closer. The partially inflated bed, unaccustomed to bearing the weight of two people, dipped under her weight. One hip met cold concrete, separated only by a few millimeters of vinyl.

"Peter, we have to inflate this bed. I'm touching the floor and it's going to give me frostbite."

"Let's try this instead." Peter scooted to the center of the bed and rolled Lia on top of him. Her hair curtained their faces, shutting out what little ambient light there was and creating a deeper void in the darkness, broken only by tiny twin reflections where he knew her eyes to be. He pulled his sleeping bag over her.

"Better?" Peter asked.

"Now you get to have frostbite."

"I'm used to it."

"You're going to get sick, even if you are bundled up like Nanook of the North."

"I'll be fine."

"Tell me that next week when I have to ply you with chicken soup and Kleenex."

Lia slid her hands under Peter's sweatshirt to find the furnace that was Peter's skin.

Peter flinched. "Talk about frostbite!"

"Sorry." Lia started to pull away.

Peter pressed his hands down on hers to keep them in place. "Leave them. They'll warm up soon enough."

Lia stretched her legs out along Peter's under the covers, feeling the tops of his shoes with her stockinged feet.

"You're wearing shoes? In bed? Seriously?"

"You want me chasing crooks in my socks? Then I really will have frostbite."

"You've been sleeping in your running shoes for six weeks?"

Peter found the appalled tone in her voice reassuring to his manliness. He supposed it was a throwback to adolescence when doing things that disgusted his sisters was proof of testosterone.

"The insulation is great. My toes are never cold."

"Peter—"

Over in the corner, Viola whuffed, a soft sound that Lia ignored. Peter placed a finger on Lia's lips, signaling her not to speak. Stealthy like a panther, Peter wrapped his hands around her waist and moved her off him. He took Lia's hand and pulled her up, feeling his way to a camp chair and silently urging her into it.

LIA SAT WARILY. She sensed more than heard Peter moving in the darkness. Peter's phone lit up, briefly illuminating his face as he tapped something into it.

She heard a loud snap coming from the bulkhead doors, which led from the back yard to the basement. Peter tapped one more button on his phone, then put it in his pocket. His lips brushed against her ear. "Bolt cutter," he breathed. "Stay here and don't move."

Lia's basement consisted of three rooms. The room they were in was the size of a bedroom and formed an ell on the side of the main room.

Peter left her as the doors creaked on rusty hinges, a dim silhouette against the faint, ambient light bleeding in from the cellar windows. Peter crossed the floor and took position beside the doorway, his gun in one hand.

Muffled noises emerged from the short stairwell as two sets of feet climbed down the wood steps. Voices drifted in from the other room.

"I tell you, I saw a light in here."

"You're nuts. Ain't no light. Ain't nobody here."

A whump sounded, followed by a clanking noise that must have been a bag of tools landing on the concrete.

"Shhhh!"

"Oh, fer Pete's sake. Who's going to hear us? The woman next door is eighty if she's a day and the other side is apartments. They can't hear us down here. You're paranoid. Cover the front windows while I look at the pipes."

An indistinct grumbling followed that Lia interpreted as "why don't *you* cover the windows while *I* look at the pipes," but in less polite terms that included "kiss" and "ass."

"There's nothing to stand on."

"Get the ladder out of the truck. Just be quiet about it."

"Get the ladder out of the truck. Yes sir, Mr. Bossman, sir. Coming right up." A moment later, Lia heard a muttered, "your ass."

"I didn't have to bring you. I could have brought Jamie. At least he knows when to keep his mouth shut."

Footsteps sounded on the wood steps, fading away. Lia

now heard a shushing noise of cloth against cloth. The 'whump' must have been some kind of canvas or block out drapes. Tension built as she kept her eyes on Peter. Viola now stood beside him, quivering, a black upon black blur, her nose pointing into the next room.

*How do they not know we're here?* Lia couldn't stand the suspense. She got out of her chair and padded across the floor, thankful she was only wearing socks.

"What are you going to do?" she whispered into Peter's ear.

Peter nudged Lia behind him. He turned toward her, felt along her shoulder for her neck and pulled himself to her ear and whispered. "Stay. I mean it."

The sound now drifting through the door was metal against metal. *Crowbar? Pipe wrench? When is Peter going to do something? Those are my pipes!*

Peter ducked his head around the corner and drew it back quickly. The sound of footsteps drifted back through the door accompanied by a thumping sound, like someone dragging something heavy down the steps. This was followed by the sound of someone dropping what was probably the aforementioned ladder on the floor.

Peter reached over to the wall. Light flooded the basement as he stepped into the glare.

"Surprise." He said it in the calm, low-key way so typical of Peter.

"Shit!"

"Told ya!"

Feet pounded across the floor and up the steps to the yard. Peter launched himself after the intruders, Viola bulleting at his heels. Lia followed in time to see Peter leap over an ancient wood stepladder, then disappear into the yard.

Lia hesitated for a tense moment, taking time to assure herself that the pipes were still intact. *Should I follow? Peter told me to stay. To hell with that! This is my house!* She grabbed her shoes.

The "whoop" of a police siren sounded outside as pulsing red and blue lights lit up the basement. Muffled shouting and curses followed. *Looks like Peter arranged reinforcements.* She took off at a trot.

A police cruiser, rack lights rotating, penned in a Chevy Silverado parked in the alley behind the house. Both intruders lay face down in the yard. Officer Brainard had his foot on the back of one of the thieves while Peter cuffed the other. The bigger man spewed filth at Brainard while the other spewed worse filth at his partner in crime.

"That's it," Lia announced. "I'm getting an alarm system."

Brainard spotted her and grinned. "Hey, Lia. Come to watch the show?"

"I don't get to see Peter in action very often."

"Did you catch his tackle? It was epic."

"I missed it. I had to put my shoes on."

Peter looked up and tossed her a look that was a combination of annoyance and concern.

"Babe, I'm a little busy right now."

She tossed her head at him and approached.

"Those jerks were going to tear my new house apart for a lousy two hundred dollars of scrap metal. I want to see their faces and I'm entitled to gloat."

Peter leaned down. "Hear that, punk? The lady wants to see your face." He took the man by the shoulder and rolled him over. "Have at."

The larger man was attempting to get up. Officer Brainard shoved him back to the ground with his foot.

"Brainard, stop playing with your food," Peter said.

"I wasn't hurting him. He should know better than to get up."

Peter shook his head and moved to cuff the second man.

Lia came closer to the smaller man, staring down into a defiant face peppered with acne. *He's not even old enough to drive.* She took in the shaggy, overgrown mullet, the stained flannel shirt, the greasy jeans hanging on a gangly frame.

"I knew you was in there." He turned his head, yelling at his partner. "But jackass wouldn't listen. Oh, no. I didn't know what I was talking about." He spit in the direction of the older man. "Ma's gonna kill you."

The older man growled. "Shut up. Shut the mother-loving fuck up."

Brainard hauled him up and pushed him toward the cruiser.

"Pat him down," Peter said. He stooped by the boy and pulled him into a sitting position then dragged him to his feet.

"Tell the nice lady you're sorry, Joey," he said.

"You know him?" Lia asked, shocked.

"We don't trade Christmas letters, but we've met. I picked Joey up for possession of stolen merchandise last year. The other guy's his uncle Bill. Graduated from breaking into cars, have you, Joey?"

"Fuck you."

"Unlike you, I have a girl."

Joey leered at Lia. "You doin' the cop?"

Lia stepped back, shocked.

Peter shoved Joey in the direction of the cruiser, where

he made the boy assume the position. "You really don't want to be here, babe."

Brainard pushed the older man's head down, forcing him into the patrol car while Peter patted Joey down for weapons. Joey jerked away from Peter and ran at Lia, hands still cuffed behind his back. Peter dived, grabbed his legs. Joey slammed face-first on the ground three feet from Lia. She could see blood seeping from Joey's nose.

"I just wanted a kiss," Joey whined.

"You'll get plenty of kisses where you're going." Peter grabbed him by the collar and pushed him stumbling toward the cruiser. Joey turned his head and stared at Lia as he stumbled ahead, licking his lips with lascivious intent, unaware or unconcerned that blood was now dripping on his shirt.

"I'm filing police brutality and entrapment!"

"That'll go far. In the car." Peter was less than gentle shoving Joey in next to his uncle. He slammed the door, then addressed Brainard. "Get them booked. I'll start the warrant." Peter started to walk away, then turned back. "And take your time about it."

"Yes, boss," Brainard said.

Lia's gut roiled with confused feelings. She wondered if he would have hit Joey if she hadn't been watching. And she wondered why she felt so aroused.

"Now I know why you didn't want me to get an alarm system. You weren't sleeping in the basement to keep anyone from breaking in. You were there to trap them. You used me."

Peter wrapped his arms around her. "Don't think too hard on it. We finally have cause to get a warrant on the carriage house behind Bill's place. I bet it's full of interesting stuff, in which case the houses in Northside will be safe, at least until someone else moves in and takes over."

"I guess that's a good thing. Thank you for saving my pipes."

"You're welcome."

"You called me 'babe.' Twice."

"I was in front of a cop and two criminals. I would have lost too many manliness points if I called you anything else."

"You were in extremis. I guess you can be forgiven."

"Heat of the moment, Woman Who Creeps in the Dark." He tipped up her chin and kissed her, adrenalin heating the kiss until her toes clenched and her knees dissolved.

Peter's voice was full of regret. "I've got to move if we're going to get into that carriage house before Bill's family has a chance to clear it out. Don't wait up for me."

He crossed the yard, heading for his car, then turned back. "And stay out of the basement. It's a crime scene."

Lia called after him. "The alarm goes in tomorrow!"

Peter held one hand over his head with the thumb up and continued walking.

A screen door slammed. Alma stepped into her yard wearing shearling lined scuffs and a floor-length chenille robe under a puffy parka. Her normally tame cap of raven hair spiked in a spectacular case of bed head.

"Is this what it's going to be like, having you next door?"

"I hope not."

"Good thing I don't sleep much anymore, or I might regret selling the house to you."

"How much did you see?"

"I heard them opening the basement doors. I looked out and saw what they were up to and called 911. I guess it wasn't necessary."

Lia looked at the gaping doors. "Dammit, they cut the lock. Now I don't have a way to lock it back up and I can't go into the basement because it's a crime scene. I'm not about to sit out in freezing weather and watch that door until Peter comes back."

"Come on in and have some tea. I imagine I have something you can use."

## 14

## TUESDAY NOVEMBER 15

LIA OPENED THE DOOR TO PETER'S BLOODSHOT EYES AT THREE p.m. She backed away when he snuffled inelegantly. "Don't kiss me."

"I love you, too," he said, bending down to pet Viola, who wriggled violently between Lia's legs. "I'm not coming in. I'm just here to get Viola. Then I'm crashing for the next eight hours. After that I'm going back to the basement."

"The hell you are." Lia grabbed the front of his jacket and pulled him inside. She brushed the hair off his forehead and laid her palm on it. "You're hot."

"I've been telling you that for years."

Lia shook her head, rolling her eyes. "You're sick."

"That's what Brent says."

Lia huffed in disgust. "You have a fever. You're staying here and you're going to bed."

"I've got to watch the basement."

"The crooks are in jail, in case you don't remember. I imagine word has gotten around about your trap."

"And the rest of Bill's relatives know I'm off my guard because he's in jail."

"Seriously?"

"They may not be smart, but they sure are cagey."

"If you're so sure the crooks of Northside are after my pipes, Brent can do it for one night."

"I asked. He said I was out of my mind."

"He's right."

Peter sneezed, then hauked something into his fist. He stared at the ugly glob in his hand. "Uh, excuse me while I wash."

Lia followed him into the kitchen. "I'll watch the basement. Then I'm having a security system installed. Tomorrow."

"No."

"No, don't sleep in my own basement, or no, don't get a security system? Not that it matters because both are going to happen."

"What would you do if Bill's ugly cousin showed up with all his friends?"

"Call the cops, what else?"

"By the time they arrive, you'll be tied up and bouncing around in the back of a rusty pickup, headed for a fate worse than death."

"What's Paul's number?"

"Brainard? I thought you had it."

"For exactly five minutes, six months ago."

"Why do you want it?"

"He's going to cover for you."

"Oh, for the love of—" Peter's rant was interrupted by another coughing fit.

"That's it." Lia shoved Peter toward the bedroom. "You're

staying. The last thing you need right now is pneumonia."

Peter braced an arm against the jamb. "Hang on a minute. I'll rest here this evening if it'll make you feel better, but I want a shower first. And I'm going to the house later."

Lia considered her options. Arguing would only make Peter dig in his heels. At least he'd agreed to lay down. It would be harder for him to get out of bed once he was in it, especially if, as she suspected, he was about to keel over. "Okay, take a shower. I'll get you some soup."

"I don't need any soup," he called to her retreating back.

She continued to the kitchen. "You wouldn't if you listened to me about your diet. Junk food is killing your immune system."

"Junk food is killing your immune system," he mimicked in an irritable sing-song.

Peter was never irritable.

She pulled one of her grandmother's Revere Ware saucepans out of the cabinet, added a quart of water, and turned on the burner. She considered adding a second quart but decided against it. *It'll take too long to boil. I want this ready when he comes out of the shower.*

She stirred in chicken base, fresh ginger and Thai chilies, then considered Peter's high tolerance for spicy food and added more chilies and ginger. While the soup was heating, she whisked two eggs until they were frothy. After that she peeled four cloves of garlic, picked a sprig of fresh cilantro off the bunch in her crisper and cut a lemon in half.

When the soup boiled, she turned off the stove and whisked the broth to get it circling. She poured in the eggs, whisking until they separated into white bits. Last she ran the garlic through her press and stirred it in. She ladled the broth into two large mugs, squeezed a quarter lemon into each and topped them with sprigs of cilantro.

Steam poured into her hall as the bathroom door opened. *Just in time.*

She found Peter sitting on the side of the bed, head in his hands.

"I feel better. If I can catch a few hours sleep, I'll be fine."

"Uh huh." She handed him a mug. "It's hot. Sip, don't gulp."

"I'm not hungry."

"I spent all day making it. The least you can do is try it."

Peter grumbled, but lifted the cup to his lips, took a sip, raised his eyebrows. "What's in this?"

"Many things that will cure what ails you. Don't you like it?"

"It's great. Clears the sinuses."

"I'll get you some tissue and a spit cup. You're going to need it."

"Yes, Bossy Woman."

Lia had intended to drink the second mug of soup herself, but handed it to Peter after he drained the first. He settled back against the pile of pillows, back propped up to help him breathe. She tucked the covers around him.

"Thanks, Mom." He closed his eyes.

Lia kissed his forehead and left Viola guarding him, curled at his feet. She called Cynth from the living room. Cynth answered on the third ring. Lia explained the situation.

"Brent's such an ass. Paul can't cover for Peter. He's on patrol tonight. Knowing Paul, he wouldn't mind spending most of it parked in your back alley, but that would just scare them away for the night. I'll talk to Parker. After the haul Peter made today, she should be willing to give him some consideration."

"Haul? What haul?"

"Didn't he tell you?"

"He looked so awful, I shoved him straight into bed."

"They raided Bill's carriage house at the crack of dawn. I hear it was the fence's version of Ali Baba's cave. The DA's office is very happy."

"Oh," Lia said.

"It should be all over the internet. I'm surprised you haven't seen it."

"I was busy. I haven't even looked at my email. If Peter arrested them, why does he still think someone is going to break in? Surely they know they'll get caught?"

"These guys are from down in Kentucky. Nobody knows how they think better than Peter. If he says there's a good chance they'll show, he's probably right. It's a big family and we don't know all the players. Added to that, Bill is out on bail. They might think it a fine thing to finish the job Bill started just to say 'F you' to Peter."

"Peter can't go back tonight. One more night in that basement and he'll wind up in the hospital."

"Parker's still here. I'll talk to her. Peter's the golden boy in District Five. That ought to count for something."

SOMETHING TURNED out to be not much. Rumors that gang members planned to make fake calls so they could ambush officers meant the uniforms were doubling up for safety. There wasn't anyone to spare for Peter's pet project. Parker generously thanked Cynth for volunteering to fill the gap, giving her no way to back out without losing major points with Parker, a woman she was determined to impress. *Me and my big mouth.*

Cynth huddled in the dark basement, wearing silk thermals under her sweats and wrapped in Peter's three-season sleeping bag, which smelled of Peter. Not unpleasantly so, but sheesh, when was the last time he washed it?

*Hell of a duty.* She had to maintain pitch black, so she couldn't fool around on her phone. She would listen to an audiobook, but then she wouldn't hear the idiots when they came. *If* they came. She sat on the air mattress and leaned against the wall, the chill of the concrete seeping through the sleeping bag and into her back. She couldn't afford to fall asleep. She considered moving to a camp chair.

Lia had offered her Viola, but Cynth was unused to dogs and wasn't sure Viola would perform with her the way she did with Peter. For all she knew, Viola would let the bastards in and lead them to her sleeping body after serving them a cocktail.

She was reduced to a half-gallon of black coffee and one of those idiotic female urinals. Between mainlining caffeine and peeing it away, she should stay awake until four a.m. Bill and friends were unlikely to show after that.

At least she'd had the satisfaction of calling Brent and telling him what an asshat he was. She only wished she'd done it on an old-school landline so she could have slammed the phone in his ear. Someone really needed to make an app for that, a widget you could tap to make that slamming noise when you disconnected a call. The person who came up with that would make a million dollars. Not that a million dollars was all that much anymore. *A lot more than I've got, though.*

And now she was spinning off into la-la land. If she had to stay awake all night staring into the dark she'd go nuts. This was like those sensory deprivation tanks her sister liked to float in at those chi-chi spas she went to, only Cynth wasn't floating in warm water. She heard people had hallucinations in those things.

She stared into the pitch dark. Colors started to appear in odd patterns as her eyes attempted to make sense of the nothingness. *I'll start seeing things if this keeps up much longer. How did Peter manage this for six weeks?*

She felt her phone in her pocket. Really, she was tucked away in an ell where she couldn't be seen from the main room. What could it hurt if she logged into Facebook? The thieves shouldn't be able to see the glow of her screen from outside, and she'd hear them coming before it would be an issue. Peter wanted total darkness in here, but he'd been sleeping. He could be such an old school hard-ass sometimes. It was one of the things she liked about him, but right now, not so much.

She jumped when she felt her phone vibrate. She checked the screen. *Brent. Asshole.* What did he think he was doing, calling her at—she checked the time—a quarter till one? She tapped the red button to refuse the call and stuffed the phone back in her pocket before she remembered she wanted to check in on Facebook.

Bam! Someone slammed a fist against one of the basement windows. *Someone's breaking a window to get in.* The sleeping bag fell away as she popped up on her feet.

Bam! Whoever it was, they weren't doing a very good job of breaking the window. She moved on stealthy feet into the next room. A thin beacon passed through the window and danced on the floor. She stayed out of the beam.

Brent hissed at her. "Cynth! I know you're in there. Let me in!"

"Are you trying to wake the neighborhood, asshat?"

"No, I'm trying to talk to you, but you refused my call. I'm not going away. Either let me in or I'm going to scare away everyone within three city blocks so your stakeout is a waste."

Cynth stomped upstairs, guided by her own LED flashlight and opened the front door.

"Get in here before I think better of it and shoot you for a prowler."

Brent slipped in the door, beating his arms with his hands.

"Damn, it's almost as cold in here as it is outside."

Cynth smirked. "Maybe you should have dressed for the occasion. What the hell are you doing here?" She said. She led him to the stairs, her light trained on the floor in hope that no one had seen Brent prowling the place. *With my luck, Alma was up and called it in and five patrol cars are going to pull up with their sirens blaring.*

"I couldn't sleep, thinking about you stuck down here. This has to be the fifth circle of Hell."

Cynth wondered why it had to be the fifth. Why not the fourth? Or the third?

The stairwell was a black hole that sucked in her Maglite so that it was a pale dot illuminating nothing.

"Watch the steps. Walk on the outside of the treads so you don't make noise, just in case. And watch your hands. You grope me and I *will* shoot you."

She felt a tug on her braid. She slammed an elbow into Brent's stomach without thinking.

"All right, all right. Hands off. I promise," Brent said.

They felt their way down the steps without speaking.

Cynth broke the silence when she reached the bottom. "I only let you in because I was about to start seeing things in the dark."

"Glad I could be of service."

Cynth rounded a corner and turned off her flashlight. There was just enough illumination from the streetlights to cast gray rectangles on the floor of the main room, alleviating the utter darkness.

"Turn to your right when you get to the bottom. You'll be able to see again."

The dark blur that was Brent emerged into the room.

"I don't exactly call this 'seeing.'"

"Wuss. There's nothing in here to trip over. Give me your hand."

She led him through the main room, into the ell with Peter's air mattress, mentally thanking God she'd taken time to top off the inflation, or she'd wind up sliding into Brent when the bed dipped in the middle.

"The bed is dead ahead. There's a blanket and a sleeping bag. You take the blanket. The sleeping bag is mine."

"You could share that sleeping bag."

"I could also wrap your balls around your neck."

"Don't I know it," Brent muttered.

Cynth sat down. The bed rocked as Brent sat down next to her. She gathered up the blanket and shoved it at him, using the move as an opportunity to create space between them.

"Seriously, what are you doing here? You can't be here to back me up."

"Considering that you once broke my nose and dislocated my shoulder, no one is more qualified than I am to say that you can take care of yourself."

Cynth smirked.

"And I will say that I have never in my life experienced such intense and exquisite pain as I did in those minutes before you agreed to reset my shoulder. I sorely wish that in the years since, you would have found it in your heart to decide I'd suffered enough so you could give it a rest."

"You hurt me once. Nobody gets the chance to do it twice."

"I get that. I get it a thousand times over, loud and clear. For once, will you listen to my side of things?"

"I can't afford your side of things. Your *side of things* almost turned me into the laughing stock of the CPD. What kind of career would I have had after that?"

She shifted irritably, wrapping the sleeping bag around herself. "It was really asinine of you to blow Peter off, as sick as he is. He's your best friend."

"He *is* my best friend. He's also a hard-ass and you know it. There's no damn reason to sit down here with no heat when Peter has an infrared camera set up in here, and you can pull it up on his laptop.

"I offered to sit in his nice warm apartment, not fifty feet from here and watch for his friends. He said no, they could damage Lia's pipes before I got here to stop them. I then suggested he leave the dogs down here, especially that yappy schnauzer of Lia's, and let them scare the boogeyman away. He wouldn't do that either. He said if anything happened to the dogs it would be the end of life as he knew it. This is a miserable set up. Admit it."

"Miserable, yeah, but it worked."

"That's the only thing it has going for it."

"Dammit, being pissed at you was keeping me warm. And focused."

They sat, saying nothing.

Brent broke the silence. "Do you still hate me so much?"

"I despise you with the white-hot passion of a thousand burning suns."

"*Taming of the Shrew*. How appropriate."

"Shakespeare never said that. It's from *Ten Things I Hate About You*. And you'll never be as hunky as Heath Ledger."

"He's dead, you know."

"You'll never be as hunky as Heath Ledger's rotting flesh."

"Ouch. If you hate me so much, why do you always hang around with me and Peter?"

"Don't think it has anything to do with you. Peter was the best friend I had at District Five before you showed up. I wasn't about to let you ruin that for me, too."

"I never said anything to him."

"I figured. Thank you for that."

"Simple self-preservation. If he found out, he would have felt obligated to kick my ass. It wouldn't have mattered that you'd already taken care of that little detail."

Cynth said nothing.

"Have you ever stopped to think what I went through?" Brent asked.

"Is there a reason I should?"

"I never thought it was you, you know."

"Brent, I—"

Brent elbowed her in the ribs. He leaned over and whispered in what he probably thought was her ear but was in fact her cheek. "Voices."

Cynth stopped to listen.

"... I've been thinking about this ever since that big bastard shoved his foot in my back. Nobody closes the barn door after the cows are gone. There's gonna be one big surprise tomorrow morning."

"I'll be damned," Brent hissed. "They were stupid enough to come back. Give Brainard the high sign and hang here. I'll go out the front door and circle around so we have them penned in. Don't show yourself unless they go after the pipes before I come up behind them." He pulled something out of the bag. "Put these on." It was a pair of ear protectors.

"What—?"

"Flashbang," he hissed.

Despite a perverse desire to fling the ear protectors after Brent, Cynth slid them on and waited for several tense minutes while the copper thieves cut the lock off the bulkhead door and hauled their equipment into the basement. She was standing around the corner of the ell with her Taser drawn and eyes averted, cursing Brent for taking so long when the stun grenade flew through the bulkhead doors in an explosion of light and sound.

The intruders howled in surprise.

Cynth slid the ear protectors down around her neck and stepped into the main room, her Taser leading. Bill, his brother-in-law and two underage males she presumed to be more nephews—Joey apparently having bowed out of a repeat performance—lay on the floor, holding their ears and screeching obscenities.

They had to call in a wagon to transport everyone. Cynth and Brent stood in the yard and watched as the officers hauled their catch away.

"Shit. Do you know what this means?" Brent asked.

"More paperwork?"

"Aside from that."

"Tell me."

"Someone will have to cover tomorrow night. There's no way Peter will let this go now. He'll figure as long as the hillbillies have decided to feud with him, he'll wait here and pick them off. Which would be fine if he wasn't sick as a dog and could do it himself."

"Don't you like being a hero, Brent?"

"I'll do it if you keep me company."

Cynth snorted. "You're pathetic, do you know that?"

## 15

# WEDNESDAY, NOVEMBER 16

THE SUN DANCED ACROSS PETER'S FACE, WAKING HIM. HE opened his eyes and gathered himself, wondering why this felt wrong. He was leaning on a pile of pillows. That felt wrong, too. He felt beside him on the bed. Lia wasn't there. He looked at his watch. Nine-thirty. *Damn.*

He'd slept through the night and never made it to the basement. Anticipating the mess waiting for him at the new house, he swung his legs over the side of the bed. And began an epic bout of coughing, sending the head he just realized was pounding into jackhammer territory.

"Peter?" Lia called from the kitchen. She walked into the room, carrying a cup of coffee. "You're awake."

Peter took the cup and inhaled the steam. It was almost enough to make him feel human. "You should be a detective." He took a careful sip. "You didn't wake me. Your pipes are gone by now."

"I didn't wake you because you needed to rest. Cynth

and Brent covered for you last night. I called your captain this morning. She said to come in at noon if you're up to it."

Peter nodded slowly in the vain hope that it wouldn't send his head pounding again.

"How'd you get Brent there?"

"I didn't. Cynth called him to chew him out on her way to the house and he was shamed into keeping her company."

"I take it nothing happened."

"It did happen. Bill decided to celebrate being out on bail by trashing my house with three of his relatives. His bail has been revoked and Cynth is hopeful that with so much of his family in custody, one of them will crack and hand over the rest."

"Bill won't stop. They won't let him back out now that he's violated his bail, but he has an endless supply of kin."

"I'm not worried about them. Cynth showed Bill and company your infrared security camera before they were hauled off to jail. You neglected to tell them they were on *Candid Camera* the other night."

Peter groaned in frustration. "That setup was fish in a barrel. I could have picked up another half-dozen of those idiots."

"And there's no telling how far they'd take it, just out of spite. They might never stop."

Peter fell back against the pillows, his mind working. "They might still vandalize the house, even if they don't break in."

"Don't sound so hopeful. I'm meeting with the security company at one. They've assured me they'll have my new system up and running this evening. That includes security cams, outside lights set on motion detectors, and a great big yard sign that says the property is protected. If you're really worried, I'll get your laptop and you can watch the footage live from bed."

"Dammit, Lia—"

"Dammit nothing. We've spent enough time talking about it that I knew what to order. You broke the copper ring. You don't have to handle everything yourself."

He shoved himself upright. "I have to help interrogate those guys."

"You need to stay in bed. Evil will just have to wait. Drink your coffee and rest while I whip up more soup." Lia stood and headed for the door.

"You said you spent all day cooking that soup yesterday."

Her voice drifted back over her shoulder. "I said that so you'd feel obligated to eat it."

Peter thumped back against the pillows. *Damn.*

Peter tried to sleep. He'd eaten the soup and coughed up lots of green goo and taken Tylenol in the hope that it would kill the headache. He'd let Lia tuck him back in. He didn't know how he slept the day before propped up like he was. He must have been half dead. He cracked his eyes at noon to find Viola staring at him from her spot by his feet.

"Not you, too," he muttered. He threw on a robe as he padded into the kitchen, noticing along the way that his headache was gone.

Peter found Lia sitting at the kitchen table, progress photos of the Hopewell frieze parading across her computer screen. "Updating your website?"

Lia glanced down, sighing. "I'm trying to keep you alive. The least you could do is put on some socks."

He dropped onto a chair, propping his feet on the rung. "Is that better?"

"No. What are you doing out of bed."

"Trying not to go crazy. Why are you still home?"

"Looking after you. The frieze can twiddle its thumbs with Evil for today."

"I thought I'd go with you to talk to the alarm company."

"No. The world will come calling soon enough."

THE WORLD CALLED AT THREE-THIRTY. Peter dove for his pants, fumbling the phone as he fished it out of his pocket.

"How are you feeling?" Captain Parker asked.

Peter snuffled.

"That bad?"

"Please tell me you have something for me. Being sick is driving me crazy."

"You're in luck. The director of Hopewell called. There's too much tension at the school with Hannah and Leander both refusing to take time off and the board fears potential lawsuits if they force either one of them out. Marshall's lawyer—"

"Culler?"

"You know her, then? She's proposing a reenactment."

"You can't be serious."

"Wingler is all over it. He participated in gestalt empty chair therapy back in the 70s and thinks it would be cathartic for the school. He's very enthusiastic about the idea."

Peter rolled his eyes, thankful Parker couldn't see him. Roller would have blustered at this idiocy. Parker's tone was always so cool you could never tell what she thought about anything, though he suspected her opinion of the idea mirrored his.

"They want you at six-thirty."

"Doesn't the cemetery close at six?"

"Spring Grove isn't happy the case is still open. They've offered to do everything in their power to aid resolution."

"Do you support this?" Peter asked.

"What I think is immaterial. They're having a reenactment. We have been invited to observe. It's in our best interest to be there."

"Why aren't Heck—Hodgkins and Jarvis covering this?"

"They are. But Hannah refuses to participate unless you're there, and she wants Lia, too."

"What do Hodgkins and Jarvis think about it?"

"Since they haven't been able to make an arrest, they're in no position to turn down anything that may help shed light on Lawrence's murder. Culler pulled out the Ryan Widmer case and pointed out that a reenactment could forestall the kind of juror experimentation that cost the city a very expensive mistrial. The brass wants you there, if only to ensure the cooperation of one of the suspects."

Peter was silent, weighing his desire to get back to work against the frustration of being sucked further into the Hopewell morass while being stuck on the sidelines.

"How sick are you? Can you handle a couple hours this evening?"

Peter's inner sense of duty won. "I can if I can do it indoors."

"That's not a problem. They want you to play Geoffrey Lawrence."

Lia sat with Hannah on a low bough under a sweeping

magnolia tree outside Norman Chapel. Lia tapped the screen on her phone, checked the clock. 6:52. *Almost time.* "Is this exactly where you were sitting?"

Hannah pointed through a gap in the leaves. "I remember seeing the door between those branches. At the time I thought it was like peeking between curtains before a performance. Ironic, don't you think?"

"How are you holding up?" Lia asked.

Hannah looked down, restless fingers combing through the fringe on her long, silk scarf. "Leander hates me. Everyone is taking sides and telling outrageous stories. I'm Lizzie Borden; I had a secret yen for Geoff and finally lost it; Leander and I planned it all out; Constance paid us to do it. I'm hanging in there. My lawyer—Michael hired a serious bad-ass for me—says to stand my ground and don't let anyone push me out. That, and don't respond, don't say anything to anyone. It's been rough. If we find answers, maybe everyone will calm down."

"I'm so sorry. How will you handle doing this with Leander tonight?"

Hannah lifted her head, chin up. "That's the mark of a professional, leaving everything personal behind when the curtain goes up. You'll see. By now everyone is on their marks, waiting for the show to begin."

The Messenger app on Lia's phone dinged. Peter's icon appeared with a request for a video chat. The sight of color in his face reassured her. "Hannah's ready. How about you?"

"We're good. Constance is at the organ and Brent is lurking by the door off the utility room. Cynth is stationed on a bench across the street. The students are in place on the dais and their coats are piled on the pews. Our esteemed counselors are sitting in the front pew with Wingler and

Thomas, waiting for the show to begin. We're trying to time it so that everyone leaves at 7:15."

"How about Heckle and Jeckle?"

"Hodgkins is sitting across the aisle from the lawyers, losing his patience. Jarvis is outside somewhere." A voice murmured in the background. Peter's face flew out of view as he set his phone down. Lia found herself staring at the chapel rafters.

Lia turned on the video app on Hannah's phone, one of several drafted into use to record the reenactment.

Seconds ticked by, then a minute. Toby's voice drifted through Lia's phone. "We can't get started until you yell at the roof."

Peter's face appeared in Lia's phone again, his eyes rolling heavenward. "What do you want me to yell?"

Voices chorused, "Where is the God damned *HEAT!*"

"Before that you have to tell us how awful we are," a female voice called out.

"And then you have to tell us to get lost," someone else said.

Lia exchanged a look with Hannah. "They think this is a joke."

Hannah screwed up her mouth. "They're kids."

Peter's voice drifted through. "And how awful are you?"

Toby drawled, "Awful enough to destroy culture as we know it." This was accompanied by titters and mutters of assent.

A voice roared. "Stop screwing around and get ON with it!"

"Hodgkins," Lia said.

The two women listened as Peter went through the motions of yelling at the students while they coached him.

A bout of coughing interrupted Peter's tirade. Once it subsided, he yelled—croaked, really—at the roof before dismissing them. The clomping of a small herd of buffalo came through the phone followed by a stream of students pouring out the side door. They pulled on coats as they headed briskly to the parking lot.

Peter's voice drifted through again. "Accuracy is one thing, but I'm not kissing you."

"Your loss," was Toby's saucy reply.

Murmurs, then Leander's voice, raging and unintelligible. Toby exited the side door and hurried off, heading into the cemetery.

"Where is Toby going?"

"He went to the family mausoleum. He told me he thought his dad might visit his mom before the concert, but he wasn't there."

"Then nobody saw him after he left."

"I doubt it. Everyone else went the other way."

"Which means he could have doubled back."

"Toby? I just don't see it." Hannah closed her eyes and said nothing more. Lia imagined she was trying to immerse herself in the event. Lia remained by her, silent as a minute passed, then two.

"Now," Hannah said softly, cued by some internal clock.

Leander stormed out of the chapel. Hannah called to him. He stopped and looked around for a moment as if confused, spotted Hannah, then ran to the magnolia tree. He fell on Hannah's lap, weeping and moaning in the darkness under the tree. "Oh God, oh God, oh God. I'm sorry, Hannah. I'm so sorry!" he cried.

*Oh, yeah, these are actors.*

After several minutes of Leander wailing and Hannah

calming him, Hannah, her voice brisk, said, "Okay, that's enough." She gently urged Leander back. "I'm going to see if 'Dr. Lawrence' needs help."

"You can't help, Hannah. Don't go. ... Don't leave me." Leander whispered, still in character.

Peter made a 'Heaven help me' face in the tiny screen on Lia's phone.

Hannah looked skyward as if praying for patience. She mouthed something at Lia as she passed by. Lia decided it was "Such a diva."

Hannah strode to the chapel, determination marking every step. *Leander's not the only actor on stage tonight.*

Leander sat next to Lia, still crying. Lia realized he was no longer acting and placed a hand on his. He gripped it tightly as a minute, then three, ticked by. Hannah emerged from the chapel, kicked the shim out of the door and returned to lead Leander into the cemetery grounds. Lia followed, taping their progress through shadowed monuments and hundred-year-old trees.

At one point the trio stalled as Hannah and Leander argued about which way to go.

Hannah checked a worn brochure in the light of Lia's phone, tracing a finger along a tiny map. "We go right. The waterfall is this way."

They crossed a wood bridge over a pond. The walkway continued on the far side, bordered by a serpentine wall containing tiny crypts for cremains. It ended at a waterfall splashing over boulders on an artificial hill.

They watched the water while Hannah pretended to toss a glove into the pond and reassured Leander that she would not let him be punished for killing Geoffrey. Hannah looked at her watch and said, "We have to go back."

They found everyone assembled under the porte cochère. Leander stayed just beyond the glow of the exterior lights while Hannah passed through the crowd to the door. She turned on the steps and addressed the officers. "Well? What now?"

CULLER, Wingler, Thomas, and Jim Madden, Hannah's newly-minted attorney, stood in the vestibule of Norman Chapel with the contingent of detectives.

"What a freaking farce," Jarvis said to no one in particular.

"What do you think?" Wingler asked Peter.

Peter glanced at Hodgkins, wondering how he was reacting to the slight. "From the time Leander left till Hannah entered was twelve minutes," Peter said. "Detective Davis had plenty of time to stave my head in with the candle stand and leave before she arrived."

"Well," Culler said, looking at Madden, "I smell reasonable doubt. What about you?"

"This certainly raises questions," Madden said, perfect teeth gleaming through a predatory smile.

Wingler moaned. "This doesn't solve anything, does it?"

Peter raised his eyebrows at Hodgkins. Hodgkins glowered back.

Brent leaned closer and spoke so only Peter could hear. "I smell a new career flipping burgers for our friend."

"We can hope," Peter said.

# THURSDAY, NOVEMBER 17

P<small>ETER SAT IN HIS</small> B<small>LAZER OUTSIDE</small> S<small>ANDY</small> A<small>LICH'S MODEST</small>
brick house, taking a moment to blow his nose and pop a
cherry-menthol cough drop. *Hacking all over Alich will do
wonders for her cooperation.* He glanced at the thermos of
nuclear soup Lia sent with him that morning. He suspected
it was the only thing keeping him alive but if he drank one
more cup of it he was going to start clucking.

*This is probably a waste of time.* Culler's gloating of the
night before had them scrambling to play catch-up,
grasping at all possible straws to find something that would
shore up a case, any case, against someone. They had found
no blood evidence on the clothes and now they had a ten-
minute gap where a third party could have slipped in
behind Marshall and finished Lawrence off. Hannah was in
and out too quickly to have done it. *Have to ask Marshall if
the timing from last night matched his memories. Strike that. It's
not my case. I don't get to call those shots and nobody's asking my
opinion.*

Peter took inventory of the property. It was a starter home, a no-frills brick box with closet-sized bedrooms built after World War II. A cement goose sat on the tiny porch while mums the color of fall leaves struggled to survive a few more weeks in carefully mulched beds.

Thanksgiving was a week away, but a wreath of pine cones and red and green plaid ribbon already hung on the door, something skirting the lines of the country-cute decor Peter's sisters cooed over. Everything about the exterior said Alich cared about her home and was invested in maintaining it.

Peter rang the bell. When it looked like no one would appear, he turned to walk around the property. He was on the steps when the door cracked open.

The man who came to the door looked worse than Peter felt. He was unshaven and red-eyed, his dark hair hanging in unwashed hunks, his expression both groggy and annoyed.

"What?"

"Are you Joe Alich?"

The man narrowed his eyes. "What do you want?"

Peter flipped his badge case open. "I'm Detective Dourson with the Cincinnati police."

"Have you found her yet?"

"I'm looking for Sandy—"

"I know that. Have you found her and Chelsey?"

Peter backpedaled. "She's missing?"

"Give the man a cigar," Joe muttered. "If you didn't know she was missing, why are you here?"

"She may be a witness to a crime."

The man rubbed his face then shoved the screen door open. "C'mon in."

The living room continued the "Martha Stewart meets Holly Hobby" theme but was overlaid with a patina of recent neglect and an abundance of fast food wrappers. *This must be urban-cute. Is there such a thing? There has to be.*

Joe dumped a pile of dirty clothes off a chair and offered it to Peter. He dropped down on the couch, behind a barricade of Old Milwaukee cans erected on a coffee table. Peter counted two LaRosa's pizza boxes, a sack from White Castle, another from KFC. *She's been gone at least four days.*

"Sorry 'bout the mess. Kinda accumulates without the wife. What's this about a crime?"

"Two weeks ago a man was murdered at Spring Grove Cemetery while your wife was in the area, waiting for a bus. We think she may be able to corroborate the movements of some of the people we're looking at."

"She took the kid and the car Thursday evening, said she was going grocery shopping. Never came back. I thought she'd left me."

"Did she have reason to leave you?"

"I dunno. ... Maybe."

"You don't know or maybe?"

Joe's eyes cut away. He stared out the window, raking his fingers through his hair. "After she was gone for a couple days, this old biddy across the street said something to me about a visitor I had while Sandy was working. If she told Sandy, then yeah, I guess she did." Joe shook his head, snorted. "I miss the little mutt. I didn't think I would."

"She took the dog, too?"

Joe looked puzzled for a moment, then his face cleared. "Naw, that's what I call Sandy. Little Mutt. Can't remember where I came up with it, but she liked it. There's no dog."

"Did she go grocery shopping?"

"The other guy asked that. How would I know? What difference does it make?"

Peter wondered what Missing Persons had been doing since they got this case. *Not a heck of a lot.* "Have you checked your bank account since she went missing? If she charged groceries, that would give us her last known whereabouts. If she withdrew a large sum of money, that would tell us she planned to leave. If she used her debit card since then, it could tell us where she is. Didn't the detective in charge of your case go over this with you?"

"I guess he didn't take it too serious."

"Why wouldn't he?"

"I kinda told him I bet she was at her sister's. He acted like I was wasting his time."

"Yeah, if you called me over to take a missing person's report when you didn't know if she was with relatives, I might blow it off, too."

"Hey, I called that bitch sister of hers. She yelled at me for five minutes because I hadn't reported Sandy missing yet. I just didn't think she was telling me the truth."

"Who is the officer in charge of your case?"

Joe dug a stained business card out of the pile of cans on the coffee table, glanced at it and handed it to Peter. "Schmidt—he said his name was Schmidt."

"Has Sandy tapped your bank account?"

"I wouldn't know. She did all the banking online. I don't know the password."

It took all of Peter's training in 'cop face' not to roll his eyes.

"Let's go to your bank and find out."

Joe sniffed his armpit. "Do you mind if I shower first? I kinda smell."

PETER TOOK a beer from Lia's fridge and sat at the kitchen table. Lia was playing with virtual paint chips in a decorating app on her computer. She clicked on a picture of a living room and a light brown color flooded the walls. She turned her face for a kiss. "What do you think?"

"About what? We already painted your place."

"For you, silly."

Peter took a pull of his beer. "Whatever you think. You're the artist."

She gave him a long look.

"What? I'm a simple guy. Whatever you want to do will be fine."

She narrowed her eyes. "Screaming fuchsia polka-dots on atomic-urine yellow."

Peter nodded at the computer. "Show me what it'll look like. Maybe I can get curtains to match."

Lia closed her laptop. "Think you're cute, don't you. How'd it go with Sandy Alich?"

Peter told her.

"If she left him, why wouldn't she empty her bank account?" Lia asked.

"That's a head scratcher."

"It bothers me that she and her child went missing a few days after Bailey and I talked to her."

"Yeah, me, too. But she had good enough reason to go."

"Whose house was it?"

"What are you talking about?"

"The house was cared for," Lia said. "Someone tended the lawn. She put up a Christmas wreath weeks early and the inside was decorated."

"And?"

"How long were they married?"

"Not sure. A few years."

"I got the impression Joe wasn't in the picture until after she left Hopewell. Allowing a year for courtship, she got pregnant almost immediately after they married."

"Possibly," Peter said.

"A wreath, all that decorating, those are female touches and they take time. A newly-married woman is more focused on her husband than her house, and a mother with a toddler doesn't have a minute to breathe."

"You think she lived there before they got married."

"Before she met him. Women who do a lot of crafts aren't in the throes of romance."

"What the hell is a throe?" He waved off the question. "Never mind, I get your point. Where are you going with this?"

"I bet you a fish log with all the trimmings she bought the house before she met Joe. And if that's true, why wouldn't she just toss him out?"

"Interesting question." Peter rubbed his chin. "Not all women think like you. Usually they want comfort and consolation, someone on their side. He's probably right, she's holed up with her sister and her sister is lying so he'll suffer more."

"If she wanted him to suffer, why didn't she clean out the account?"

"That guy has no clue how to fend for himself. Maybe she didn't want him to starve before he came to his senses."

"Maybe she has fixer-upper-itis."

"She has what-is?"

"She's in love with his potential, and puts all her energy

into helping him become the man she knows he's meant to be so he can take care of her in the manner to which she'd like to become accustomed."

"You act like it's a real thing."

"Mom and her friends all had it. I had a touch of it with Luthor but I got over it quickly. Plenty of women treat a guy, well, like a house. Slap some paint on, update the gutters. Not only do you have the husband you've always wanted, he will reward you with lifelong devotion and new kitchen appliances every five years."

Peter grunted. He'd never thought of himself as a "fixer-upper," but Lia's description sounded too much like his relationship with Susan. "So he doesn't respond the way she wants him to. What happens next?"

"Depends. Either she digs her heels in and pushes harder or she bails for a better prospect."

Peter winced inwardly. Susan had bailed, dumping him for the furniture king of Southwest Kentucky. "So, what's for dinner?"

"Bailey's coming over. We're having leftover vegan chili from Alma's."

"With zucchini noodles? I thought you loved me."

Lia snorted. "Relax. I'm frying up ground beef for yours."

"That's okay then. What brings the Queen of Woo here?"

"I didn't know it but she and the guys were lurking on the grounds last night. They couldn't resist watching the reenactment, even if it was from a hundred yards away."

"Oh?"

"Now that she's absorbed vibes from the scene, she wants to do a Tarot reading to find out who the killer is."

Peter laughed. "It should only be so easy."

"I'm sorry."

Peter waved a hand. "Don't be. You're the one who has a problem with it. ... What the hell, the stuff they have me doing now is barely a step up from consulting psychics. Who knows, maybe she'll turn something up."

LIA CLEARED dishes from the table while Bailey unpacked what Lia called her "woo-woo kit." This was kept in a hatbox from a craft store. Lia had painted the box for Bailey, covering it with mystical symbols designating the four suits of the Tarot and glyphs representing planets and astrological signs.

Bailey unfolded a large square of upholstery fabric in a lovely, Renaissance-inspired, floral pattern and laid it on the table. Then she brought out a silk-wrapped block, laying it in the center of the fabric before setting a dish beside it. The dish had an oriental motif and was the size of an ashtray. It held a burnt stub of white sage tied with criss-crossing red string.

*This is like a magic trick. Now she'll pull out a rabbit, or maybe a hundred silk scarves.*

Next came three miniature skulls carved out of a stone that looked like turquoise but lacked veining. After that, a large calcite orb with an ornate brass stand emerged from the depths of the box. Despite her cynicism about Bailey's New Age tendencies, Lia enjoyed the colorful array of objects. Peter sipped his beer and said nothing though Lia could tell he was intrigued.

Bailey unfolded the silk, revealing a worn deck of cards.

"Do you think this will help?" Peter asked.

"I don't see why not. The reading I did about Leroy was

good, I just missed the interpretation of one card for a while."

Lia set a fragrant cup of ginger tea on the table for Bailey. Bailey claimed ginger turned you into a conduit for Spirit, with a capital "S." Lia ate tons of ginger and had never noticed Spirit knocking at her consciousness.

"I imagine you can make anything fit after the fact," Lia said. "Peter counted nine suspects. How are you going to make that work? Or will you pull out a Ouija board next?"

"Oh ye of little faith. I'm going to do an options spread. We take our list of suspects, and pull one card per person. Upright cards are yes responses, reversed cards mean no."

"You expect to get eight upside down cards and one that's right side up? That will be a trick."

"Watch and learn. Do you have any matches?"

Lia shook her head.

"I'll use your stove."

Bailey held the burned end of the bundle of sage over the front burner as she turned on the gas. It flamed up when she dipped it in the fire. Bailey removed the bundle from the burner and the flame died. She blew softly on the still-glowing end. Smoke curled up in mesmerizing arabesques. The pungent scent wasn't to Lia's taste but it wasn't unpleasant.

"What are you going to do with that?" Lia asked.

"It's for purification."

Bailey blew on the bundle again to keep the herbs burning, then passed the deck through the smoke several times. She drew the bundle through the air, creating a cloud of smoke before setting it back in the oriental dish. Bits of fire struggled and died while Bailey stepped into the smoke, fanning it around herself in graceful movements.

The dogs circled around her, sniffing, their default response to odd things. Peter lured them back under the table with biscuits. Bailey's strangeness was no competition for treats.

She returned to her seat and closed her eyes while she held the cards in both hands, silently mouthing something. *A spell? A prayer?* Lia wondered about the tiny skulls but refrained from interrupting.

Lia continued to watch as Bailey shuffled the cards three times, casino-style. *How many people can still do that? Nobody plays card games anymore.*

"Hand me the list," Bailey said.

Peter set it by her elbow. Bailey turned over the cards one at a time, reciting the names as she did so. "Toby Grant ... Constance DeVries ... Kari Bennett ... Leander Marshall ... Michael Wingler ... Hannah Kleemeyer ... Suki Thomas ... Nigel Porter ... and for fun, let's add Sandy Alich."

"Why Nigel?" Peter asked. "We eliminated him."

"He's the control. I always add a null option to the mix." Bailey flipped the deck over, exposing the bottom card, then frowned as she surveyed the row of images. "They're all reversed. That shouldn't have happened."

"They look right side up to me, except for the one in the middle," Lia said. She stroked the card, then jerked her finger back, guiltily. "Sorry. Hope I didn't mess up your vibe. They're just so pretty. The colors are much brighter than the deck you used last time."

"It's the Radiant Tarot. Same drawings as the Rider-Waite, but someone redid the color."

"I like it. I don't believe in it, but the art is wonderful."

"What does it mean if all the cards are upside down?" Peter asked.

"It means none of our suspects did it."

"Uh huh," Lia said, still examining the cards. "What about the last card, the one from the bottom of the deck? You didn't give it a name."

"That's the root card. It's the underlying issue. Getting to the bottom of the question, so to speak."

"They mean that literally?"

Bailey smiled. "Spirit responds well to puns."

The final card featured a figure on a throne holding a set of scales. "What does it mean?" Lia asked.

"That's Justice. It's the karma card. It's also about balance."

"So upside down, it would mean injustice?"

"It could."

"What happened to Geoffrey Lawrence was an excellent example of karma. Where would the injustice come in?" Lia asked.

"As the root card it means he was killed over an injustice."

"Huh," Peter said. "Nothing like narrowing the field."

Lia tapped a card that showed a wealthy man doling out coins to a beggar. "What's this one? Is it about charity?"

"Six of Pentacles. See the scales he's holding? It's about sharing what you have with those who need it so things balance out."

"So someone refused to share? How does that relate?"

"It doesn't. An upright card has meaning in an options spread, but the 'no' cards are just 'no.' They don't mean anything else."

"The images are so evocative. There's a heart stabbed with swords, that guy laying on the ground with a bunch of swords in his back, another guy with a bandage on his head and a bunch of long sticks—he looks like someone hit him in the head with one of those sticks—and that angry guy on a horse, waving a sword, he looks like he's attacking the guy with the bandage. They all look like murder to me," Lia said.

"Not necessarily. The three of swords is about betrayal and the ten is hitting rock bottom. The nine of wands is an old soldier who is pushing on, even though he's at the end of his reserves."

"What about the guy on the horse?"

"He's a hothead. He acts without thinking."

"Someone sure did that, all over Geoff Lawrence," Peter said.

"And this guy doing ballet with his hands behind his back?"

Bailey tilted her head, considering the card. "I never thought of The Hanged Man that way." She turned the card around. "He's actually hanging from one foot. It means taking time out to see things from a different point of view."

Lia traced a finger across the cards. "It's like they want to make a story."

"So," Peter said, "You don't think any of our suspects killed Lawrence."

"Not according to the cards," Bailey said.

"Can you ask who did?"

"I can, but the likelihood of getting a helpful response is limited. That's why I like to work with specific options."

"Give it a shot," he said.

"Just a minute." Bailey used her phone to take pictures of the layout and Peter's list. "For future reference." She riffled the cards three times, then dealt the top card. It showed a man with his arms full of swords, tip-toeing away from a group of tents.

"Seven of Swords," she said.

"What does it mean?" Peter asked.

"He's a liar and a cheat." Bailey looked up. "I'm sorry, I don't think this is what you were looking for."

"Sounds like Joe Alich," Lia said. "Is it possible he had anything to do with this? Maybe he killed Sandy, too."

Peter made a pained face. "And his kid? The only thing I see him killing is brain cells." He nodded at the card. "Can you tell me anything else about our guy?"

Bailey took a deep breath and stared at the card. Finally she looked up. "I'm sorry. Nothing else is coming to me. I can't tell you any more about him."

"Can you ask for more details?"

"I could, but I won't. A big part of establishing a relationship with Spirit is trusting the message they send and taking the time to understand the message. If I don't get the answer I want and keep asking for more information, I'll start getting gibberish."

"How about this. Ask how I can catch him."

Bailey went through her ritual again. This time the card displayed a naked woman dancing on top of a globe. Again the card was upside down. She looked at Peter. "The World, reversed. It means lack of completion or resolution. I'm sorry, but you're not going to catch him."

Lia walked with Bailey to the front door. "So you're giving up gardening for this?"

"I'm going to try it out over the winter. It will give me something to do while John is at work. If I'm able to get steady business online, I'll start scaling back on gardening next spring." She set her box down and gave Lia a hug. "Sorry I couldn't be more help. I'll see you in the morning."

Lia watched through the front window as Bailey walked

to her truck. She felt Peter walk up behind her. "You shouldn't encourage her like that. I know she means well, but this is just silly."

"Oh, I don't know about that. My granny has seen some strange things."

"Bailey isn't your granny."

"You never know. She may have told us more than she realizes."

"Such as?"

"I don't know. I'll tuck it away. Something may come bubbling up."

"Why bother? She said you aren't going to catch him."

Peter wrapped his arms around her from behind, pulled her to him. "You're such a pragmatist for an artist. She said I'm not going to catch him. She didn't say he won't be caught."

# FRIDAY, NOVEMBER 18

"Hannah, what is it?" Lia set down her mug of afternoon chai and held her hand out.

Hannah passed her phone to Lia. "What would you do about this?" A text from Toby screamed out from the screen: "It's all my fault. I killed Geoff. I can't stand it anymore. I'm sorry, I'm sorry, I'm so sorry."

Lia tapped in a message: "Where are you?"

Lia stared at the phone willing Toby to respond. "He killed Geoff? I thought he was nowhere near the chapel."

"You once thought I was nowhere near the chapel," Hannah said.

"It sounds like he means to hurt himself."

"It does, doesn't it." They continued to stare at the phone as a minutes slipped by. The dogs whined, sensing their distress.

"Can I send him another message?" Lia asked.

"Be my guest."

Lia keyed in: "This is Lia. Talk to me. Let me help you."

A minute later, the phone vibrated.

"Nobody can help. Time has run out."

"Shit, shit, shit," Lia said. "Do you think he's serious?"

"Toby? No telling."

"I need to call 911." Lia grabbed her phone and punched in the numbers. She related the problem to the operator, reciting Toby's number off Hannah's phone. Duty done, the women sat, staring at each other. "I feel like we need to be doing something."

"I'll call his father." Hannah picked up her desk phone and flipped through the Rolodex.

The pitch of Hannah's voice raised and thinned as the conversation progressed, sharpened by frustration to a razor edge. "You have to be able to reach him. If your bloody company exploded, you'd be able to reach him—" Hannah was silent for a long moment, then slammed the phone into the cradle.

"Stupid, supercilious—"

"I'll call Peter."

"Thank you. It may just be histrionics, but I couldn't live with myself if I ignored this and he hurt himself."

Lia got Peter's voicemail. She left a message, then sent a text. Peter was probably in one of those meetings where he couldn't be disturbed. Ironic, since the meeting would be about the lack of progress in identifying Geoffrey Lawrence's killer. She tapped her fingers rapidly against Hannah's desktop then caught herself. She was picking up this habit from Peter.

"Even if they triangulate his phone, it's not going to give them more than a general area. You know him as well as anyone. Where would he go?"

Hannah's expression was bleak. "I don't know."

Lia cast her mind back to all the conversations she'd had with Toby, starting with their night at the chapel. Surely she'd picked up something? What do people do when they're stressed? *They find a hidey-hole, a place they feel safe.*

She'd always had such a space during her mother's more tumultuous marriages, a corner carved out of a storeroom, or a space under the stairs like Harry Potter. Where would a poor little prince go when the entire castle was closing in on him?

Something about the text nagged at her. She picked up Hannah's phone and read it again. "Time has run out ..." *Something about time. Time. No time. There's a place where time doesn't matter.*

Lia stood up, grabbed her phone. "I know where he went. He's at Spring Grove, at the clock tower."

"What are you going to do?"

"I'm going after him. By the time I get their head of security on the phone, I could be there."

"Should I call?"

Lia paused in the doorway. "No. ... If he's not there you'll raise a ruckus and nobody will thank you for it. If he is there, being approached by a stranger who knows nothing about the situation could push him over the edge —literally."

LIA THOUGHT she caught a bit of movement in the clock tower when she pulled into the parking lot at Spring Grove Cemetery, but the angle was too steep and the interior of the tower was cast in shadows. *Probably pigeons, and this is a waste of time.*

The building was an architectural mashup. The main portion was a lovely example of Romanesque Revival, but the enormous tower rode on the back of the building like an obese monk on a donkey. The tower was open like a belfry, each side featuring a pair of slender, pointed windows under a medallion engraved with the hours of a clock around the rim and a hole in the center where clockworks would fit. The roof of the tower was square and steep, angling to a flat top fitted with a railing in a style Lia associated with New England widow walks.

The pièce de résistance was a small structure resembling a miniature Greek temple on the peak of the roof at the end next to the drive. It was intended to honor Mausolus, for whom the first mausoleum was built and whose burial place was one of the Seven Wonders of the Ancient World. An unintelligible sculpture meant to represent flames topped the roof of this mini mausoleum. In a cemetery full of nineteenth century wonders and oddities, this cupola-like structure was one of the most wonderful and odd.

Lia eyed the building and wondered how she was going to get in. *Should I call Toby? No, he's not likely to answer.* She looked at the modern offices across the drive. *He could kill himself in the time it takes to get someone to let me in. ... Toby had a key. Maybe he didn't lock up.*

Sometime in the last fifty years someone had added a utilitarian cement stoop on the back of the building with a steel door. As Lia sat in her car and thought, it kept drawing her eye in a kind of mental nudge.

The door was unlocked. She eased it open a crack and found herself looking into a hall, a modern addition lined with offices and a kitchenette. Soft voices emerged from an open door, a meeting of some kind. If she could just slip past, maybe she could find Toby without a lot of explanations. She edged up to the door and risked ducking her head so she could see in. Everyone was paying attention to a speaker at the other end of the room. She blessed the very solid, silent, wood floor and stepped past.

The hall opened into an enormous room full of workstations and conference tables. She looked to the left. A restroom—more retrofitting—sat where she expected to see the base of the tower jutting into the room.

*This is what I get for having expectations.* A glance around the room revealed no clue to accessing the tower. The murmur of voices became louder. Chairs scraped on the floor as the meeting ended. In seconds they would see her. Out of options, she ran for the restroom. *Bad idea. Where do all women go after they've been stuck in a room for two hours?*

She dove into the room. On the facing wall a series of wood rungs led to a trap door fifteen feet overhead. The two women who entered moments later chattered about their Thanksgiving plans, oblivious to Lia's legs dangling through the ceiling above them.

Lia held her breath as she drew her legs through the trap door and into the dusty tower space. She froze for a long moment as her desire to find Toby battled with her need to avoid discovery. Finally a toilet flushed. She used the noise to hide the sound she made as she lowered the trap door in place.

Safely concealed, she looked around the dust mote filled gloom. The tower felt pregnant around her, anticipating. This room was much shorter and contained only a set of wood steps leading to an opening in the ceiling, the only source of light. Lia took a deep breath and started to climb.

Toby sat on a low ledge in the chill air, wearing an

incongruously cheerful neon green puffy coat, loose curls hiding his face as he looked out over the grounds. *Playing in his imagined kingdom? Is he battling foxes or zombies?*

"Toby," She said softly.

Toby spun around, then stared at her and said nothing as she climbed the last few steps and sat on the icy floor. His eyes were full. Full of fear, full of shame, full of anguish. He was still, but for the fingers of one hand. They rested on an object, stroking it. She came to the sudden realization that it was a gun.

"Talk to me," Lia said, her voice unthreatening.

He shook his head, mute.

Peter once told her that silence was often the best tool for getting people to open up. Silence and time. She waited.

"I didn't know," he said finally.

Lia remained silent.

He shook his head again, this time looking down. "He did it because of me."

"Who did it?"

"My father."

Lia swallowed her surprise.

"Your father killed Professor Lawrence?"

Toby nodded, still looking down. "He—he said horrible things."

"What things?"

"I never had the nerve to tell my father I'm gay. He's so old school. Hopewell, things are different there. I know a lot of people don't like me, but at least it's not because I'm gay. And Geoff—" His mouth worked as tears spilled down his face. "Oh, God, Geoff."

"How did you find out?"

"A few days ago, my father went through my things. He

found a strip of photographs. I was clowning with Tom at The Comet—you wouldn't know Tom, we were a thing for a while—and we went into the photo booth there, and took some pictures. We're kissing in some of them.

"Dad shoved those pictures in my face and screamed at me that no son of his was going to be a faggot. He said, 'I killed that filthy faggot teacher of yours because I thought he turned you gay. Turns out I was wrong and you've been an abomination all along.' Then he took a baggie out of his pocket and handed it to me. It was one of his handkerchiefs, crusted over with blood from wiping his fingerprints off that candlestick."

"Oh, Toby." It was all Lia could think to say.

"Then he—he told me that Geoff was just using me to get to his money, that Geoff told Leander I'd never be Faust. He said I was useless and too stupid to know when I was being played."

Lia's heart ached. However clueless Toby had been, his sense of betrayal was real—betrayal by the father who'd never loved him as well as the lover who only pretended to. She remembered the shock of discovering the truth about Luthor after he died. *Can I talk him down? Will listening be enough?*

Toby's index finger traced the trigger guard of the gun.

"What do you want to do?"

"I want to die!" he howled, startling a trio of pigeons roosting under the roof. They flew out with an agitated fluttering of wings. Toby watched as if more than anything, he wanted to fly away with them.

Lia didn't dare look away from Toby. She didn't dare reach for her phone. Anything could break the fragile bubble that contained them, that kept Toby talking. *Where's*

*Peter? Where are the cops? Why, why, why, didn't I call 911 before I spoke to him? Why didn't I turn on my voice recorder? I am such an idiot!*

"I always loved this place," Toby said. "I brought Tom here. This is where I lost my virginity. We sat up here naked and I never felt so free. I wanted it to last forever."

Toby knocked a fist against the ledge.

"What happened to Tom?" Lia asked.

Toby shrugged. "I guess he didn't love me."

*Keep him talking.* "Yeah, I hate when that happens."

"You know the worst part? He left me for a girl."

"I'm sorry."

"Then he pretended we were never together."

"That sucks."

"Big time." Toby's index finger trailed the length of the gun barrel.

*I should have brought the dogs. He'd never shoot himself in front of the Fur Boys.*

Lia considered her options. Grappling with a disturbed person holding a gun was not her favorite pastime. Too easy to turn it on her. Hit him with pepper spray, then take the gun away? It might tip the odds in her favor, or he could start shooting blindly. Besides, it seemed like a rude thing to do when he wasn't threatening her. And he was sitting on that ledge, next to a fifteen-foot drop that would land him on a steeply sloped roof. If he fell, he'd slide off the edge. If he defended himself successfully, Lia might be the one heading for the pavement. *Where are the damn cops?*

"Toby, I know things look dark right now—"

Toby scoffed. "Things will look better in the morning? Don't you get it? This is my *life*. The only people who ever loved me are dead, and the only happy place I know is in my head with the badgers and foxes. They hate me at Hopewell. Anyone who's nice to me wants my father's money. My father wishes I'd never been born. I *hate* being me."

"Aren't I nice to you?"

"You're just temporary. You'll finish the frieze and go away."

Toby picked up the gun. Lia drew in her breath, but he put it in his jacket pocket and zipped it shut. Lia exhaled, thanking God she would not have to watch him shoot himself.

"You're a really nice lady. Have a nice life." He swiveled around, and with his hands gripping the inside edge of the ledge, dropped over the side. His hands held for a second, then two, and disappeared. Before Lia could react, she heard the thud of Toby's body hitting the roof below. She dashed to the ledge. He'd landed where the tower met the roof in a protected "vee." It was a long drop but he'd never been in danger of rolling off.

Toby looked up and grinned. "Damn, that was hard on the ankles. Surprised you, didn't I?"

"Toby, what are you doing?"

"See that funny little Greek house at the end of the roof? I've been staring at that funny little house most of my life. I guess you could say it's the last thing on my bucket list. I'm going to climb inside and when I'm ready, I'll shoot myself. You can make your calls now."

Lia whipped out her phone and dialed 911. She outlined the situation to the operator while she watched Toby scramble up the roof in that blind spot where only she could see him. She stayed on the line with the operator. By the time Toby gained the ridge line, she could hear sirens.

"Are those for me?" he yelled.

"I hope so," Lia called back.

Toby laughed. "Do you think the cameras will come? They really played up Geoff's death. What do you think they'll do for me? I could lead on the six o'clock news. That will put a burr up the old man's ass."

"Toby, please come back." Lia was stunned by Toby's excitement. Perhaps he felt in control for the first time in his life. Or was this what it was like for all performers when the curtain rose?

"How would I get back in the tower? You know, I wanted Hannah to come, but you're doing great." Toby walked slowly along the spine of the roof, favoring one ankle. People in the lane below spotted him. They gathered and pointed. Toby took a bow. He turned back to Lia and yelled, "Look at me! I'm a star! Mama would be so proud." He turned again, targeting the little mausoleum and stepped forward.

"Toby!" Lia screamed. "You don't need to do this!"

Toby tossed a negligent wave over his shoulder.

In Lia's ear, the operator asked, "What's happening?"

A fire truck with a ladder followed two police cars into the cemetery.

"The police are here," Lia told the 911 operator. "Thank you for staying on the line with me. I'm hanging up now." She jabbed the little red phone icon, then dialed Peter. One ring, two, three, keeping eerie time with Toby's careful steps across the rooftop.

"Hey, Babe—"

"Where the hell *are* you!"

"Whoa. I just got out of a meeting. Where am I supposed to be?"

"Toby is getting ready to shoot himself on top of the

cemetery offices because his dad killed Geoff Lawrence. The police just pulled up. Stupid people on the ground have their phones aimed at him. I bet he's already lighting up Facebook."

"Where are you?"

"I'm inside the clock tower."

"There's a clock tower? Never mind. I'm on my way."

"Hurry!"

"Ten minutes. I'll be there in ten minutes. Stay on the line."

Lia looked at her battery indicator. Seven percent power. "If my phone lasts that long."

A bull horn squealed as the Channel 12 news van pulled in, followed by Channel 7.

"Toby Grant," the tinny voice called.

"That's me," Toby called. "Make sure you spell it right." He was now less than five feet from the little mausoleum.

"Careful, son. We're going to get you down from there."

Toby laughed. It was a harsh sound, lacking the glee of moments earlier. "I'm not your son. As of today, I'm nobody's son." He reached out and grabbed the roof of the little structure and climbed in.

"That's good," the tinny voice said. "Sit tight and we'll get you down."

Toby crawled into the tiny temple and sat, dangling his feet over the edge.

"Don't you get it?" he screamed down. "I'm exactly where I want to be. You can't make me come down."

He unzipped his pocket and removed the gun, holding it up in the air so everyone tuned in on Facebook Live could see it. "This is for me," Toby yelled. "But if anyone comes after me, I'll shoot them first."

Two officers pulled their guns and aimed at Toby. Toby shoved the gun back in his pocket. "See, I put it away. You have no excuse to shoot me. You can lower your guns now. Quick, quick, you have an au-di-ence." He sang out the last word, a taunting reference to the news cameras and cell phones aimed in their direction. The officers looked around and lowered their weapons.

"I have a statement to make before I kill myself." Toby reached into his other pocket and pulled out the baggie containing the incriminating handkerchief. He removed it from the baggie, waving it in the air. "My fa-ther," he sing-songed, "the *estimable* Tobias Grant, shoved this handkerchief at me last night and told me he used it to wipe his fingerprints off the candlestick he used to bash Geoff Lawrence's head in less than three weeks ago in Norman Chapel, the lovely building behind you."

"Why did your father kill Dr. Lawrence?" This was Aubrey Morse, the pretty blonde reporter from Channel 7.

"He did it because Geoff Lawrence had the nerve to be gay, and he thought poor Geoff was corrupting me. I've been as queer as a three-dollar bill since I was born, and he was too STOO-pid to notice."

An ambulance pulled into the drive. Toby yelled down, "You aren't going to need that!"

"Where is your father now?" the competing Channel 12 reporter asked. "Why isn't he here?"

"He isn't here because he thinks I'm an abomination who never should have been BORN!"

"Why are you killing yourself?" Aubrey asked. "Why not let us help you?"

"What's left for ME?" Toby screamed. "The only person who loved me is dead and my father has disinherited me. I have nowhere to go. What do YOU think I have to live for?"

"Stay alive so you can testify against your father!" Aubrey called out. "Live for justice!"

"This is my dying testimony!" Toby screamed. "It counts, and it's too public to hush up."

Toby pressed the gun against his chest and fired.

PETER BADGED an officer at the police barricade blocking the entrance to Spring Grove Cemetery, then circled a fire truck positioned against the old office with its ladder raised. A pair of medics climbed the ladder while firemen rigged a Stokes basket to carry Toby's body down from the roof. The milling array of first responders, witnesses, and media parted as he drove to the parking lot behind the building.

He'd been frantic when he'd heard the gunshot through Lia's phone. There was nothing he could do about what she'd witnessed, but he could take care of her now.

Following directions Lia had given him before her phone died, Peter parked his car and slipped through the back door. The offices were empty. *Everyone's out front watching the show.* He climbed the odd, built-in ladder and the tower stairs. Lia sat on the ledge, watching the medics wrestle Toby out of the strange little temple and into the dangling Stoke's basket.

"Hey," he said softly.

Lia jerked around. "Peter," she said, tears streaming down.

Peter crouched down and gathered her in his arms, stroking her hair and saying nothing.

Lia shook her head against his chest. "He just shot himself. I couldn't do anything to stop him. I—"

"Shhhh." He tilted her chin up and looked into her wet, green eyes. "That's it, focus on me. It's going to be okay, but we need to get you out of here. Can you stand up?"

Lia nodded into his jacket. Peter took stock of the tower. It was empty of everything except dust and pigeon droppings, containing nothing he could see that would be of interest from an evidentiary perspective. He stood, pulling Lia up with him.

"What happens now?" she asked.

"If I can sneak you out of here, I'm taking you home."

"Shouldn't I be talking to someone?"

"They'll be busy for hours. Everyone's focused on Toby."

"Do you think he'll live? I watched them working on him. A medic stuck a giant needle into his chest. It was awful."

Lia was steady enough on the stairs but faltered when they reached the trap door. Peter went down first, waiting several rungs below for Lia to get her bearings. Her foot slipped, missing a rung. Peter extended a hand to steady her, then backed down step by step to ensure she didn't fall. He continued to hold onto her when they reached the floor. Lia stared around, blinking as if she didn't know where she was.

"Shouldn't you be helping instead of taking care of me?"

"Not my case. If they want me, they'll call."

"I'm such an idiot. I could have recorded the whole thing if I'd been thinking."

"You were thinking. You were thinking like a compassionate human being. You weren't thinking like a cop."

"Are Heckle and Jeckle going to grill me like tuna?"

"Probably. If I can get you out of here, they'll have to do it on your turf."

It was easy to slip out the back to the Blazer. Peter had Lia lay across the console with her head in his lap while he drove back through the police barrier. He took a moment to appreciate his decision to drive an SUV. The height that allowed officers to see down into cars—a trick that brought evidence into plain sight that would be hidden when viewed from a normal car—kept people on the ground from seeing in.

Hodgkins and Jarvis would catch up to them, but he could at least get Lia settled first. He spotted the newly arrived detectives inside the crowd of onlookers, dogged by news media and too busy to notice Peter. *Better them than me.*

PETER LED LIA into her apartment and settled her on the big Mission couch with Honey and Chewy.

"I'm going to pour you a big glass of wine, but first I need to take your statement and send it to Hodgkins. That should keep them off your back for now."

He turned on the voice recorder on his phone and walked Lia through the events of the preceding hour while she buried her hands into Honey's fur, her fingers clenching as she recited the difficult parts. She slumped back against the couch when she was done. Peter doubted she had the energy to move under her own steam.

"I'm getting you that wine now, and while you work on that, I'm running you a hot bath."

"What did I do to deserve you?"

He winked at her. "You haven't done it yet."

"Asshole," she called after his retreating back.

"Is that one of those person-specific terms of endearment you were telling me about?"

"Absolutely."

Peter sat on the closed toilet with water thundering into the tub beside him and sent the audio file off. There would be fallout, but it would land on him and not Lia.

# 18

## SATURDAY, NOVEMBER 19

"How sharper than a serpent's tooth it is to have a thankless child," Terry said. Morning sun glinted off his Teddy Roosevelt glasses as he raised an imperious finger to punctuate the sentiment.

Jim looked up from the fire he was coaxing to life and shook his head, his lips compressed behind his beard.

Bailey fed a dog biscuit to Kita. "You can hardly blame him for ratting out his father after the old man disowned him."

Lia sat next to Peter on the bench in front of the fire, absorbing all the comments while she lobbed tennis balls down the hill for Honey. She still felt fragile from the day before and didn't need to listen to her friends rehash Toby's spectacular suicide attempt. But deviating from her routine would make her feel even more—rootless? Disoriented? She didn't know how to describe the way she felt. She was disconnected, a step back from everything as if she saw the world through a pane of glass.

The other dogs raced Honey to the tennis ball, chasing her after she caught it, trying to take it away. *Honey loves this game. I wish life could be that simple.*

"Tobias Senior, eh? Has he been on anyone's radar before now?" Terry asked.

"No," Lia said. "Toby told me he expected to find his dad at the family mausoleum before the concert, but he wasn't there."

Jim addressed Peter. "What does the father say?"

"Senior says Toby is disturbed and fabricated the entire story to get attention. He owns handkerchiefs like the one with the blood on it, but he has dozens just like it and Toby sometimes borrowed them. He claims he's never had an issue with his son's sexual preference and has been aware of it for years."

"Do they know whose blood is on the handkerchief? Maybe it's not even Lawrence's," Steve said.

"Wouldn't that be a twist," Peter said. "The blood type is right, but DNA will take weeks."

"Can't they get DNA from fingerprints now?" Bailey asked. "That would prove who handled the handkerchief."

"If they can find skin cells," Peter said. "That's not a given. We know Toby handled it because he took it out of the bag to wave it at everyone while he was on the roof. For all we know, Toby took it after his father handled it and used it to mop up Lawrence's blood. That's if his father's DNA is on it."

"The fact that Toby had it is evidence that one of them killed the professor," Terry said.

"If it's the professor's blood, all it proves is that Toby got it from the killer," Bailey said. "The killer could have been Toby, his father, or someone else."

"Bah," Terry said. "Occam's Razor. A third party is too convoluted."

"Why would Toby kill Lawrence?" Jim asked.

"If he knew Lawrence lied to him about *Faust*, that could be reason enough," Steve said.

"Lia, is there any chance Toby knew?" Bailey asked.

"I don't know. I'm sure other people figured Dr. Lawrence was stringing Toby along about his potential, but I don't think Toby would believe it unless it came directly from Dr. Lawrence. If he doubled back before the concert, he could have overheard the argument."

"The lad did it," Terry decided.

"If Toby killed Dr. Lawrence, why would he implicate his father?" Lia asked.

"You question family dynamics with your history?" Bailey asked.

"Truth," Lia said.

"We need a witness," Terry said.

"Yeah, that would be handy," Steve said. "Lia, you can conjure one up, can't you?"

A TERSE PHONE call had Peter heading to District Five despite his plan to spend his day off in bed. He had to kill the remainder of this cold before Thanksgiving if he wanted to spend the long weekend moving Lia into the new place. *Later. I can rest later. If I'm still alive.*

Captain Parker faced him across her desk with an impassivity suitable for Mount Rushmore. "Did you or did you not remove a key witness from a crime scene without advising the detective in charge?"

Peter prevaricated. "There didn't seem to be anyone in charge while I was there."

Captain Parker gave him a steady look. "This skirts very close to obstruction of justice."

Peter had his points ready. "There are at least a dozen video records of Grant's suicide attempt on Facebook Live and more on YouTube, not to mention Channels 7 and 12. You don't need Lia to know what happened."

"She spoke with him prior to his performance on the roof. That isn't on Facebook."

"No, sir. I took her statement and forwarded it to Hodgkins."

"You stood between a witness and the investigating officers."

"Lia has a history with Hodgkins and Jarvis. She doesn't trust them and wasn't likely to open up with them, not after she'd been traumatized. It was my judgment that I would be able to get the full story from her with less anxiety on her part, and faster. I sent the audio file to Hodgkins hours before they could have interviewed her. If they have any follow-up questions, she'll be steadier today."

Parker sighed, a rare expression of emotion. "You're a good cop. Is this beef between you, Hodgkins, and Jarvis going to haunt this district?"

"Not on my part, sir."

She gave him another steady look. "Your lack of objectivity is a problem."

"Yes, sir."

"How is Lia doing?"

"She blames herself because she didn't know how to stop him."

"From the performance I saw on YouTube, I don't think

a freight train carrying an atom bomb could have stopped him, not after he had an audience."

"How is he?"

"He shot himself with a .22 target pistol. The bullet lodged in a wallet he had in the chest pocket of his parka. The impact cracked a rib, and the rib punctured a lung. He was in critical condition after his surgery, but it's been upgraded to serious."

"He shot himself in the wallet?"

"Not surprising. It's hard to tell what's where under one of those puffy coats."

"Has anyone been able to interview him?"

"He's still under heavy sedation. It may be tomorrow before he's able to talk."

"What about his father?"

"Hiding behind a wall of suits. Hinkle has been standing guard over Junior and says Senior has yet to show at the hospital."

"That's cold."

"Can you blame the man for circling his wagons? Junior's public declaration is damning."

"Grant hasn't responded?"

"His lawyer issued a statement to the effect that his son was troubled and the allegations are false."

"Sounds like fun for everyone."

Parker snorted. "This is going to be a world-class case of he said/he said complicated by social media. Thank God it's not our problem." Parker looked directly at Peter, examining his face carefully. "Or is it?"

"It's like an itchy scab, sir."

"Whatever you do, don't pick at it. I'll convey my opinion that your actions, while not within protocol, have not harmed the investigation and do not warrant disciplinary action beyond our chat. Get out of here. Now that all the copper pipes in District Five are breathing easier, you've got package thieves to collar."

A HELPFUL NURSE pointed Lia in the direction of Toby's room at Good Sam. Cal Hinkle looked up from his seat outside Toby's door and waved. "How is he?" Lia asked.

"Asleep now. He was feeling good enough to go bonkers when his dad showed up a couple hours ago."

"No! What happened?"

"I was under orders not to let Senior in the room, but the kid was awake and saw him standing in the doorway and started screaming. I thought he was going to rip his IV out and come after him. The old man didn't bat an eye. He just looked all concerned and told Toby he hoped he recovered soon so they could put this behind them. Had his lawyer with him. Told me to take good care of his son. Can you believe that?"

"Why do you think he brought a lawyer?"

"Kid accused him of murder. I imagine that lawyer's been by his side twenty-four/seven ever since. I heard the old man's arranging home care for him." Cal shook his head. "Don't know why the two of them would want to be under the same roof, considering."

"What did you think of Toby's dad?"

"If you'll pardon the expression, he's got gonads of steel. Can't tell which one of them is lying. You talked to the kid. What did you think?"

"I know he's hurting."

"You think he was telling the truth?"

"I did, but the way he was soaking it up when the cameras arrived made me wonder if it was all an act."

Cal rubbed his chin. "I had this dog when I was in high school. He went everywhere with me. Loved riding in the car more than anything in the world. Got hit by a car. Broke his leg so the bone was sticking out. The neighbors helped me load him into my car. I was driving to the vet like a maniac while he bled all over the back seat. Do you know, he sat up and poked his head between the front seats. Creepiest thing I ever saw, that bone sticking out of his leg, blood pouring out, and he's sitting there grinning, he's so happy because he's going for a ride. I bet it's the same with a performer. Give them an audience and it doesn't matter that they're dying inside."

Lia stared at Cal, at the freckles and haystack hair that gave the impression of being earnest but none too bright. She hadn't expected insight from him. "Did you catch any of the video?"

"Facebook and YouTube pulled the clips by the time I heard about it, but I saw the video on the Channel 12 website. They didn't show him pulling the trigger. Gotta protect the public's sensibilities."

"Nobody needs to see that." Lia glanced into the room. Toby still slept. "Looks like he's not waking up anytime soon. I'm going to write him a note and take off."

LIA EXITED the elevator on the ground floor of Good Sam to find Tobias Sr. coming toward her, flanked by a man in a suit that had to be his lawyer.

"Ms. Anderson, I hope you'll do me the courtesy of having a word with me," Senior said.

"I—I don't know," she said.

"Please. You were the last person to talk to my son before he shot himself. Won't you have pity on a grieving parent?"

Torn between compassion and Toby's vile accusations, Lia said nothing.

"A short chat, nothing more." He nodded to a grouping of upholstered chairs by the giant lobby windows. "We can sit there if you like."

"Toby accused you of murder. Someone could call this witness tampering."

"There's no case, Ms. Anderson," the smarmy little man said. "No charges. What is there to interfere with?"

*No charges yet, you little piece of navel lint.*

Senior took her hand and held it gently in his. "Please. He's my *son.*"

Lia withdrew her hand, resisting the urge to wipe it on her pants. "I can give you five minutes." She pulled out her phone. "Do you mind? I need to send a quick text to let someone know I'm going to be late."

Senior waved a hand in a be-my-guest gesture. Lia activated her voice recorder, then locked the screen on her phone before she dropped it back in her pocket. Ohio was a one-party consent state. Recording her conversation was not only legal, it was admissible.

Lia took a seat with her back to the window, leaving Senior and his mini-me blinking against the sunlight. The small act of malice would normally be beneath her. She figured they deserved all the discomfort she could create for them. She tilted her head in a "Well?" gesture.

"What did my son say to you?"

"I'm sorry, that is between him and me. I won't repeat it without his consent."

"You repeated it to the law."

"You aren't the law."

"Ms. Anderson," Smarmy said, "if this becomes a court matter, we will have the right to depose you."

"I'm perfectly happy to wait until that happens. Is there anything else?"

Senior sat with his hands on his knees. He tapped them several times in a nervous gesture as if trying to make a decision. "Perhaps we should rewind. I don't want this to be an adversarial conversation. I just wanted to understand what was going on with Toby before he shot himself. He's my only child. Have pity on an old man."

"I'm sorry, I can't help you."

"Perhaps you can listen?"

Lia sat back, folding her arms against her chest. "I'm listening."

"Toby and I have always had a difficult relationship. He was his mother's child. She lived through him and I let her. When she died, Toby and I had little to hold us together. It's been an uneasy year."

"Why are you telling me this?"

"I want you to understand. Toby blames me for his mother's death. I think he made that horrible accusation to strike out at me."

"Why would he blame you?"

"Do you know how she died?"

Lia shook her head.

"She had a bad cold and took an ill-advised combination of pills while drinking vodka. Such a combination is like playing Russian roulette. If it hits your system the wrong way, you can die. There were some whispers she did it on purpose."

"Why would she kill herself?" Lia said.

"I don't believe she did. It's more to the point that Toby does. He's certain I did something to make her unhappy but he's never said what. Perhaps she said something to him that he's never shared with me. Ms. Anderson, I'm just a parent trying to do my best for a troubled child."

"I repeat: why are you telling me this?"

Senior leaned forward, holding Lia with gray, flinty eyes. "I think Toby killed Geoff and decided to use the situation to get revenge for his mother's death."

# 19

## MONDAY, NOVEMBER 21

"At least you and Leander are off the hook now," Lia told Hannah as she sipped her latte. She bent over and petted the dogs.

"Not really. This situation is tearing the school apart. Senior's financial support has been critical to Hopewell and they're terrified of losing it. Michael and Suki are saying Toby is prone to hysteria and his story isn't credible. That he made the whole thing up, including the evidence. The students are furious. They don't want to be in a school where they can be dismissed so easily."

"His father could have made the whole thing up for his own purposes," Lia said.

"Do you think he'd do something like that? Toby's the attention seeker."

"The kind of control Senior showed at the hospital was abnormal. I felt a kind of oily righteousness under the surface. He gave me the creeps. In my book someone like that is capable of anything."

"I hope they figure it out fast. Otherwise people will start looking at me and Leander again, and Leander will be out of a job."

"Leander and not you?"

"They'll keep me because I'm their key to Geoff's estate. They toss Leander out as the sacrificial lamb and eventually everything goes back to normal. Only now I've got the sword of Damocles hanging over my head while my Fur Boys live out their very long and useless lives." She picked up Dasher and nuzzled him. "I'm sorry, sweetie. Mommy didn't mean that. I wuv you very, very much, even if you hold my life hostage simply by existing. You can't help that."

"But how can they fire Leander? Couldn't he sue?"

Hannah shook her head. "No tenure. They won't have to fire him. They just won't renew his contract."

A TAP on the window of Lia's Volvo caused her to jolt. She reached across and opened the passenger door. Bailey slid in, handing Lia a cup of hot chocolate. "I thought you might be cold, sitting out here."

Lia accepted the cup, wrapping her hands around it, absorbing the heat. "Thanks." She returned to staring out the windshield. The car sat in the Salway Park parking lot, across Spring Grove Avenue from the cemetery. The Volvo was angled to provide the best view of Norman Chapel.

"Didn't Peter ask you to butt out?" Bailey asked.

"Of course he did."

"Then why are we here?"

"Peter's not inside my head. He's not the one sitting in

that office every day, watching Hopewell fall apart. How am I supposed to leave it alone?"

"Just checking. How is surveilling the cemetery supposed to help? Do you expect the doer to return to the scene of the crime?"

Lia shook her head and took a sip of chocolate. "Wouldn't that be handy? Peter says a lot of things fall into place if you understand the logistics of a scene. He'll go to a scene and absorb it until whatever is bothering him floats to the surface."

"And I'm here because?"

"Because talking things out with another person opens them up. I can't talk to Peter because he asked me to drop it."

"Okay, so what's bothering you?"

"The whole business is like sticking your hand into a pond full of minnows and expecting to catch one."

"Maybe you're not looking for a minnow," Bailey said.

"What if you're right? What if it's someone nobody is looking at?"

"Wouldn't someone have seen them?"

"Hannah and Leander backed each other up. What if some of those kids who said they went to Frisch's never made it there? What if Hannah and Leander weren't the only ones who made up alibis?"

"How would you figure that out?"

"Heckle and Jeckle are supposed to be coordinating everyone's statements," Lia said.

"Don't you trust them to do that?"

"Like they're going to create a timeline that involves two dozen people?"

"I see your point."

"Peter went to see Sandy Alich today in case she recognized some of the students coming and going at Frisch's while she was waiting for the bus. Turns out she had enough of her cheating bastard of a husband and left him. Nobody knows where she is."

"Weird timing."

"I thought so." Still staring at the chapel, Lia narrowed her eyes. "What do you see in front of you?"

"A chapel, a street, bushes, an iron fence. What are you looking at?"

"On this side of the street."

"I see a bench," Bailey said.

"Uh huh. There's a sign on the telephone pole next to it. Bet you a fish log it's a bus stop sign."

"I'm a vegetarian. No bet."

"That must be the bench Peter was talking about during the reenactment. Cynth sat there because it gave her a good view of the chapel." Lia exited the car and walked out to the curb, looking north along the avenue. "Can you see Sandy's bus stop from here?"

"What are you thinking?" Bailey asked.

"Horseshoes and hand-grenades. Sandy was too close for comfort. Can you pull up the bus schedule on your phone? I'm curious how long she had to wait."

"I don't get it."

"There's a bench here because of the park. There's no bench in front of Frisch's. Think about it. You've been on your feet for eight hours. Do you really want to stand for fifteen minutes while you stare at the place where you work? I would rather walk five minutes to a place where I can sit down."

"And where the bus arrives sooner."

"And is almost directly across the street from Norman Chapel."

Bailey downloaded a map of bus routes, then fiddled with the pdf, zooming and dragging it across the tiny screen to find Spring Grove Avenue. "These are not ideal conditions for this."

"Yeah, yeah, yeah. What bus is she taking?"

"Do you know where she lives?"

"Winton Road, toward Northbend."

"Either the Sixteen or the Twenty will get you there." Bailey switched back to the Metro website and downloaded schedules for the two routes. "The Sixteen shows up at 7:28. ... The Twenty comes at 7:32."

"A minimum twenty-minute wait after she left the restaurant. She was sitting right here and she saw something."

"I knew she was acting funny. Why do you suppose she lied to us?"

"Don't know. But we need to find her. What's Trees up to tonight?"

## 20

# TUESDAY, NOVEMBER 22

Lia and Bailey sat in Lia's Volvo behind a red Ford Focus parked at the Remke's in Lawrenceburg, watching for the Ford's owner, a woman named Sherry Pace.

"How long do you think she'll be?" Bailey asked. "Is there time for me to grab a couple things? I still need to shop for Thanksgiving."

"You aren't leaving this car," Lia said. "We can shop later."

"Can I be bad cop when she shows up?" Bailey asked.

"No window to hang her out of. You can be stern cop. We'll both be stern cop. I hope Trees is right about this."

"Relax," Bailey said. "He was right about her shopping after work on Tuesdays, and why else would baby food and diapers suddenly appear on her shopper card? Sandy has to be staying with her."

"I wish we didn't have to threaten her," Lia said.

"Do you want to explain to Peter's boss how we used a

hacker to find Sandy and get Trees tossed into prison? Our plan is dicey enough as it is."

Lia spotted a cloudy mass of russet hair on a woman pushing a shopping cart in their direction. She nudged Bailey. "I think that's her."

They waited until the woman popped the hatch on her car and began loading in bags of groceries. Lia and Bailey walked up on either side of her. Lia pulled a package of Luv's Pull-Ups off the bottom of the cart and set them inside the hatchback beside a case of Diet Mountain Dew.

Sherry jumped, banging her head on the hatch. "Ow! Who are you?"

"I'm always forgetting the stuff on the bottom of the cart. How about you, Bailey?"

"I said, who are you?"

"We're your best friends, Sherry," Lia said. "You lied when the police asked if you knew where Sandy and Chelsey were. You're guilty of obstructing a police investigation. We're giving you a chance to get out from under it."

Sherry grabbed more bags from her cart, keeping her face averted. "What are you talking about?"

Lia leaned on the diapers. "Go ahead, tell us these are for your incontinent German shepherd. Oh, wait, I don't see any dog food."

"What business is it of yours if she doesn't want her dirtbag of a husband to know where she is?"

"Is that what she told you? That she ran away from her husband?" Lia shook her head. "Forget her husband. They put Amber alerts out for Chelsey. What about all those strangers who are looking at every toddler they see, hoping to find her? What about them?"

Sherry shifted bags around in the back of her car. "That's Sandy's business, not mine."

"Sandy isn't hiding from Joe," Bailey said. "Sandy's hiding from the man who killed Geoffrey Lawrence."

Sherry pulled her head out of her groceries and stared at Lia. "What are you talking about?"

"Sandy saw someone she knew at Norman Chapel when Geoffrey Lawrence was murdered," Lia said. "Instead of telling the police, she ran."

Sherry's face went mulish. "I don't believe you. You made that up. … Joe sent you."

"Joe didn't send us," Lia said. "Have you asked Sandy why she didn't toss the dirtbag out of the house she owns?"

Sherry bit her lip. "She doesn't want to talk about it."

"She had another reason for getting out of town and leaving no forwarding address," Lia said.

"I'd say telling a killer you saw him at the scene of the crime rates right up there," Bailey said, widening her Marty Feldman eyes to great effect.

"Do you want us to call the police now and tell them where she is, or do you want us to follow you back to your house so Sandy can have a chance to explain first?"

"'Raffe has a boo-boo," Chelsey said, shoving the limp toy into Sandy's lap. Sandy set her crocheting aside to look at a tear in the stuffed giraffe.

A key rattled in the front door. Sandy set 'Raffe aside. "Aunt Sherry's back with the groceries, honey. Would you like to help put them away?"

Sherry wasn't carrying groceries. And she wasn't alone.

"What are you doing here?" It was the only thing she could think to say.

Sherry narrowed her eyes. "You know them."

"No, I uh …" Caught, the words died before she could utter them. Sandy ducked her head.

"I'm hurt," Lia said.

"Dammit, Sandy, don't lie to me. What have you gotten me into? I thought you were teaching Joe a lesson. These ladies say you're running from a murderer!"

Sandy's head popped up, her mouth working like a fish, nothing coming out.

"We need you," Lia said. "If you've seen the news you know Toby Grant accused his father of killing Dr. Lawrence and the case is a bigger mess than ever. We need you to tell who you saw outside the chapel that night."

"I didn't see anything. I already told you that."

Lia sighed. "Looks like I call Peter."

It was eleven before Peter made it to Lia's house. He caught Lia's questioning look as he knelt to give Viola a hello scratch. "No joy. Sandy insists she boarded the bus across from Frisch's and saw nothing. Even when Heckle and Jeckle insinuated she was in on it and double teamed her with the possibility of charging her with accessory to murder—" Peter stopped petting Viola at Lia's appalled expression. "It was an empty threat and I think she knew it."

He headed for Lia's kitchen and his stash of Grolsch, woman and dogs trailing behind.

"How could she have been in on it? She didn't even know Lawrence was dead until Bailey and I told her."

274

"Their theory is that she watched to see when everyone was gone and gave Grant the high sign—texted him with a burner phone that has since been destroyed." Peter pawed through groceries—Lia must have gone shopping—and pulled a bottle out of the fridge. He twisted the cap and took a long swig.

"Idiots," Lia said. "Whatever Sandy saw, she had no clue what it meant till Bailey and I told her Lawrence was dead."

"Then they came out and expressed their frustration that I wasted their time with a non-witness."

"Weren't they the ones who sent you after her? Now they're upset because you found her?"

"Technically, I didn't find her."

"Why do you think she's lying?" Lia said. "Do you think she's covering for Grant—whichever one it was—in an accessory after the fact kind of way?"

"That, or she's terrified of him. Damned if I know which one it is."

"Let's look at it from a different perspective," Lia said.

"What's this 'let's'? As if 'we' are conducting an investigation, Woman of Long Nose?"

"Too late for that. You're dying to hash it out. Admit it."

Peter set his beer on the counter and folded his arms. "What perspective are you proposing?"

"You're a rich killer. You know Sandy saw something, because she thought you would give her money if she told you about it."

Peter raised his eyebrows.

"Think about it. If the killer had seen her, he would have acted before Bailey and I talked to her. So if he knows, it's because she told him. And she'd only tell him if she thought there was something to gain."

"I'm a killer," Peter told Viola soberly. "Check."

"Did Sandy hide out because you paid her off to stay out of sight until the case calmed down—which would explain why she didn't need to empty her bank account when she left town—or was she on the run from you because her blackmail scheme went bad?"

"Good question. What difference does it make?"

"Not sure," Lia said. "Now Sandy's turned up and the police have her. What's your next move?"

"I'd want to make my presence felt. If I paid her off, I need to remind her what she has to lose. If I didn't pay her off, I let her know there's still time to make a deal."

"You saw her interview. Is she keeping quiet because she's scared of the consequences if she speaks or because she hopes there's money on the table?"

"Maybe both," Peter said. "If our killer has sources, he already knows we're talking to her. If not, Sandy may give him a nudge. That's if she's looking for a payday."

"So your best bet—as a detective, not a killer—is to keep an eye on her and see what she does."

"She's back in Indiana. Even if I could get Parker to approve the time, it's out of my jurisdiction."

"I have no jurisdiction," Lia said.

*Better poke a stick in her spokes before she gets going.* "No. Uh-uh. She knows what you look like."

"She knows me. She doesn't know my friends."

# 21

# FRIDAY, NOVEMBER 25

CHELSEY TODDLED ACROSS THE GRASS IN THE PRE-DAWN, waving her favorite, worn-to-a-rag, floppy giraffe. "Play slide! Play slide!"

"What's going on, Sandy?" Sherry scowled at Sandy from her seat on a bench at Ludlow Hill Park. The playground sat on a lonely road bisecting the woods that surrounded them, illuminated by a single post light intended to discourage vandals.

Sandy blinked, an attempt to act innocent that hadn't worked on Sherry since childhood. "What do you mean?"

"I mean why are we here?" Sherry waved her hand at the surrounding gloom. "It's Black Friday. We're supposed to be in line at Walmart. That Samsung wide-screen will be sold out before we get through the doors. Then what are we going to do for Mom's Christmas? This is the most ridiculous thing I can think of."

Sandy enunciated carefully, as if Sherry was dense. "I

told you. Joe came crawling back and said he wanted to meet me at the gazebo. He's trying to soften me up."

"Sunrise on the lake was your idea. Joe's idea of romance is popping the tab on his own can of beer so you don't have to do it for him. It doesn't wash. You're not telling me something."

Sandy huffed. Acting indignant was always her next line of defense after innocence and acting as if Sherry was stupid didn't work. "Look I just need you to watch after Chelsey while I talk to Joe. I don't want her seeing him and getting all excited until we've had a chance to work things out. That's all."

She picked Chelsey up. Chelsey patted her mom's face and gave her a kiss. "I've got to run for a little bit, baby doll. Play here with your auntie and I'll be back soon. Then we'll go for pancakes."

Chelsey clapped her hands together. "Pancakes! Pancakes! Pancakes!" She wiggled down and ran over to her aunt. She slapped Sherry's knees with both hands. "You come to pancakes! More pancakes! Mmmmm!"

Sherry gave Sandy her best fisheye. "Fine. We miss that sale and you're buying Mom's present."

Sandy threw up a hand before she turned away. "Whatever."

Sherry's voice followed her down the path. "We're going to talk later."

*Always have to have the last word, don't you?*

SANDY WALKED down Old Clerk Road towards the pond Lawrenceburg called a lake. If Sherry would cooperate for one damn minute everything would be fine and it would all be over.

She'd known if she could hang on everything would work out. Then the package arrived, a padded envelope containing a cheap flip phone, already charged. The note said, "I'll call at eleven p.m. Be sure to answer." When the call came, the number was blocked. *Covering your ass, are you?*

"I thought I might be hearing from you," Sandy said. "I bet you wish you'd been nicer to me."

"I'm hoping we can come to an understanding," the voice said.

Sandy took a chance. "The price has gone up. I want a million."

"And what do I get for my million dollars?" the voice asked. He sounded amused.

"You get silence. I take the money. I leave town and nobody ever hears from me again. That includes you. Or you can double it, and I'll tell the police anything you want."

"Such a deal," the voice said.

Sandy was more careful this time. He wasn't going to get a chance at her again. She'd told him to put the money in a diaper bag and leave it at Ludlow Hill Park, in the gazebo where she'd married Joe. The gazebo sat on piers out on a tiny lake. You had to cross an open field and a bridge to reach it. She would be able to see if the money was there and if anyone was around before she exposed herself.

The drop was set for sunrise, when few people were around. Her plan had been to get in, grab the money, and get gone. Then Joe called from his mother's house—she'd given him an earful over Thanksgiving dinner—and it occurred to her that it was time Joe made himself useful.

You never knew with a man like jackass Lawrence's killer, what he was really thinking and whether he meant to keep his end of the bargain. So she told Joe to meet her at the gazebo at dawn. He could go first and be her decoy. If anything funny was going on, he'd run into it before she did. As for her and Joe, he could do this one thing for her and then she would see.

The sky lightened, revealing a man walking down the road toward her. He had a grizzled look, with a long beard and shaggy eyebrows and he walked with a staff made from a tree branch with the bark stripped off. A little mop of a dog ran fast on stubby legs to keep up with him. *I know how you feel, little dog.*

The man nodded at her, then turned and fell in beside her. "Nice morning to be out in the woods."

"I guess so," Sandy said, impatient. She increased her pace, hoping to move beyond the man. He had to be 70 if he was a day. You'd think it wouldn't be hard to get away from an old guy who needed a stick to walk, but he kept up. "Look, I don't want company right now."

"It's not going to work you know."

"What are you talking about? Do I know you?"

"I know you. I know you made a deal with a killer and you're digging yourself in deeper and deeper. Time to get out, Sandy."

"I don't know what you're talking about and I want you to leave me alone."

Sandy's phone chimed, her regular phone, not the burner. She held up the phone, glancing at the screen while the old man continued to walk beside her. It was Joe. *Better answer.* "Hi, baby. Where are you?"

"I'm heading into the gazebo now. Where are you?"

"I'm almost there. Baby, I came out here yesterday with Chelsey and I think I left her diaper bag. Can you see it?"

"I see a purple something under a bench. Is that what you're talking about?"

Sandy relaxed, only now aware how tense she'd been. "Good, it's still there. I'll be there in a minute."

"I can't wait to see you," Joe said. "I've been such an ass. We've got a lot to talk about."

"And we will, baby. I promise."

A rifle shot echoed across the lake.

JOE FROZE, staring dumbly at the splintered pillar until sense kicked in and he dropped to the floor of the gazebo. A second shot zoomed over his head. He could barely hear Sandy screaming through the phone, now several feet away on the deck. He bellied over to the phone as another shot zinged by like a nuclear mosquito. *Jesus. This is Afghanistan all over again.*

"Joe, answer me!"

"I'm here, Mutt."

"I hear shots. What's happening?"

"This is crazy. Someone's shooting at me."

"Grab my bag and get out of there!" Sandy screamed into his ear

"What the hell are you talking about?"

"Just grab my bag," Sandy used that voice, the voice that told him he'd better not ignore her if he knew what was good for him. "Grab the fucking bag and get out of there. If you come back without that bag, we have nothing to talk about."

*Women.* Joe wormed over to the purple bag. *I could get killed over a bunch of nothing.* He snagged the strap of the bag and inched his way backwards. The bag dragged, heavier than expected. *What the hell are you putting on Chelsey? Lead diapers?*

"Joe, are you there?"

"I'm busy right now. For Christ's sake, hang up and call 911."

Joe shoved the phone into a pocket and lifted his head just enough to scan his surroundings. He could see the shooter through the gazebo balusters, rifle braced on the railing of a bridge crossing the creek that fed the lake. The shooter was a hundred yards away, too far for Joe to get a good look at him. Far enough that the gazebo railing with its closely set balusters provided decent cover.

The railing was a double edged sword. It protected him from the shooter, but it also prevented him from escaping the gazebo. If he could, he'd roll off the deck and into the water—though in November, that meant hypothermia. Still, it was a risk he would take if he could. *And Sandy will raise hell if I get her precious diapers wet.*

He'd have to belly crawl backwards over the little wood bridge. When he reached the sidewalk, he'd be in the open for fifty yards or more. He could try to run for it. But whoever was shooting at him had plenty of time to line up a kill shot before Joe exposed himself at the end of the bridge. Maybe the shooter wasn't that good. *And maybe I'm not that fast anymore.*

Splinters flew from the railing a foot from Joe's head. *Nope, not gonna risk it.* He pulled the diaper bag between him and the shooter—*what the hell was in there?*—and continued to inch backwards until the toes of his boots scraped concrete.

Joe rested while he rehearsed his next move in his head. He had to pop up and duck around the end of the railing, then drop under the bridge. A stone wall supported this end of the bridge. There was enough bank between the wall and the lake for him to be comfortable while he waited for rescue. If he timed it right, he'd be exposed for less than three seconds. *Three seconds too long.*

JIM MCDONALD GRABBED his phone and stabbed at the screen. *Should have left the line open. Should have brought Terry and Steve.*

Sandy knocked his hand away. "What do you think you're doing?"

Jim backed up two long steps, accidentally dropping Chester's leash in the process. "I'm calling 911," he growled. "What do you think I'm doing?"

Chester reacted to Sandy's aggression, dancing around her while he yapped ferociously.

"The hell you are." She pulled a stun gun out of her pocket. "I don't know who you are or why you're here, but this isn't your business." She stepped on Chester's leash, then bent down and picked up the end. She pulled him to her while he tugged violently in the opposite direction. "You drop the phone or your dog gets it."

Jim opened his hand. The phone bounced on the pavement, landing by Chester's paws. Chester continued snarling while Sandy dragged the phone toward her with one foot, then stomped on it.

"There. You can have it back now."

"To hell with the phone. I want my dog."

"Your dog is insurance. You can have him when I get back." Chester quit tugging and was now chewing on the leash to get away. Sandy took off her jacket, tossed it over Chester, and scooped him in her arms. The bundle writhed as Chester tried to escape. She backed away, rearranging her hold on Chester so she held both him and the stun gun securely. "You're not going to mess this up for me."

Another shot echoed, the fourth? Fifth?

"You hear that? It's already gone to hell. If you have any sense, you'll get your child and get out of here."

"Don't you talk about my baby. I'm doing this for her!" Sandy screamed. She cut into the woods.

SHERRY GRABBED her phone and jabbed the little green receiver under Sandy's picture while Chelsey tugged on Sherry's pants. "Slide! 'Raffe wants a slide!"

"Shh! Give me a minute, cutie-pie." *Pick up, pick up, pick up! C'mon Sandy.* It wasn't unusual to hear a shot at odd hours, but there'd been five of them in a few minutes. *That's just wrong.*

"Hello?"

Sandy sounded perfectly calm.

"You hear the shots? Someone's hunting deer up here, and you aren't wearing orange. You need to get out of there."

"Such a worrywart. Those shots aren't anywhere near here. I'll be fine."

"What about Joe? Have you seen him yet?"

"I just talked to him."

"You need to get back here. I'd leave you stranded, but you took the car keys."

Sandy hung up.

Sherry gripped her phone as if she wanted to strangle it. *Stupid, stupid Sandy, doesn't she care about Chelsey?* She beckoned to the little girl. "Come here, cutie-pie, come sit on Aunt Sherry's lap. I'll tell you a story."

"A story about 'Raffe?"

"A story about anything you want."

*WHERE ARE THE SIRENS? There should be sirens by now.*

Joe huddled under the bridge, cradling his phone in his hands. He hit speed dial for Sandy and didn't wait for her to speak. "Did you call 911?"

"I'm on the line with them now. You just hang tight, baby. Everything is going to be all right."

"Where's Chelsey? You gotta make sure Chelsey is safe."

"Chelsey's with Sherry. I sent them away."

"You should have gone with them."

"I won't leave you, baby."

"I love you, Mutt." He hadn't said it enough, not nearly enough.

"I love you too, baby. I've got to hang up now."

Joe dropped his head against the wall. How long does it take to get a freaking patrol car in a town that's barely five square miles?

Joe hated being pinned down. It had happened more than once in Afghanistan, and he'd been damn lucky to escape without injury. He wanted to poke his head out, just enough to see if the shooter was still on the bridge. But it was like Sandy told him about peeking between the curtains before a performance: If you can see the audience, they can see you. *Only the audience isn't trying to blow your head off.*

The diaper bag was a boxy purple thing. He imagined Chelsey liked the cute elephants blowing bubbles on the front. It was now scuffed and muddy from being dragged. Sandy was going to be pissed. She was like that. The roof could be falling in and she'd start fussing because Chelsey had oatmeal on her face.

*Maybe there's a granola bar inside. No telling how long I'll be stuck here.* Joe pulled the top open as he tugged at the zipper. He stared at the inside of the bag, finally understanding. They weren't shooting at him. They were shooting at Sandy. *Or the idiot she sent to pick up her payoff.*

The troops weren't coming. Sandy hadn't called 911. She wasn't going to call 911, and if he wanted out of there, he was on his own.

The bag was filled to the top with stacks of hundred dollar bills. *Sandy, what are you mixed up with?* It had to have something to do with the cop who came to the door a week earlier. What was his name? Dourson?

The cop thought Sandy had seen something. Obviously she had. *Bitch. You didn't leave because I cheated on you. You were hiding out until you could collect your payday.* He wished violently for a wall he could punch, one that wouldn't break his hand.

Joe pulled a stack of bills out of the bag, revealing a bundle of newspaper underneath. He shook his head. *Girl, you were played. He lured you out here to kill you.* He riffled the end of the stack of bills. He snorted, then started laughing. There was a hundred on top, but the rest were all ones. He ran the numbers in his head. Six stacks, probably fifty bills each. Six hundred dollars, plus six times forty-nine ... *Jesus, Mutt, you set me up for target practice and your big payoff is less than a grand.*

Joe continued to laugh until he convulsed, until tears ran down his face, cutting rivers through the grime covering it. Then he reached for his phone and dialed 911.

WHEN SHE FIRST HEARD THE sirens, Sandy thought it was a coincidence. But they drew nearer. *Who called? Joe thinks I called and the old man doesn't have a phone. Sherry thinks it's just hunters. Who called? Think, think, think!*

The stupid dog finally stopped wiggling. Maybe she should just let him go. *Not yet.* She looked behind her. The old man was keeping her in sight from a distance. She reached the edge of the woods and looked out on the water to the gazebo. Joe was gone. *Freaking S.O.B took off with my money. I'll kill him!*

Sandy looked back at the old man. He was too far away to see if she still held the stun gun on his dumb mutt. She juggled the squirming dog and the stun gun so she could hold her phone and dial Joe. Sandy stared stupidly at the phone as her call was rejected.

The dog growled. "Oh, shut up," she said. She released the dog and ran, her coat caught in one fist, flying behind her like a flag. *I've got to get back to the car.* She blew past the old man, who had dropped his walking stick and was chasing his dog.

She was too late.

A patrol car, red and blue lights flashing, had her car

blocked in. A pair of cops peered in her window. One looked up, spotted Sandy and nudged his partner.

Chelsey fidgeted on Sherry's lap while Sherry glared at Sandy at with a look that could annihilate a mid-sized city.

"Looks like shopping is out today," Sherry sneered.

The cops were now walking toward Sandy, hands on their holstered guns. The taller cop spoke, hard and mean. "Sandy Alich, drop the coat. Let us see your hands."

Sandy froze, a deer in headlights, unable to process the cop's instructions.

Chelsey fought to get away from Sherry. "Mama! I want mama!"

The cops were now twenty feet away. The tall one drew his gun. "Drop. The. Coat."

Sandy watched the gun barrel come up. She looked down at her hand and willed the fingers, fingers that were no longer hers, to open. She looked up. The gun was now trained on her head from fifteen feet away. Chelsey broke loose from Sherry's hold and tumbled to the ground, scrambling, running to Sandy, running in the path of the gun.

She opened her hands, raising them to warn Chelsey off, screaming, "Noooo!" The coat drifted over her feet a second before Chelsey collided with her legs. Sandy collapsed, falling over Chelsey, sobbing, begging, screaming, "Don't hurt my baby!"

Chelsey erupted into a full Chernobyl meltdown, stiffening and shrieking under Sandy's crouching body. Sandy stroked Chelsey's head, making shushing noises.

"It's okay, it's okay. Be mama's good baby," She crooned,

tamping down the hysterical edge threatening to creep into her own voice, wishing she could just hide with her head down like an ostrich until everyone went away.

Hard, rough hands dragged Sandy up, pulled her arms behind her back, snapped cold steel cuffs around her wrists. Chelsey clung to her legs, her fit exhausted, chanting a distressed mantra, "Mama-mama-mama-mama-mama ..."

Sandy heard the hard, mean voice ask Sherry to take Chelsey.

Another voice, closer to her, spoke softly. "We're going to walk over here and sit down. We just want to talk. We're not going to hurt your little girl. Nod if you understand."

Sandy's head, another part of her body that no longer belonged to her, jerked up and down again like a clumsily manipulated marionette.

The world came back into focus as the short cop urged Sandy toward a bench. The tall cop now reached into the patrol car, rack lights painting him red, then blue, then red again. The car's radio squawked and the hard-voiced cop spoke into the receiver, "We have her now. She's unarmed."

Sandy felt the tightness across her chest, in her shoulder blades, of her arms wrenched behind her. She watched the tiny, retreating back of her whimpering child as Sherry led her away. She wondered if she would ever get to hold Chelsey again.

*This wasn't supposed to happen.*

Sandy and her escort reached the bench.

"Sit down."

She sat. Sandy tried to gather her tumbling thoughts and failed. She looked at the soft-voiced cop. He was older and stocky. He didn't look kind, but he didn't look like he would shoot her, either. *Polite, be polite, don't make them angry.* "Why am I handcuffed?" she asked.

"Someone shot at your husband down by the lake. He said you had something to do with it."

Sandy's eye's widened. Shock. Fear. Guilt. "Me? I wouldn't hurt Joe!" *I came to meet Joe. We were having problems. That's all you need to say.* Her mouth would not obey her. It said nothing.

"You know who and you know why. You need to tell us what's going on before someone gets killed."

Sandy shook her head, a hopeless denial of reality.

"What does that mean? Why are you shaking your head?" he paused, then tried again. "Lives are at stake. Do you understand this?"

She looked at the flashing rack lights atop the police car. The old man had his dog again and was now talking to the hard-voiced cop. They looked over at her. *That old man knew things. What does he know? What is he saying?*

"No." A tear trickled down her cheek. "I don't understand any of it." She wasn't lying, not much.

A new siren wailed in the distance. It was a faint sound drifting on the wind. Sandy worried about it. Better than thinking about the cops in front of her and the handcuffs biting into her wrist. *Better than thinking about Chelsey.*

Sandy couldn't help herself. She glanced over at the other bench. Chelsey sagged on Sherry's lap, asleep with a thumb in her slack mouth. Sherry's lips pressed tight under narrowed, deadly eyes. Sherry was loyal, but only to a point. Right now Sherry was deciding exactly where that point was.

"Where's Joe?" Sandy asked. "Is he okay?"

"You don't need to worry about him," the cop said.

*Why not? What did Joe tell them?*

The old man and his dog left the hard-voiced cop to go sit in a car, a black station wagon now parked just beyond the patrol car. The hard-voiced cop headed for Sandy's bench. He loomed over her and addressed his partner. "She say anything?"

"Not yet."

The siren grew louder. Sandy looked down the road. Whatever was coming, it was beyond the curve, hidden by trees. Sandy's resolve crumbled to dust inside her, leaving only fear and defeat.

"What do we have?" This was the soft-voiced cop, talking to the tall one.

The tall one spat on the ground. *Habit? Or contempt?* "Digby found a guy lying on the bridge. Unconscious. There's a rifle with him. ID says he's Tobias Grant. Junior." He turned eyes as hard as his voice on Sandy, drilling down into her. "Young guy with a bandaged chest. Mean anything to you?"

The fog of Sandy's stress-induced confusion lifted, to be replaced by genuine incomprehension. "Toby? Not his father?"

# 22

## SATURDAY NOVEMBER 26

PETER SUCKED THE DREGS OF HIS MORNING PEPSI AND TOSSED the can in the passenger footwell as he pulled into the dog park. Viola's nose poked out the passenger window, the feathers of her tail brushing his arm as it wagged. He took in the row of cars, noting the make and model of familiar vehicles, checking off his mental roster of usual suspects.

*Nobody wants to miss this one. Too bad I can't sell tickets.*

Peter exited his Blazer, looking up the hill as he held the door open for Viola. A half-dozen faces seated around Lia's favorite picnic table were trained on him as he headed for the service road leading to the park entrance. He knew those faces would follow him up the drive and across the park. They wouldn't be satisfied until they extracted every detail from him. He supposed he owed it to them.

Making sense of the Ludlow Hill shooting had been a debacle lasting into the wee hours. He still wasn't sure the case was resolved. Thank God he wasn't in the homicide unit, or those insane hours would be his life.

Unknown to him—thank God—Jim, Steve, and Terry had snuck a GPS tracking device on Sandy's car Wednesday night and had been taking shifts in a room at the Lawrenceburg Quality Inn while they waited for Sandy to move.

Jim alerted Terry and Steve before he approached Sandy at the park. With his phone smashed he'd been unable to contact anyone when the shooting started. Terry called Peter when he couldn't reach Jim.

Peter was on his way to Indiana—thoroughly resenting the need to abandon Lia to her packing while he made the twenty-mile drive—when Parker tagged him about the shooting. She and Arseneault wanted him to liaise with the Lawrenceburg department due to his knowledge of the involved parties. And there went his day.

Knowing Jim was talking to the Lawrenceburg guys cracked Sandy's defenses. When she found out Grant cheated her on the payoff, she was so furious she started spilling faster than the Exxon Valdez. She admitted she'd been waiting for the bus on the bench across from Norman Chapel—as Lia had suspected—and had seen Grant Senior enter and leave the chapel. When Lia told her about the killing, Sandy decided it was a good opportunity to create a nest egg. Her attempt at blackmail went sideways, sending her on the run.

Initially Grant denied everything—rather his lawyer denied everything for him. Grant's mistake was paying for the diaper bag with a credit card. Some fast action nailed the purchase with the store's security footage. A little more digging and they would find the bank where Grant got the cash for the payoff.

Confronted with the damning video, Grant issued a statement through his lawyer, that he entered the chapel through the back door the night of the murder, wanting to discuss last minute details about the concert with Lawrence. Lawrence was dead when he got there.

Not wanting to be tied to the investigation, he played along with Sandy when she called. Then he tried to scare her off by waving a gun at her but he never intended to kill her.

This part of his story differed from Sandy's. She said he fired the gun. Peter wasn't sure it would be worth the effort hunting for the slug, but it might come down to that. Now she wanted to press charges against Grant for the shooting she claimed happened at Mount Airy Forest. *Good luck with that.*

Toby's injured lung collapsed again while he was taking potshots at Joe Alich from the bridge at Ludlow Hill Park. They'd finally been able to talk to him twelve hours after he was rushed to the hospital.

Ironically, Toby made up the story about Grant's confession. He concocted the show at the cemetery, figuring if his father would never be held to account for his mother's suicide, maybe he could be made to pay for Lawrence. Toby didn't appear to care whether or not his father had actually killed Lawrence.

The bloody handkerchief was one he'd loaned Lawrence when Lawrence cut a finger while cooking dinner for Toby. Toby kept it as a memento (When Hodgkins curled his lip at this, Toby said that if Jane Austen could do it, so could he). He later realized it could be used to implicate his father.

Toby intentionally shot himself to make sure his accusation was newsworthy and could not be ignored. An experienced shooter, he expected the low caliber target round to lodge in his wallet. He hadn't expected the impact to crack a rib and for that rib to puncture a lung.

Grant admitted to telling Toby about the blackmail. Outraged that his ruse to get his father convicted for Lawrence's murder was not working, Toby realized his only chance to make his father pay would be to scuttle the payoff.

He slipped out of the house in the middle of the night and set himself up on the bridge, planning to scare the person who tried to collect the money. He figured the blackmailer would think Grant was trying to kill him and expected them to run to the cops.

Toby faced charges for the shooting. Indiana wasn't sure what they were yet, though Peter suspected the resolution would involve a psych eval and a stay at a pricey treatment center.

Grant Senior had been released. As his lawyer maintained, it was not illegal to pay blackmail. That Grant had another agenda, Peter had no doubt. You don't short a blackmailer unless you plan to shut her up some other way.

As for the murder, they had a dubious witness and no physical proof. *Not yet.* Peter wondered if Grant would ever be arraigned. *Not my case, thank God.*

Lia perched atop her favorite picnic table, watching Viola drag Peter up the drive. *My guy is whipped.* She nudged Bailey and scooted over to make room.

The gang was silent as Peter released Viola and crossed the park. He passed wordlessly through the group standing around the table, then leaned in to give Lia a brief kiss before he clambered up beside her, snugging his arm behind her back.

"Who am I today, Kentucky Boy?"

Peter tilted his head and narrowed his eyes, considering. "You are ... Woman with Too Many Friends."

Lia handed him the white bag she'd been guarding on her lap. "Before everyone pesters you to death, I brought breakfast."

He opened the bag from Bonomini Bakery. It held a trio of freshly baked yeast donuts. "I changed my mind. Today you are Goddess Above All Women."

## 23

## SUNDAY, NOVEMBER 27

BAILEY EXAMINED LIA'S MISSION COUCH, GIVING IT WHAT LIA would forever more think of as "Rory eye." The couch was centered against the far wall of Lia's new living room and flanked by a pair of matching end tables. Finally Bailey spoke. "It's too symmetrical. It kills the flow."

Lia looked sideways at Peter and smirked. "Told you so."

"I surrender in the face of overwhelming forces. I'll head back to my place and let you ladies gab."

"Don't go," Bailey said. "I took another look at that Tarot reading I did for you."

"Oh? Did you come up with something interesting?"

"Something odd. I don't know what to think about it."

Lia headed for the kitchen, happy for the opportunity to roll her eyes in private. "You're in luck. I unpacked the kitchen. I'll make tea."

Bailey followed, seating herself at the kitchen table. She drew her deck out of a pocket. Peter shoved an empty packing box aside with his foot so he could reach the opposite chair.

"Are we in for a reenactment?" he asked.

"Reproducing the spread will help me explain," Bailey said.

"What's the point?" Lia asked as she set a pair of mugs on the table and handed Peter a beer. "You didn't draw a card for Toby's dad. I thought the reading was a wash."

"So did I," Bailey said as she turned over the cards one by one. "I wondered if I was missing something. Sometimes you ask Spirit a question and the answer doesn't follow the layout you created, so Spirit sends the answer the best way it can. I recreated the reading and meditated on it. I realized you could read the entire layout as one story instead of each card saying something about one person."

"What kind of story?" Peter asked.

"Let's start with the root card. We talked about that before." Bailey pointed to the upside down woman with scales. "Every card has several meanings. One interpretation of this card is 'an injustice,' another is 'turning a blind eye to an injustice.' So the killer knew an injustice had been committed and was complicit in some way, possibly pretending they didn't know what they knew."

"There was a lot of that going on. Lawrence's behavior was an open secret at Hopewell," Lia said.

"Now look at the cards in the main reading. If we ignore them as yes or no cards and just read them in a line, first we have the reversed Six of Pentacles. You have a wealthy man doling out coins to a beggar."

"That sounds like Grant," Peter said. "He did a lot of charitable giving."

"That might be right if it were upright. Upside down it's

about unequal relationships, using money and power to control people."

"Who do you think it refers to?" Lia asked.

"That was the professor's whole modus operandi, wasn't it?" Bailey asked. "Doling out favors to his pets, but only bits and pieces, and never given freely?"

"True. What's next?" Peter asked.

"The reversed Nine of Wands. An old soldier who is wounded and leaning against a staff for support. This is someone who is burdened and burned out by a situation and not sure they can hang in there any longer. After that you have the reversed Knight of Swords. Impulsive action and aggression."

"Those first three cards could describe Marshall's situation," Peter said. "He's oppressed, he can't take anymore and he cracks."

"And bonks the evil professor in the head."

"Okay, what next?" Peter asked.

"The reversed Two of Swords. This card says you have no good choices and whatever you do will lead to suffering. The next card is the reversed Tower. It means a catastrophe has been averted."

"So someone did the best they could do in a bad situation?" Peter asked.

"And it worked." Bailey tapped the following card. "The Hanged Man, reversed."

"Reversed? He's right side up," Lia said.

"You'd think so, but when this card is right side up, the man is hanging upside down."

"Oh."

"This card has several meanings. One is about impotence or a period of inactivity. When the card is reversed, the inactivity has ended. This is the card that drew my attention. Your root card refers to someone turning a blind eye to an injustice. Here, they stopped doing nothing and took action."

"But by this time the only choices left were bad ones," Peter said.

"Now look at this. Reversed Devil, end of enslavement. Ten of swords is hitting rock bottom. Reversed says the bad times are over. And the reversed Three of Swords means the end of pain and suffering."

"So killing Lawrence ended someone's pain and suffering."

"Yes, but the person who did it wasn't the person who was suffering. It was someone who knew about the suffering and regretted their part in it and took action."

"Where's the regret? You didn't say anything about regret," Lia said, fascinated in spite of herself.

"I think it's implied," Peter said.

"I could feel the regret pouring off the cards when I was meditating," Bailey said. "Regret may be the wound on the old soldier."

"I thought that was Leander?" Lia asked.

"Cards often refer to more than one thing. In this case, it could refer to Leander as well as the killer, who would be the rescuer."

"That's if this is about Leander," Lia said. Geoff oppressed plenty of people. Look at Constance. They divorced and she still couldn't get free of him."

"True," Bailey said.

"If we're talking about Grant, then he was tired of Lawrence using his son," Peter said.

"But that would mean he knew about it and let it go on,"

Lia said. "If he's the kind of man who could do that, where's the guilt?" She turned to Peter. "You said Dr. Lawrence's killer acted in a primal rage. It doesn't fit."

"Maybe he fooled himself into thinking the professor's attention would ultimately help Toby. He overheard differently and acted." Bailey said.

"We're going in circles," Peter said. "We'll never have all the answers. Even if Grant confesses, there will still be gaps in the story."

Bailey gathered up the cards and stood to leave. "I'm sure you're right. It was just such a compelling story."

Lia followed Bailey to the door and gave her a hug. When she returned to the kitchen, Honey, Chewy, and Viola lined up by her shelving unit, waiting for treats. "Such good dogs you were while Bailey was here." She broke a giant biscuit into thirds and doled them out while she gauged Peter's mood.

"Peter, what dress did Hannah give you when we took her home?"

"Something black. Why?"

"Did the material have a pattern woven into it? Black on black?"

"Something flowery. Does it matter?"

"Maybe. She wore a long coat that night and it was buttoned the whole time I was with her. I could only see the hem of her dress, but it was this gorgeous silk jacquard in a fleur-de-lis. I didn't think anything about it. But if she killed Professor Lawrence, she wouldn't have wanted anyone to see her dress, and she would have given a different black dress to you for testing. Fleur-de-lis is a stylized iris but a lot of people wouldn't recognize it as a flower. Were the petals pointed?"

"I didn't look that closely. What brought this on?"

"Bailey's reading. What if the story she saw in the cards is the truth?"

A corner of Peter's mouth twitched as he arched an eyebrow. "So there's more to Bailey's woo-woo than random cards and wishful thinking?"

Lia narrowed her eyes. "Don't you dare tell her I'm even thinking this."

"My lips are sealed. What about the reading makes you think Hannah did Lawrence?"

"You remember, Hannah told us she missed her chance to get Dr. Lawrence fired years ago. She felt awful about it."

"So when Leander told her he snapped and killed Lawrence, she felt responsible?"

"And was left with bad choices, but ultimately fixed the situation."

"Which card was Hannah's?"

Lia bit her lip, calling to mind the layout, mentally counting out the cards. "It was the one I thought was right-side-up, the Hanged Man."

"The one Bailey said meant 'taking action after a period of inaction.'"

"That's the one," Lia said. "The other meaning was 'a sacrifice that doesn't have the expected results.'"

"If she did it, it could have been seen as a sacrifice, putting herself at risk that way. If so, it went sideways when Leander confessed. I hate to say it but you may be right about Hannah."

"What makes you say that?"

"Hannah was with the Renaissance Festival for more than a decade," Peter said.

"Yes, I know. She told me."

"Did she tell you she was their combat choreographer?"

"No ... but that's just fake fighting."

"Those shows are as physically demanding as real fights and you need to know how real fighting works if you're going to avoid injuries. I'll bet Hannah is much stronger than she looks."

"And she would know how to cause a fatal head wound."

"Exactly."

"What will you do about it?"

Peter shrugged. "What do you have? Some Tarot cards and a hinky feeling? She's not the only one at Hopewell experienced in stage combat. Even if you're right about her —and you may be—you know how it works. What can you prove? It won't be enough to prove she swapped the dress, we'd have to find the real dress and you can bet it's long gone."

"Leaving no evidence." Lia sighed. "Hannah played me. The whole time, she was playing me to manipulate the investigation and I didn't see it. Won't I ever see it?"

Peter brushed Lia's hair aside and cupped her chin. "She played both of us. I didn't see it either."

"What do you mean?"

"Who do you think our anonymous tipster was?"

"Hannah? But she knew nothing about Sandy."

"Misdirection," Peter said. "All of it, the emails and the things she told you. If it makes you feel better, I think she genuinely likes you. And there was a lot of truth mixed in with the lies."

"I can't believe she fooled everyone."

"You have to admire her nerve. If she killed Lawrence, she talked to you, me, Cynth, and all those bigwigs while she was walking around in a bloody dress."

"Don't you care about justice?"

"If Hannah killed Lawrence—and that's a big if—she did it after years of being ground down by the man and watching him destroy the people around her. She did it in the heat of the moment after Lawrence pushed Leander over the edge. If your theory is correct, she was protecting Leander. It's not quite a burning bed situation, but it's close. I'm not so sure the letter of the law would deliver justice to Hannah."

"But she killed someone."

"I know a lost cause when I see one. Wingler will confess to killing Lawrence himself if that's what it takes to keep Hannah from going to prison and violating the terms of the bequest."

"You're not going to do anything?"

Peter leaned back in his chair and grinned. "Not my case."

# EPILOGUE

THE ARENAL VOLCANO LOOMED OVER THE CANOPY OF TREES, obscuring the night sky in an ominous silhouette. Rivulets of lava glowed against the dark slope in a delicate and deadly tracery. Zephyrs carried the heavenly scent of ylang ylang trees, caressing Hannah's skin and playing with her too-fine hair as she sipped wine on the balcony of her hotel room. She set her glass down and leaned against the rail, closing her eyes to better hear nuances in the cacophony of nighttime birds.

Finally, she could relax. *Bless Toby and his melodramatic ass.* She hadn't known what to do when Leander cracked. Then Toby did his faux swan song at the clock tower and it was a new game.

Everyone was convinced either Toby or Tobias Senior killed Geoff, assuming one of them had to overhear the argument in the chapel for Toby to know Geoff was leading him on about *Faust*. *As if Leander could pass up the temptation to taunt Toby with this tidbit.* She wished she'd been a fly on the wall during that conversation.

Now the investigation into Geoff's murder was so bolloxed, no DA would ever touch it. And while everyone might believe Tobias Senior killed Geoff, all his charities would still take his money. He would stay on everyone's A lists. The hint of murder, especially now that Geoff's dirty little tricks were coming to light, would probably give him an interesting cachet at parties.

When she'd left Leander to check on Geoff that night, the one thing she'd been sure of was that Leander's life was over and it was her fault for not protecting him years earlier. Geoff would dedicate his life to destroying Leander, piece by piece through every means at his command. It was up to her to fix it.

She'd spent the walk through the magnolia trees to the chapel ransacking her brain for an answer: a bribe, or some blackmail that she could use to protect Leander. There had to be a way. By the time she entered the family chamber, she knew she was kidding herself. Leander was doomed, and there was no telling who would be caught in the fallout.

The solution hit her as she bent over Geoff to check his pulse. She could fix the entire mess and rescue the school from Geoff's clutches if she had the nerve. Leander just had to keep his mouth shut. She'd thought the idea of going to prison would be enough to keep him silent.

Even so, if he somehow wound up convicted of killing Geoff, a few years in prison for manslaughter with time off for good behavior—she could count on Leander behaving well—would be an acceptable tradeoff for a lifetime at the mercy of Geoff's manipulations. If it had come down to that, she wouldn't feel guilty. Leander created this mess. She shouldn't have to pay for cleaning it up.

Despite the bumps, everything worked out better than she'd planned. Leander didn't have to carry guilt for a crime he hadn't committed. Tobias Senior could handle the suspicion and probably profit from it—People never accumulated that much wealth without committing a crime or fifty along the way. A little karma wouldn't hurt him. With a punctured lung, Toby could let go of his mother's delusion that he would follow in her enormous footsteps. Now he could find a life of his own.

She'd had a close look at Geoff's will before she'd agreed to take on guardianship of her Fur Boys. She couldn't benefit from the trust, but she was allowed to hire whatever household help she needed. That enabled her to bring Constance and Leander on board at outrageous salaries to make up for the injustice of Geoff's final wishes.

Hannah wondered if Constance would break down and admit she knew about Geoff's bi-sexuality if she lived with Leander long enough. Maybe they would carry the pretense forever.

Meanwhile, she'd let Michael and Suki bribe her with this lovely Costa Rica vacay, a last bit of freedom before she assumed her new duties. She had a tour of the hanging bridges lined up for the morning. She heard it was like being in a Tarzan movie, or Indiana Jones. Then there was the eco-boat tour, the one that sold her on coming to Costa Rica. After that, a trip to Bribri and the coast, where she'd see the indigenous people and do some snorkeling.

It was going to be an excellent trip.

# FUR BOYS THEME

Is there a lap that needs snuggling?
A treat for my stomach?
Do you need some loving?
We got what you need.
We're the Fur Boys
We'll make you happy.
Guaranteed.
Cause that's how we roll.
Yeah.
That's how we roll.

# AUTHOR'S NOTES

In fur Boys, the Ryan Widmer trials are used as justification for the reenactment at Norman Chapel. Widmer was convicted of drowning his wife, Sarah, in 2009. The verdict was overturned due to juror misconduct after it was learned that some jurors conducted home experiments and shared their findings with the rest of the panel, influencing the verdict.

Sarah's skin was dry when the EMTs arrived six minutes after Ryan called 911 to say he'd found his wife drowned in their tub. Two jurors tested how long it would take for a body to air dry after bathing. They concluded that Widmer waited to call 911 after removing his wife's body from the tub, contrary to Widmer's statements during the 911 call (In a later trial, a fan of Widmer's testified he told her he killed Sarah by drowning her in the toilet after she hit her head during an altercation. This would explain why Sarah's skin and the bathtub were dry but her hair was wet when the EMTs arrived).

Widmer's second trial ended in a hung jury. He was convicted in his third trial. He has since been denied an appeal.

Spring Grove Cemetery is a fascinating historical site five minutes from my house and my favorite place to bike. I have attempted to be as true as I can to the architectural details of the original buildings but needed to fudge a bit for the plot of *Fur Boys*.

I added an exterior door to the utility room in Norman Chapel. The rest of the chapel is as described.

I expected a creepy locked stairwell leading to the timeless clock tower in the original office building. Instead I discovered a trap door fifteen feet off the ground in what is now a bathroom. It is impossible to reach without a very tall ladder and a great deal of trouble. I added rungs nailed to the wall so that Toby and Lia would have a way up. The tower windows are now covered with netting to keep out pigeons.

While Hopewell Music Conservatory is entirely fictional, I have been assured by people who would know that the sordid activities within the school have occurred in many music departments.

There are several references to package thieves in *Fur Boys*. Increases in online shopping in recent years mean packages are frequently left on doorsteps while the recipients are at work. Local criminals have taken to following delivery trucks and scooping packages off porches. It is quite natural that pursuing these miscreants would be next on Peter's agenda.

Bailey's beliefs about Tarot cards and how they work are her own, drawn from many sources. Her style of reading and interpretation owes much to Brigit Esselmont's wonderful web-site, http://www.biddytarot.com. This is a fabulous, down-to-earth resource for anyone who wants to learn how to read Tarot.

The Johnny Lee Miller reference comes from an episode of *Elementary*, where he plays a modern-day Sherlock Holmes.

Captain Ann Parker is inspired by Colleen Belongea, an exceptional officer with 22 years' experience and one of the reasons The Writers' Police Academy is such an amazing experience.

The Taliband (not Taliban) was a Northside gang that was dismantled by the Cincinnati Police several years before this book was written.

Lucy balls are real.

Elmer and Old Timber Inn are also real. Like Lia, I drove by it for years, imagining it to be a scary place. I am now a fan. Along with the fish and raspberry cheesecake, Elmer's hot slaw and mac and cheese are highly recommended. I keep missing meatloaf day but I hear it's wonderful.

# ACKNOWLEDGEMENTS

When it comes to writing books, no author is an island. On the home front are the friends and colleagues who provide the moral support necessary to completing such a huge undertaking. Thanks go to Anna and Pat, and to my dog park friends.

My virtual support network is legion. The self-publishing industry is made of generous people who have come together to build this brave new world. First and foremost is my Facebook writers' haven, The Retreat. Author Taylor Stevens (who took me to school when I was writing this book) and her podcasting partner, Stephen Campbell, keep me on my toes with my writing and have become special friends.

I am humbled and blessed by the efforts of my Beta team, people who are strangers to me (at least initially) who volunteer time in often busy lives to read my manuscripts with a critical eye and comb through them for errors. It is no small thing.

Thanks go to Sandy Wilson Alich for allowing me latitude when I asked to base a character on her in Fur Boys. Real life Sandy is a lovely lady who is much smarter and possesses none of the character flaws attributed to fictional Sandy. Those are purely a product of my imagination for the purpose of this story. She adores dogs and would never consider harming one.

Thanks to Leander Marshall, Geoffrey Lawrence, Michael J. Wingler, Joel Girgenti, Sherry Pace, Jim Madden, Cathy Kleemeyer, and Suki Korp for lending their names to the book.

Thanks for technical assistance go to Irene Brown for her help with Spring Grove Cemetery architecture (any mistakes or discrepancies are my own); Randall Lindsay for firefighter details; and Pat North for details about music schools.

Special thanks to Elizabeth Mackey of Elizabeth Mackey Graphics for always making me look classy.

**A Shot in the Bark**
Detective Peter Dourson is convinced the suicide of Lia's
deadbeat boyfriend is not what it seems.
**Drool Baby**
Peter's search for the truth behind Luthor's death brings Lia
into the cross hairs of a killer increasingly out of control.
**Maximum Security**
Lia's loyalties are tested when Peter arrests the wrong
woman for murder.
**Sneak Thief**
Lia's kindness to an orphaned beagle draws the attention of
an obsessed stalker.
**Muddy Mouth**
A Fourth of July parade, 89 feral cats, and a missing author.
It's nothing Lia and her schnauzer can't handle.
**Fur Boys**
There's no end to the drama when Lia stumbles on a
dead diva.

Like what you've read? Sign up for C. A.' s News at
http://canewsome.com and receive Lia's second mystery,
**Drool Baby,** as your special gift. Members of C. A.'s News
are the first to know about upcoming releases. Other perks
from the dog park: dog tips, Lia's recipes, book recommen-
dations, exclusive giveaways, and access to Carol's online
file of deleted scenes, all delivered at the whim of the
author.

# ABOUT THE AUTHOR

Carol Ann "C. A." Newsome is an author and painter who lives in Cincinnati. She spends most mornings at the Mount Airy Dog Park with a zombie swamp monster named Gypsy Foo La Beenz.

*Carol loves to hear from readers.*
*Contact her at*
gypsy@canewsome.com

*Would you like to stay in touch?*
*Sign up for Carol's newsletter at*
CANewsome.com

f facebook.com/AShotInTheBark